CA

# THE CARDINAL AND THE CROOK

AN INSPIRATIONAL FAMILY SAGA OF UNSHAKABLE
FAITH & COURAGE IN THE MIDST OF TRAGEDY & CRIME

SAL TOCCO

Published by Aim High Books
Editing, design, and distribution by Bublish

ISBN: 978-1-647047-63-4 (paperback)
ISBN: 978-1-647047-64-1 (hardcover)
ISBN: 978-1-647047-62-7 (eBook)

To my wife, Rosalia for her unconditional
love, support and encouragement.

# Contents

## PART THREE: THE SEMINARIAN

## PART FOUR: THE MOTHER

## PART FIVE: CANCER IN THE CHURCH

## PART SIX: GOD'S PLAN

## PART SEVEN: TRANSFORMATION

# The Call

**Archbishop John Donnelly**
**Saint Joseph's Cemetery | 2016**

THE GOVERNOR AND archbishop finished their monthly lunch meeting at the statehouse on Beacon Hill. It was a picture-perfect fall day in Boston. The leaves on the trees in the Boston Common had turned a brilliant red, the sky was a deep blue, and the temperature was a very comfortable seventy degrees. During these meetings, they would discuss various social programs where the Boston diocese and the state government could collaborate; however, at times, they became lobbying sessions, especially when there were bills being discussed in the legislature around late-term abortions. But overall, Archbishop John Donnelly enjoyed his visits with Governor Stephen Ruffo, whom he'd met nearly thirty years prior when he had been a seminarian and the governor an assistant district attorney in Boston.

Over the years, they had developed a strong bond, both personally and professionally. Both were highly respected for their compassionate leadership, unwavering integrity, and strong connection to the Boston community. Despite their powerful positions, each remained humble and respectful to others. They were both in their midfifties now but—as far as Archbishop Donnelly believed, at least—could easily pass for men in their forties. The archbishop was tall and slim with deep-blue eyes and a tan complexion. His wavy black hair was just starting to thin and turn gray. The governor was not as tall but had a broader, more powerful physique. While it had been several years since he played college football, it appeared he could easily fit into his old uniform. His brown hair also had a few specks of gray.

The governor turned and smiled at his friend; his piercing green eyes especially bright against the rust-colored autumn backdrop. "So, John, I hear rumors that you may be getting a red hat. Any truth to that?"

The archbishop grinned. "I hear that *you* have been approached about running for president, Stephen. God knows we could use an adult like you in Washington." He paused to see if he would get a reaction, but the governor just laughed. "Stephen, rumors are simply that. Until I get a call from Rome—or you tell me that you are running for president—I won't believe either."

At that very moment, there was a knock on the governor's door. His chief of staff walked in and said, "Governor, I'm sorry to interrupt, but it is the archbishop's office. They said they need to speak to him immediately. He has a call from the Vatican."

As the archbishop was being driven to the rectory at the Cathedral of the Holy Cross, he glanced out the window. He was in deep thought, remembering a night over half a century ago. Then he turned to his driver and said, "Paul, I'd like to drive out to western Massachusetts tomorrow morning, right after breakfast."

Paul had been a street cop in Boston before retiring seven years ago, at the age of fifty-two, when he arguably should've decided to embrace his retirement for all it was worth—but that wasn't the sort of man Paul was. After one year of trying to relax, he'd already been looking for something else to do, for a way to keep his mind and body busy. His former police captain was friendly with someone at the archbishop's office and made the connection. The archbishop needed a driver, and they hit it off immediately, leading into Paul's now six-year employ as John's personal chauffeur. However, given his six-foot-tall frame and prior experience, he also doubled as protective security whenever necessary, which he took as a pride point since he was approaching sixty. Aside from those qualities, the archbishop appreciated Paul's sense of humor and willingness to give him honest feedback—both solicited and unsolicited.

Paul glanced at his rearview mirror briefly, meeting the archbishop's gaze. "Will we be spending the whole day there, Your Excellency?" Then with a wink and a smile, he added, "Whoops . . . I suppose I should say 'Your Eminence.'"

The archbishop grinned back. "I want to visit the cemetery where my father and brother are buried." He paused at that, as though tempted to justify the desire to still visit regularly, after all these years, only to think better of it. Any desire to disguise the truth was a futile effort within the confines of this vehicle, this friendship, for Paul knew John all too well to fall for anything but the truth. "Afterward," he carried on, "we will pick up Father Jason and bring him into town for lunch. And, Paul, 'Your Excellency' is fine for now."

It was another gorgeous fall day as Paul drove the archbishop to western Massachusetts. The leaves on the trees in the Berkshire Mountains were at their peak. Even after all these years, the archbishop never ceased to be amazed by the natural beauty of these mountains. He and his brother had taken numerous hikes in the Berkshires, and he remembered how they always agreed that they felt very close to God there.

The two men covered various topics during the drive, including their disappointment with the Red Sox and their hopes for the Patriots, as well as a good dose of Washington politics.

"So, when will we be traveling to Rome?" asked Paul.

"It sounds like the Holy Father wants to conduct the consistory on All Saints' Day, so we will be leaving during the last week of October. Is your passport up-to-date?"

"Yes, and so is my wife's. She is excited about going to Rome. More importantly, she is overjoyed for you. Last night, she said to me, 'Paul, do you realize that Archbishop John could become the next pope?'"

The archbishop said, "Tell Catherine that she is getting way ahead of herself. I'm extremely humbled by this recognition. There are many excellent bishops who are more worthy than me. Likewise, there are a great number of cardinals who are much more qualified to be pope than I am." Then he paused, thinking of something that made him laugh.

"What's so funny, Your Excellency?"

"I was just imagining what you would look like in one of those Swiss Guard uniforms if I ever did become pope."

That comment got a hearty laugh out of Paul.

They pulled into the entranceway of the cemetery. The archbishop got out of the car and said to Paul, "I'll be here for a while."

Paul nodded, unsurprised. "I kind of figured that, so I brought a good book to read. Take all the time you need."

The archbishop walked down the path that led to his father's grave—a monument composed of dark granite with a life-size statue of Saint Joseph next to it. There was a picture of his father on the headstone, which had been taken the day the archbishop had been ordained as a priest. The picture captured the essence of his father, who always had a welcoming smile on his face. The archbishop read the inscription:

*Reverend Patrick J. Donnelly*
*"Father Pat"*
*1907–1997*
*Priest Father Friend*

Archbishop John smiled and thought back on what that evening— over fifty years ago—must have been like from Father Pat's perspective.

# PART ONE
# THE EARLY YEARS

# 1

# The Beginning

IT WAS A damp, dreary Saturday evening—the type of night that chills every bone. The heavy rain and thunder had stopped, the temperature dipping to a brisk sixty degrees. A young woman in her early twenties stepped out from the darkness. Her hooded raincoat and woolen scarf could not hide that she was extremely attractive. She had long brown hair and a beautiful olive complexion. Her eyes, which were a brilliant green, were swollen and red from crying. The young woman looked up at the house, which was only a few steps away.

Inside the house was the pastor, Father Pat Donnelly—a warm and friendly priest in his early fifties. He'd just poured himself his nightly two fingers of single malt scotch, sat down in his favorite leather chair, and looked forward to continuing the crime novel he'd started a few nights before. He thought to himself that a good book and a glass of scotch in the warm, comfortable rectory were perfect on an unusually cold and damp summer evening.

Meanwhile, outside, the young woman carried two baskets and struggled both physically and emotionally. She carefully placed the baskets by the doorstep and gently lifted the woolen blanket from one, revealing a beautiful baby. She lifted the child, held him closely, and kissed his forehead as tears fell from her eyes. The child looked up and smiled at her. It seemed he was reassuring her that everything would be all right. She put him down, covered him with the blanket, and then turned to the second basket, where there was another baby—a twin. This child stared at her with intense eyes. He almost seemed angry. She held him close and felt his strength as he stiffened in her arms. Her tears continued flowing as she placed him back into the basket. She rang the bell of the rectory and hurried into the bushes, waiting for someone to answer the door.

Father Pat heard the bell. Putting down his book and walking to the door, he wondered who would be out on a night like this one. His journey from his favorite leather chair to the front door of the rectory felt like an eternity for the young woman, and she began to change her mind—but just as she was about to go back for her babies, the door opened, and the priest stepped out.

Father Pat was confused when he did not see anyone at the door. Then he looked down, saw the baskets, and immediately assumed that one of his parishioners had wanted to surprise him with some fresh-baked cookies. Suddenly, he heard the cries of a baby. Puzzled, he bent down and lifted the blanket. He was amazed to see a beautiful infant staring up at him. Then he turned to the second basket and was completely shocked to see another child. He looked around to see who had left the infants at his door.

The young woman held her breath as she watched the priest with her babies. Father Pat carefully picked up each basket and brought them inside the rectory. The woman remained in the bushes for several minutes as she watched the house light up. Tears continued flowing down her cheeks. There was a part of her that wanted to run to the house and take back her sons, but instead, she turned and slowly walked back to her car. At that moment, there was a flash of lightning and a loud clap of thunder. It pierced her heart as she recalled everything that had happened over the past year.

Recovering from the initial shock, Father Pat picked up the phone and called the only person he thought he could—Sister Dorothea.

"Sister, I—I mean *we*—received a very special delivery tonight."

Sister Dorothea, who was just sitting down to relax with a cup of tea, was used to Father Pat's late-night phone calls. She'd worked with him for nearly twenty years and was very fond of him. Tonight, she sensed something in his voice that seemed like a combination of excitement, shock, and confusion.

"What is it, Father Pat?"

There was some uncomfortable silence, which was even more unusual for him. Then he slowly responded, "It's . . . I mean *they* . . . they are babies, two of them. Someone rang the bell and just left them. Please . . . please come over here now, Sister. We have to care for them!"

Sister Dorothea knocked on Sister Annette's door.

"Sister, there are a couple of packages for us at the rectory."

With her curiosity heightened, Sister Annette asked, "Packages? What kind of packages? And who would deliver packages this late on a Saturday night?"

Sister Dorothea simply smiled and said that it was a very special delivery from God. Now she really had Sister Annette's attention.

The two nuns had entered the convent at the same time nearly twenty-five years ago. They joined the Sisters of the Presentation. This order had been founded in Ireland in the late 1700s and was originally dedicated to serving the poor. In the late 1800s, some of the nuns came to America to teach the children of poor Irish immigrants. Both of these women came from Irish Catholic families. It was not unusual for one or more of the children from these Irish families to choose a religious life during these years.

Both nuns put on their coats and went out into the chilly night. They walked past the school in silence and went to the back door of the rectory, not bothering to knock once they got there, as there wasn't a need for it. Father Pat had been watching for them and immediately opened the door. His heart was racing as he quickly ushered them into the rectory. There, sitting on the kitchen table, were the two baskets containing the infants. By this time, both babies had started to cry. The priest was not sure if they were hungry, missing their mother, or in need of changing. This certainly added to his anxiety.

Sister Annette quickly overcame her surprise and said to Sister Dorothea, "You were absolutely right, Sister; it is a very special delivery from God!" Then she turned to Father Pat and said, "Don't worry, Father—Dorothea and I will take good care of these little angels."

She immediately reached down and picked up one of the infants, while Sister Dorothea did the same with the other child. Within minutes, both babies stopped crying. It was clear that they were missing the warmth of someone holding and caressing them. The nuns smiled at the two beautiful infants. They guessed that the babies were barely two months old. They were twins—identical twins, it seemed, though it was hard to tell at such a young age.

Father Pat's uneasiness began to dissipate. Sisters Dorothea and Annette were experienced and competent caretakers and more than capable of handling such a responsibility. As his pulse slowed and his muscles relaxed, he was able to see this for what it really was—a miracle.

"Don't be concerned, Father," said Sister Dorothea. "We will take them to the convent, give them some warm milk, change their clothes, and put them to bed." As they gathered their things, she looked up and asked, "Was there a note?"

"Oh, yes, of course." He'd almost forgotten, swept up in the moment. Father Pat picked up the envelope from the kitchen counter. "Yes, yes, a very, very touching and loving letter was left."

He felt a lump in his throat as he read the letter to them. Both nuns also found it difficult to control their emotions as they listened to the touching words in the note.

After regaining her composure, Sister Annette said, "Well, we will have to give them names. We can't simply call them Baby One and Baby Two!"

Father Pat watched as the child that Sister Dorothea was holding laid his head on her chest. Then he glanced up at the painting of the Last Supper that hung on the wall. It was the scene where the beloved apostle, John, laid his head on Jesus's chest.

"I have their names! The one that Sister Dorothea is holding will be named John. And the child that you are holding will be named James."

Sister Annette burst out laughing when Father Pat explained how he arrived at the names. Sister Dorothea, who was used to her friend, simply raised an eyebrow and looked at Sister Annette.

"What's so funny, Sister?" asked Father Pat.

The nun explained, "I was just thinking about the thunder earlier tonight and remembered that Jesus called the two brothers—James and John— 'Sons of Thunder.'"

Father Pat tilted his head back and laughed along with the sisters— Sister Dorothea demurely, with a hand over her lips, and Sister Annette with a sparkle in her eye. He felt very much as though God himself had played a role in this fateful evening. Then, the nuns wrapped the babies in blankets, placed them in the baskets, and prepared to leave. Father Pat blessed each child and could not stop thanking the nuns.

Just as they were walking out, he remembered something and said, "Sisters, bring these 'Sons of Thunder' to the church tomorrow at noon-time. We will baptize them, with all the parishioners as their honorary godparents."

Father Pat also made a mental note to speak with Frank Palmer at the Department of Children and Families. Frank was an old and very dear friend. He would definitely be at Sunday mass. The priest planned on scheduling a meeting with Frank for Monday morning.

# 2

# The Adoption

**Reverend Patrick J. Donnelly**
**Rectory | July 1961**

FATHER PAT AWOKE early the next morning in preparation for the three Sunday masses, which would be well attended. It was a beautiful sunny morning—almost the complete opposite of the previous night. As the parishioners entered the church, Father Pat was there to greet them, with an extra twinkle in his eyes because he was about to deliver a very special message.

The Gospel reading was from Mark that day. Just prior to mass, Father Pat reread the scripture to himself, knowing that this was truly a message from God. This particular reading was from chapter 9, when Jesus responded to the question about who was the greatest in the kingdom of God. The most poignant lines for Father Pat were the following:

> Taking a child He placed it in their midst, and putting
> His arms around it He said to them, whoever receives
> one child as this in my name, receives me; and whoever
> receives me, receives not me but the One who sent me.
> (Mark 9:36–37)

Father Pat was a powerful orator, but today, feeling moved with compassion, he was even more forceful as he proclaimed this Gospel passage. He was about to give his parishioners an extraordinary homily.

"Brothers and sisters, Jesus tells us that whoever receives one child in his name welcomes both him and his heavenly Father. Today, we have the opportunity to truly bring this Gospel message to life. In fact, we have twice the opportunity to do so!" He paused and gave them a broad grin. "Last evening, we received two very special packages from our Lord."

He went on to explain what had occurred the previous evening, including how he and the good sisters decided on the names for the children. Then, in an effort to reach out to the mother of the infants, he said, "Clearly, the decision to give up a child is a difficult one. We can only imagine what brings a mother to part with her children. She must be feeling very sad and lonely right now. We are not here to judge! Rather, we choose to reach out and say to that woman—just as the angel Gabriel said to Mary— 'Do not be afraid . . . God can do anything.' Our message for this mother is that we are here for you. We can help you and these beautiful babies through whatever challenges you are facing. God will provide!"

Father Pat closed his homily by inviting all of the parishioners to the baptism at noon. He suspected that many of them would spread the word. It was possible that someone might know something about the mother of these babies. Perhaps the infants could be reunited with her. Another possibility was that a young couple from the parish might approach him about adopting the two boys. While the priest had never dealt with abandoned children in the past, he was confident that a loving home would be found for these infants.

Father Pat repeated the same heartfelt message at each of the masses, and his parishioners did not let him down. The church was packed for the baptism. While Sisters Dorothea and Annette stood with him at the baptismal font, he explained to all of the parishioners that they should consider themselves honorary godparents to James and John.

Several times during the baptism, he looked out at the congregation with much gratitude. He was overwhelmed by their warm response. One time, he looked up and noticed a young, unfamiliar woman in the back of the church. She was very beautiful, with long brown hair and an olive complexion. Even from this distance, he saw that she had a sad expression on her face. It wasn't sympathy in that expression but something more . . . something that somehow felt *personal*. Could it be? Had he been speaking indirectly with the mother of these two infants all this time without even realizing it? He would seek her out after the ceremony.

As soon as the baptism was finished, he attempted to hurry down the side aisle, but he was delayed by the many parishioners who wanted to speak with him. By the time he finally reached the back of the church, the young woman was gone.

Father Pat was hopeful that she would be inspired to come forward. He discussed his suspicion with Sister Dorothea, who challenged him.

"Father Pat, how can you be sure this woman was their mother? She could have simply been at mass and stayed for the baptism. The sorrowful expression could have been for something else. She may have broken off a relationship, or she may want children of her own. I think you may be telling yourself a story, Father."

The pastor thought about what Sister Dorothea had just said. He was silent for several seconds before saying, "Perhaps you're right, Sister. Maybe it was a little wishful thinking on my part. Do you think there are any young couples within the parish who would like to adopt these beautiful infants?"

"Possibly," she replied, brows furrowed in thought. "I would hope so. I'll put thought into this tonight, Father Pat."

Monday morning arrived, and it was another bright, sunny day. Father Pat woke up at his normal six o'clock, after which he said his morning prayers, held mass, and found himself going through his typical routine (down to his cup of black coffee and bowl of oatmeal) almost perfectly. And yet, this morning was somehow different.

He couldn't stop thinking about the two abandoned babies and the upcoming meeting with the authorities. He felt many different emotions—concern for the well-being of these infants, confusion as to what would drive someone to abandon their children, frustration at not being able to fix the problem, and excitement at having these beautiful gifts left on his doorstep.

He asked God for an extra dose of strength and guidance.

The convent was more lively than normal that morning. The nuns were excited about caring for the babies, John and James, even if it was only for a brief period. The motherly instinct was clearly evident in each one of them. On Sunday afternoon, Father Pat was touched to host several parishioners who had stopped by, bringing gifts for their "godchildren" that included baby formula, blankets, clothes, plenty of diapers, and two brand-new cribs.

Later, when Father Pat's longtime friend Frank Palmer arrived, he was once again moved by the community's ability to come together for a common cause.

"Frank," Father Pat said, opening the convent's door wide for him to enter, "thank you so much for coming. I wasn't sure you'd make it today, seeing as we just spoke yesterday morning."

"Normally, I doubt I would've," Frank joked, walking inside. Following behind him were two other people Father Pat hadn't met before. "But these are special circumstances, aren't they, Father? Which is why I've brought along my trusted friends and colleagues Chuck Goodman and Louise Arturo."

Father Pat stepped forward, shaking their hands warmly. "It's wonderful to meet you."

Chuck and Louise nodded in unison before everyone's attention fell back to Frank, whose round face—framed only by a dollop of hair—broadened with a smile. Father Pat knew this was a topic near and dear to Frank's heart, seeing as his own son, Jesse, was once his fifth-grade student. When Jesse informed Frank that his foster parents weren't able to keep him any longer and he was to be transferred to an unknown home, Frank and his wife made the remarkable and loving decision to adopt him.

"How's Jesse?" Father Pat asked, clapping Frank on the shoulder amicably.

"He's excellent, Father, just excellent," Frank reported proudly. "He just graduated with high honors from college and is now working in an accounting firm in Boston . . . I couldn't be prouder of the kid, honestly."

"That's great, Frank. I'm happy to hear it."

Dr. McDonald was already in one of the bedrooms, examining the infants. The others met in the dining room of the convent—a large room with a beautiful mahogany table that could easily accommodate up to twelve people, where the sisters had their dinners. The room had white wainscoting halfway up the wall, and the rest was painted a light blue, giving the impression of a clear summer sky. The windows on the east side of the convent filled the room with warm sunlight. The walls were tastefully decorated with religious prints. Naturally, there was a larger print of the Last Supper above the buffet table. Father Pat smiled as he thought about how he had decided on the names for the children.

There was coffee on the sideboard, along with some freshly baked chocolate chip cookies.

The priest sat at the head of the table and began chewing his second cookie. Frank and his associates each took a cup of coffee and a cookie, joining the priest at the table.

They exchanged pleasantries as they waited for the doctor. A few minutes later, he entered with Sisters Dorothea and Annette, each carrying one of the babies. Dr. McDonald shared his observations. "I am pleased to report that these infants are in excellent health! I estimate they're about two months old. It's obvious these babies have been well cared for since birth."

Father Pat retold the story of the infants being left at his doorstep on Saturday evening. He then explained how he had hoped to reunite the children with their mother. He even shared his suspicion about the young woman in the back of the church, acknowledging—as he glanced at Sister Dorothea—that it may have been some wishful thinking on his part. He then asked Frank to describe the next steps.

"Child protective services takes custody of the babies and attempts to find any relatives. If none are found, we will then look for couples who are willing to be foster or adoptive parents," Frank explained.

Sister Dorothea listened intently as Frank disclosed the process. When he paused, she asked, "Frank, when you say that child protective services takes custody of the babies, who *actually* takes the children?"

"Sister, we place the children into what we call substitute care, which is usually a foster home."

The nun looked directly at Father Pat. Given their long history of working together, he already knew where she was going with her question. He smiled and gave her a slight nod, indicating his approval and support.

"So, Frank," asked Sister Dorothea, "could the sisters and I be qualified for the substitute care while you look for a relative or a couple to adopt the children?"

Louise, who had observed the eye contact between the priest and the nun, was the first to respond. "Frank, I think that would be an excellent way to care for these infants during this time. With school being out for the summer, the children would have ten wonderful women caring for them."

"And one outstanding gentleman!" added Father Pat with a wink and a smile.

Frank looked at Chuck, who nodded his agreement. Frank seemed to think about it for several moments before saying, "This is highly unusual, but given the circumstances, I think we can get it approved. In fact, this will give us the opportunity to focus the majority of our time on finding a relative or an adoptive couple for these children. We know the babies will be well cared for, and Louise can check in on them periodically."

A regular visitation plan for Louise was agreed upon, and Frank promised to have the necessary legal paperwork signed before the end of the week. When it was all said and done, Father Pat shared the news with the other nuns, and needless to say, they were extremely happy with the announcement. They understood that it was only temporary but nevertheless were elated that they would be watching over these two beautiful babies a little longer.

Soon after that, a schedule was developed among the nuns. Louise had been correct in her expectation about the loving devotion the children would receive. In fact, during her regular visits, she would often comment that she had never seen a better level of care for foster children. Father Pat was extremely pleased—but not surprised—by this observation.

Another part of the routine was Father Pat's afternoon visits to the convent. Unless he had a scheduled meeting, he would make his way over to the convent and ask to see the babies. He would then take one of the infants in his arms and walk over to the back porch. There, he would sit in the large wicker rocking chair and begin speaking to the child about everything.

"So, Johnny, let me tell you about my day. I met with the finance committee right after morning mass. And you know what they want me to do? They want me to ask the parishioners to increase their weekly donations. I really hate asking them for more money. These folks have already been so generous to the church, and I'm sure they have plenty of other expenses. What is that you just said? Yes, you are right, my boy. We do need the additional funds to repair the steps of the church. I know I have to do it; it just makes me feel so uncomfortable!"

Then, after about a half hour, he would return the one baby and take the second child to begin the same ritual.

"How was your day, Jimmy? What's that, Sister Annette kept you laughing? Yes, she is quite the jokester, that one!"

Even at this young age, Father Pat discerned a difference in their personalities. John was always very easygoing. He rarely got cranky and seemed completely comfortable being held. James, on the other hand, was in constant motion. He would often twist and turn as if he wanted to get up and take a walk. He would grab for the priest's glasses and was frequently successful in taking them off. Father Pat would enjoy these wrestling matches with Jimmy and laughed uncontrollably whenever the baby was able to pull off his glasses. Sister Dorothea would spy good-naturedly on Father Pat and the children from the large window facing the porch. She told Sister Annette and the other nuns that Father Pat would absolutely glow whenever he was with the infants.

Several weeks went by, and then on one Wednesday afternoon, Frank Palmer called Father Pat. He said that they would like to meet with the priest and the nuns to discuss the status of their investigation. Father Pat noticed that his friend's tone of voice and demeanor over the phone were much more serious than normal. They agreed to meet on Friday morning. Frank said that Chuck and Louise would be accompanying him. Father Pat immediately called Sister Dorothea to inform her of the meeting, telling her that he was not sure what to expect but that he had an uneasy feeling, given the tone of Frank's voice.

Friday morning arrived, and as Father Pat began his morning prayers, he said a special prayer to Saint Joseph, who had always been his go-to saint for special intercessions. He thought it was especially appropriate today, since Saint Joseph was the foster father of Jesus. He knelt before the lifelike statue of Saint Joseph above the side altar of the church and began to pray.

*Dear Saint Joseph, I'm feeling especially anxious today about the fate of Johnny and Jimmy. Would you please speak to your boy Jesus for me? Ask him to bless these two darling children and to make sure that they find a loving home.*

Frank, Chuck, and Louise arrived promptly at ten o'clock. Father Pat and Sisters Dorothea and Annette were already waiting for them in the dining room of the convent. The babies were in the bedroom that had been set aside for them. After some pleasantries, Frank got down to business.

"Louise tells me that she has never seen better caretaking of any foster children than what the wonderful sisters have provided!"

This brought a big smile to the faces of the two nuns. *What a pleasant way to start the meeting,* Father Pat thought to himself. *Maybe my uneasiness was unfounded.* He began to relax.

Frank continued, "Because of the excellent care of these two children, we were able to focus all of our attention on finding a suitable home for them. Chuck took the lead in attempting to find a relative or someone who might know the mother. Louise concentrated on finding suitable adoptive parents . . ."

Frank paused for a beat that stretched into a long silence, prompting Father Pat's palms to sweat and his heart to rapidly pick up its pace. Then, after what felt like an eternity, Frank said, "Of these suitable adoptive parents, many of them are very willing and able to provide a loving home."

Father Pat held his breath, sensing that there was a "but" coming.

And he was absolutely correct.

"But," Frank went on, "there is a problem. None of these families feel capable of taking on two babies at this time. They are willing and able to care for one child only."

There was another long, uneasy silence.

Father Pat felt his heart break. Separating the babies? That felt incredibly cruel, like a mistake with irrevocable repercussions that would haunt—

He couldn't finish his thought.

Frank continued, "So, we are proposing that we separate the children in order to provide the type of home that will ensure their well-being."

Father Pat, who rarely lost his temper, felt his heartbreak transform into outrage. Heat rose to his cheeks, anger and despair reaching a boiling point in his chest. Sister Dorothea glanced his way, eyes widening at his unusual and very open display of emotion, and quickly spoke up.

"Do you mean that you would allow these two brothers to grow up apart?"

Louise pursed her lips, as though carefully considering each word before speaking it aloud. "It is the only feasible option, given the circumstances."

By this time, Father Pat had regained some of his composure, and he looked directly at Louise and Frank as he stated in a firm voice, "No, that's not a feasible option! These children have already been separated from the mother who gave them birth. God only knows what led that poor woman to give up these two beautiful babies. Now you are proposing to separate them from each other. That would be a tragedy!"

Frank looked blankly back at Father Pat—as though he very much expected this reaction but not the degree of emotion with which it was being delivered.

Taking advantage of Frank's silence, Father Pat looked at Sisters Dorothea and Annette before continuing. This time, he got a slight nod from Sister Dorothea and knew that he had her full support.

"I have a much better proposal," he began, steadying his voice, "one that will keep these two brothers together, provide them with excellent care, and ensure that they will grow up in a loving environment that will afford them an excellent education and exceptional role models." Father Pat spoke with passionate determination. He'd already processed everything in his head and made the decision. "I will adopt these children!"

Frank's eyes widened a fraction before flicking to Louise at his side, who had clasped her hand over her mouth in surprise.

Before they could interject, Father Pat added, "The good sisters will help me to care for them. Louise has already given them an outstanding evaluation. When the boys are old enough, they will attend school right here. With so many wonderful families in our parish, they will have the opportunity to meet and interact with plenty of other children. Their physical, mental, and spiritual well-being will be our primary objectives."

There was another very long silence before Frank responded. "Father Pat, it's obvious that you have very deep feelings for these two infants, but I'm not convinced that you fully realize the challenges in raising these children." Father Pat opened his mouth to reply, but Frank only kept going. "Outside of that, there are legal matters to concern ourselves with. I'm not sure your bishop would allow you to take on such a responsibility, and even if he did, I'm not certain that I can get the folks in Boston to sign off on this arrangement."

Father Pat was on a mission, however, and he was fully prepared to handle any objection.

In his peripheral vision, he saw Sisters Dorothea and Annette glance at each other, each of them nodding their quiet approval. Fortified by their support, Father Pat looked his friend in the eye and calmly said, "Frank, no parent—biological or adoptive—fully appreciates all of the challenges in raising children beforehand. It would be great if children came with instructions, but they don't, and I'm sure that I will make mistakes along the way. But I'll learn from these mistakes, just as I've always learned and adapted in the past. I'll also have some very watchful eyes keeping me in check. The most important part of being a parent will be unconditional love and trusting that God will guide me. As far as approval from my bishop, I have many unpaid favors owed to me from the good bishop. I can't think of a better reason to collect on them. And, Frank, you've told me about the numerous times that you have gone above and beyond for the folks in Boston. I'm absolutely convinced that you can make this happen."

Frank nodded in silence, swallowing hard. It was impossible to tell what he was thinking. Father Pat felt the touch of Sister Dorothea's hand falling on his forearm, a silent vow of support, which was a sentiment that Sister Annette likely shared as well.

Whatever was to happen, he'd get through this. He knew that. But he wouldn't be able to live with himself if he didn't fight for Johnny and Jimmy—it was the least he could do for those two boys, and he felt emboldened by God to do so.

Finally, Frank nodded with a smile and said, "I have rarely been able to win an argument with you, my friend, and it's clear that I'm not going to win this one." Father Pat and the sisters sighed in relief and excitement, exchanging elated grins. "You raise some excellent points. I have often wished that my kids had come with printed directions. Unconditional love, learning from our mistakes, adjusting to changing circumstances, and always trusting in God seem to be pretty good guidelines. You will start off as a foster parent. After an adequate period of evaluation, you will apply for full adoption. I'll push this up the chain of command and ask you to do the same. It will take a few months to get the formal approvals. Will you be able to get the bishop's blessing within that time frame?"

Father Pat was beaming when he responded, "I'll have his approval by this afternoon!"

He thought about his prayer to Saint Joseph earlier in the morning and knew that his go-to saint had come through again. That afternoon, he placed a candle before the statue of Saint Joseph and said a special prayer of thanksgiving.

*Dear Saint Joseph, I'm so grateful for this amazing opportunity. Johnny and Jimmy are truly a blessing from God. It will definitely wipe out that complacency I was starting to feel. This is one of the happiest days of my life!*

# 3

## Raising Sons of Thunder

**Reverend Patrick J. Donnelly**
**Rectory | 1961–1975**

AFTER SOME THOUGHTFUL pushback, the bishop agreed to Father Pat's request, convinced that if anyone could pull it off, it would be this remarkable pastor. The bishop gave the priest his approval and blessing. In less than two months, Frank was also able to obtain formal consent from his superiors. The paperwork was signed, and Father Pat became the foster father of James and John.

The nuns had prepared a little celebration to honor the special event. As the cake was cut and coffee served, Sister Annette sat up a little straighter, eyes bright with happiness, and asked, "So, Father Pat, when the children are old enough to speak, what will they call you? Daddy, Pop, or Father Dad?"

By the time she finished her question, she was laughing uncontrollably, and Sister Dorothea gave her a raised-eyebrow look.

Father Pat smiled. "Well, Sister, I think 'Father' will be just fine."

It was decided that until the boys were older, they would remain in the convent. With school starting in September, the sisters established a schedule to care for the children. Father Pat continued his daily visits and, in fact, would extend them as much as possible. He even became comfortable with feeding his sons. The changing of diapers was a bit of a challenge at first, but with guidance from the nuns, he got the hang of it. He learned very quickly to cover the private area before bending down to get a clean diaper. The first time he failed to do so, he experienced a tiny shower. Naturally, Sister Annette was quick to share this humorous story with everyone who would listen.

The next few months seemed to pass very quickly. By Christmas, the boys were already teething, causing more than a few sleepless nights at the convent. And Father Pat found out the hard way when Jimmy took a bite out of his finger. It was the middle of January when James started crawling; John followed his brother the next month. This brought a whole new round of entertainment for the nuns as they watched Father Pat on his hands and knees, chasing his two sons around the convent.

By the time they reached early May, as they were preparing for First Communion, Father Pat realized it was time to consider one of the biggest milestones yet for the boys.

"Sister," he said one evening, finding Sister Dorothea taking her tea outside in the garden now that it was finally warm enough to do so. "We've got an exciting event coming up this month."

Sister Dorothea's brows shot up. "We do?"

"Indeed." He paused, relishing the suspense—only for Sister Dorothea to swat him on the arm playfully and demand an answer. "We need," he went on, smiling broadly, "to celebrate the first birthday of our boys."

Sister Dorothea beamed as she realized that this was a very special occasion. Then in the next instant, with one eyebrow raised and her forehead scrunched up, she stated, "But, Father Pat, we don't know the actual date these children were born."

"Dr. McDonald estimated that they were about two months old when they were left on our doorstep. That would mean they were born in May, the month of Mary. So, let's choose May 15."

"That's an excellent idea, Father. What kind of celebration?"

"Oh, nothing elaborate. I thought we could have it at the convent and invite Frank and his team to join us."

The actual birthday celebration turned out to be a lot more extensive once word leaked out to the parishioners, who wanted to attend the party because the two boys had become such an important part of the parish family. By the time everything was arranged, it was clear the venue would have to be changed from the convent to the much larger church hall. Larry, whose family had operated the local bakery for half a century, donated a beautiful vanilla buttercream birthday cake with a layer of fresh spring fruit in the center. Giovanni, who owned the Italian restaurant in town, catered the event and refused to accept any payment. The stuffed manicotti and the oversize meatballs were a big hit. Others brought toys and clothes for the two boys.

Father Pat was beaming and could not conceal his joy. Everyone joined in singing "Happy Birthday," and the priest bent down to help his sons blow out their candles. Johnny looked up at the priest, smiled, and said, "Fa-da." Not to be outdone by his twin, Jimmy uttered the words "fa-da pa," which would eventually evolve into "Father Pat"—their permanent name for him. The priest was overjoyed, and he lovingly hugged each child. Remembering her question about what the children would call him, Sister Annette smiled and wiped a tear of joy from her eye.

The twins quickly added to their vocabulary, and they each started walking by early summer. The next major milestone was when Frank came with the formal adoption papers. Naturally, this was the impetus for another celebration.

The years went by, and the boys started school. In reality, the nuns had been teaching them for the past four years, so the transition to a formal classroom was a nonevent for the twins. The most significant transition was interacting with other children on a daily basis. While James was slightly more outgoing, both boys seemed to enjoy being around the other students.

Shortly after the boys started school, Father Pat was in his office going through the mail when he was pleasantly surprised. He'd received a certified bank check for $500 in the mail with a typed note.

> *Dear Father Pat,*
> *You have done a wonderful job raising James and John.*
> *Please accept this gift on their behalf.*
> *Use it in whatever way you think best.*
> *May God continue to bless you and these wonderful children!*

He stared at the note and then, remembering a previous letter, smiled, with a strong suspicion of who had sent the money.

Each year, the amount increased, and over time, the checks would be for several thousand dollars. The envelopes had no return address, and the postmark was always from a different city, sometimes even a different country. Father Pat opened up bank accounts for each boy. He intended for all the money to be used for their college education.

By the time the boys were seven and preparing for First Communion, the bishop had assigned an assistant pastor to the parish. He did this for two reasons: First, the parish, under Father Pat's dynamic leadership, continued to grow and prosper. So, the bishop thought the pastor could use the extra help. Second, he believed that Father Pat would be an excellent mentor for this young priest. He was correct on both counts.

Father Jason, who was in his early thirties, had recently been ordained and was excited to learn from Father Pat, whom he'd heard many wonderful things about. He was a big man—both in height and weight—and had wavy blond hair, blue eyes, and a round, boyish face. Most people thought he was of Scandinavian descent, but his grandparents had actually emigrated from northern Italy.

Father Pat loved watching his sons play together. One of the things that amazed him the most was how well James and John got along. He could not remember ever seeing the two boys argue with each other. Father Pat wondered if there was a special connection between twins, because this was a far cry from his childhood. He had grown up with three brothers, and rarely did a day pass without an argument among his siblings. Sometimes those arguments turned quite physical. Although the four brothers became the best of friends as adults, his mother continued blaming them for turning her hair gray.

Both sons added to Father Pat's pride by doing well in school. Sister Dorothea said that they were both exceptionally bright. Johnny was the more studious of the two brothers, whereas Jimmy could easily be distracted but still seemed to readily grasp the material.

When they were in the fifth grade, Father Pat suggested that his sons consider becoming altar servers. It was his style to *suggest* rather than to *tell*.

He wanted it to be their decision, not his. He explained that participating in the mass as servers was an excellent way to honor the Lord. John was thrilled at the opportunity to serve at mass and quickly agreed to it. With some friendly nagging from his brother, James also agreed to become an altar server. So, Father Jason began the training, and on the day they celebrated their eleventh birthdays, James and John served their first mass together. Father Pat had an extra glow on his face that day.

Shortly after the two had become altar boys, Father Pat received a disturbing call from Sister Dorothea.

"Father, please come to my office immediately."

His heart began to beat rapidly as he immediately thought about his sons.

"What is it, Sister? Did something happen to the boys?"

"The boys are safe, but they have been in a fistfight."

"A fight? Oh my! I'll be right there."

Father Pat rushed to the school. When he got to the office, he saw his two sons and another boy—Tommy Smith—sitting in the hallway. Johnny looked like he had been crying. James was red-faced and appeared angry and embarrassed. Tommy looked like he also had been crying and was holding a tissue to his bloodied nose.

Father Pat simply looked at each boy with concern and confusion but did not say anything. He walked into Sister Dorothea's office, where both she and Sister Annette were waiting. He asked what had happened, and Sister Annette explained.

"It was recess, and I was on the other side of the playground when I heard a lot of yelling going on. I rushed over and saw Jimmy on top of Tommy, beating the daylights out of him. Johnny kept saying, 'I'm sorry, Jimmy—please stop!' It took all my strength to pull James off Tommy. Once I was able to separate them, I marched the three of them into the office, and then we called you."

Father Pat remembered his statement to Frank Palmer eleven years before about children not coming with instructions. *This is one of those times, isn't it, Frank?* he thought to himself. *I really could use an instruction manual right about now.*

Father Pat stared at the ceiling for a moment in silent prayer and then turned to Sister Annette. "Please bring the three boys into the office, Sister." When the boys arrived, he spoke in a low, serious tone. "Which one of you is going to explain what happened today?"

There was dead silence for several seconds, and then Johnny spoke up.

"It was my fault, Father Pat. I caused the fight." He spoke haltingly, and his eyes darted nervously from his father to the other two boys.

Father Pat's brows furrowed. Hadn't James been the one doing the fighting? How could it have been John's fault? But before he could ask John what he meant, James spoke up.

"It wasn't your fault, Johnny; it was mine. I'm the one who got mad and started hitting Tommy. I—"

Before James could finish his sentence, Tommy interrupted. "No, Father Pat—it wasn't Johnny or Jimmy who caused the fight. Please, please don't punish them! It was my fault. I said something . . . something terrible to Johnny, and it upset him. He told Jimmy what I said, and I deserved what I got."

The priest and the two nuns looked at each other with both astonishment and relief. Father Pat thought to himself that the Holy Spirit was guiding this resolution, but he was curious about what Tommy had said.

He placed his hand on Tommy's shoulder, looked directly into his eyes, and said, "What you just said took a lot of courage, Tommy. I'm curious as to why you are stepping up and taking the blame for what happened."

Tommy hesitated, looking at the other two boys, and then began to explain. "I . . . I think I was jealous. Johnny is always telling the rest of us how great you are to have as a father. He has talked about all the stuff you guys and Father Jason do together—the hikes, the movies, the games you play, the books you read." Something about Tommy's expression darkened. His gaze dropped to his feet. "I don't have that kind of relationship with my dad. Don't get me wrong, he's always good to me, and I love him . . . but with running his own business, he's hardly ever around. We aren't able to do any of the things that the four of you do together. I was especially disappointed this past weekend. My dad and I were supposed to go on a fishing trip together. We had planned it for weeks. Then, on Saturday morning, just before we were going to leave, he got a call from his plant manager. There was some problem, and he had to cancel our fishing trip. So, when Johnny started talking about the great weekend you had, I just lashed out and said something terrible."

Father Pat realized how difficult this admission was for Tommy. He asked Tommy what he had said that upset Johnny.

"I said that their mother didn't love them, and . . . that was why she left them."

Father Pat couldn't stop his intake of breath. Sister Dorothea's lips flattened into a hard line, while Sister Annette brought a hand to her mouth, as though silencing a cry. It was a hurtful thing to say, no doubt about it, but . . .

He'd known this day would come. Eventually. And as painful as this incident was, he was sure it wouldn't be the last.

Tommy's eyes filled with genuine tears. "I am so sorry . . . so very sorry! Please," he added, glancing at the twins beside him, "please forgive me, Jimmy and Johnny. That was so wrong of me to do. I was feeling hurt, and I took it out on you."

James immediately turned to the other boy, stuck out his hand, and said, "I'm really sorry, Tommy. I let my temper get the best of me."

"I'm sorry, too, Tommy," added John. "I shouldn't be bragging so much." Then, turning to his father, he asked, "Father Pat, would it be all right if Tommy came on the next hike with us?"

Father Pat, whose heart was bursting with pride at the way his sons had responded, answered, "I think that would be a marvelous idea!" From that point on, Tommy would often join them on their weekend adventures. After a friendly conversation initiated by Father Pat, Tommy's father frequently participated in their activities.

That evening after dinner, Father Pat asked the twins to sit on the living room couch while he got something to share with them. James gave his brother a questioning glance. John just shrugged his shoulders. Father Pat went into his office and came out with an envelope. He pulled out a folded piece of paper and sat down in his leather chair.

"When your mother left you on my doorstep, she also left a letter. I've been waiting for the right time to share it with you. After what happened today, I think tonight is a perfect time to share it."

The priest began to read the letter slowly and with deep emotion. Even after all these years, it still touched his heart, just as it had that first evening.

By the time he finished reading the letter, all three of them had tears running down their cheeks. The boys got up from the couch, and each put an arm around Father Pat's shoulders. He handed the letter to James, who just stared at it for several seconds.

Father Pat held each boy close to him, and in his warm, soothing voice, he said, "So, you see, boys, your mother loved you a lot. Something terrible must have happened, and she felt that she wouldn't be able to give you a good home. I know that she still loves you, and I truly believe God will reunite her with you again someday. I don't know when or how, but I do know that it will be a very, very special day!"

Father Pat told the boys where he kept the letter in his office, and he gave them permission to take it out and read it as often as they liked. From that day forward, each boy would frequently go to the office and reread the letter. That night in bed, before going to sleep, the two brothers could not stop thinking about the letter and what Father Pat had said.

"Do you think Father Pat is right . . . that someday, we will get to meet her? Where do you think she lives? Do you think she knows where we are?" Johnny asked, staring at the dark ceiling overhead, voice a whisper.

After considering his brother's questions, James responded, "I don't know. We don't know why she had to give us up. I have no clue as to where she might be or if she even knows what's happened to us."

"I know in my heart that someday, some way, God will bring us together with her again!"

"I really hope you're right," James whispered, trying to envision a future in which his mother played a role in his life. "I really, *really* hope you're right."

# 4

# The High School Years

**Reverend Patrick J. Donnelly**
**Rectory | 1975–1979**

FATHER PAT AND Father Jason were sitting on the front porch of the rectory, discussing the boys.

"Johnny has always been the more sensitive one—even when he was an infant," Father Pat said. "I remember holding him in my arms, and he would be so gentle and peaceful. Jimmy would always be squirming and kicking. It was a real wrestling match with him!"

"I can just imagine what they were like as toddlers. John is also the more spiritual of the two."

"You are absolutely correct with that observation. Johnny received the Holy Spirit, and Jimmy got the *wild* one! In fact, that's the only way I can really ever tell them apart—by their personalities."

"John takes his altar server role very seriously, Father Pat. You probably know that he is already considering the priesthood. He asks me about the seminary regularly."

"I'm not surprised. I've watched him, and whenever he is on the altar, he is completely focused—captivated—by every aspect of the mass. Johnny is the one who wants to serve a greater purpose by channeling good into the world. Who knows—maybe he'll take over for us someday." Father Pat smiled with pride as he imagined John saying mass and giving an inspirational homily. "On the other hand, Jimmy is always so easily distracted while serving on the altar."

"Yes, I noticed," Father Jason agreed, "especially whenever a cute girl sits in the front pew. By the way, I also realized that the altar wine ran out more quickly when Jimmy served at mass. So, I decided to replace the wine with bitter red wine vinegar on a day he was scheduled to serve. Since then, the wine doesn't seem to disappear as fast!"

Father Pat's hand immediately went to his forehead, and he just shook his head. "Sometimes that boy worries me!"

"Pat, you shouldn't worry. You've done a great job raising him. Jimmy has a good heart, and in the end, he'll always do what's right."

"Yes . . . yes, you're correct. In the end, he'll always do the right thing!"

"But it probably won't hurt for us to keep an eye on your scotch," Father Jason said with a wink and a smile.

The differences between the boys were apparent in school as well. While both boys were naturally very bright and gifted, John continued to be the more studious of the two. He always completed his assignments on time and was well prepared for any upcoming test. James, on the other hand, was regularly late in finishing his homework and waited until the very last day to study for his exams. Whenever Father Pat or Sister Dorothea would sit with him to discuss his lack of effort, James would always promise to do better. He actually did improve his performance for a while, but then he would slip into his bad habits again. Consequently, John was a consistent A student, and James was generally a B student.

There was also another noticeable difference between the two brothers. James had a very quick temper and could easily lose it when he felt that someone was offending him. His anger never affected his relationship with his brother because John always had a way of diffusing the situation with humor or a quick retort. He could easily come up with a witty comment or a thoughtful phrase that would disarm James. Unfortunately, John was not always around when James got angry with someone else. At a minimum, these incidents ended in shouting matches. However, sometimes there was pushing and shoving or, worse yet, an actual fistfight.

After each incident was over and James had time to reflect on what happened, he regretted the way he reacted. He would actually chastise himself over it and wish that he would have handled the situation differently. Father Pat and James had several discussions about this behavior.

"One day, that temper is going to get you into serious trouble!"

"I know! I'm really sorry! I feel like such a jerk. I don't know what gets into me. I can actually feel myself losing it, and once I sink into that hole, I can't get out. I feel so bad!"

"You're a good boy, and I love you dearly. The devil finds our weaknesses and leverages them against us. Your weakness is your temper. We all get angry sometimes. That's human! The important thing is to recognize what really got us angry and to change the way we react to the situation. Sometimes it is as simple as walking away when you sense yourself getting close to that hole you mentioned."

These conversations would usually end with James hugging his father and promising to try harder. And just like with the schoolwork, for a while, it would be better, but eventually, James would regress.

The teenage years brought a new set of challenges for Father Pat and a new set of opportunities for his sons. The parish school ended at eighth grade, so the twins attended the regional high school. They were no longer under the watchful eyes of Sisters Dorothea and Annette. This was less of an issue for John, who continued to be a serious and focused student. James, on the other hand, took advantage of his newfound freedom. This was also when puberty kicked in. The girls were naturally attracted to the tanned, good-looking twins with wavy black hair and piercing blue eyes. John was still considering the priesthood, so he was less responsive to the flirtations. James, on the other hand—who had no interest in the priesthood—fully embraced the opportunity. He dated several girls during his high school years. While things got intense at times, he ultimately treated the girls with respect, thanks to the positive influence of Father Pat and the nuns.

The high school years were also when the brothers learned to drive. Father Pat delegated this task to Father Jason.

"Father Jason, I'm afraid that I would lose whatever hair I have left if I tried teaching them how to drive."

Father Jason, who had developed a very strong relationship with the boys, was happy to help them through this rite of passage.

"No problem, Father Pat. I have plenty of hair, and this assignment will help me to work on that wonderful virtue of patience!"

James, who seemed to think stop signs and speed limits were merely suggestions, certainly tested Father Jason's patience.

Attending public school gave the boys the opportunity to try out for sports. Both had natural athletic abilities that enabled them to be solid team players. Neither was a superstar; rather, the coaches considered them to be dependable and dedicated. Except for baseball, they chose different sports. John enjoyed track and basketball, whereas James went out for football and wrestling. Father Pat made an insightful observation to Father Jason.

"There are fewer angry episodes when Jimmy is playing football or wrestling. He's able to channel his aggressive behavior in a more constructive way."

Schoolwork followed the normal pattern, with John being the more studious of the two boys. He graduated in the top ten of his class and was accepted at Boston College. James was further down in the ranking—not because of his intellect but due to his lack of effort. He was accepted at the University of Massachusetts.

John was still considering the priesthood, but he was not entirely sure at this point in his life. After several long conversations with Father Jason, he decided to do a double major—theology and general management. Boston College was founded by the Jesuits, who believed that a liberal arts education provided a solid foundation for learning. Students were encouraged to pursue double majors. Boston College was located in Chestnut Hill, about ten miles outside of Boston.

James decided he would major in business, specifically accounting. He would attend the Harvard campus on Columbia Point Peninsula, which was surrounded by Dorchester Bay. The campus, which was just five miles outside of Boston, was relatively new, and the JFK Presidential Library had just been completed next to it.

Although he was proud that both boys were starting a new and exciting chapter in their lives, Father Pat knew he was going to miss them.

A few weeks before they left for college, John approached his father with something that was on his mind.

"Father Pat, I've got a concern."

"What's the matter?"

John looked directly into his father's eyes and gently placed his hand on the priest's shoulder. Father Pat sensed the anxiety in his son and wondered what could be troubling him.

"I know college isn't cheap, and I know you haven't made a lot of money as a priest. I'm just concerned that you're taking money from your retirement savings to pay for our college. You're over seventy, and I'm worried about you."

Father Pat sighed with relief and smiled with immense pride at his son. He knew in his heart that whatever path John chose, he would always be deeply compassionate toward others.

"Don't you worry! God always provides. Everything is going to be fine."

Father Pat decided to share something important with his sons that evening. They had just finished dinner, and this was when the four of them usually spent time discussing various topics. Tonight, Father Pat had something very specific to share.

As the four of them gathered in the living room, Father Pat spoke. "Boys—I should say, *men*—now that you're going off to college, I want to discuss something with you." He smiled at his sons before continuing. "John came to me with a concern."

James turned to his brother with an inquisitive expression. John simply nodded toward Father Pat, as if to say, *Just listen.* The two brothers always had this silent way of communicating with each other.

"Johnny was worried about the cost of college and that it might wipe out my retirement savings. I told him that he shouldn't be concerned because God would provide."

Before Father Pat could continue, James wisecracked, "So, Father Pat, are you telling us that you're just going to steal the money from the collection baskets?"

Father Pat, who was used to James's humor, simply shook his head, laughed, and said, "No, Jimmy, I am not a crook! And I hope that you never think about becoming one, either. God has actually provided!"

Now Father Pat had the attention of both of his sons as he continued explaining. "Just about the time you boys started school, I began receiving checks in the mail. They came from an anonymous source and always included a typed note like this one."

Father Pat handed the most recent note to the brothers and then continued, "The checks arrive around the same time each year. The amount started out at five hundred dollars and has increased ever since. The most recent check was for thirteen thousand. I've been putting the money in a savings account for your education, and it has grown to over one hundred and twenty-five thousand. So, you see, there is no need to worry about wiping out my retirement savings." Then with a wink at Father Jason, he said, "And who said that I am ever going to retire?"

When the brothers heard the dollar figure, their jaws dropped. Father Pat could see the astonishment on their faces. James was the first to ask the obvious question.

"Who do you think is sending this money?"

The old priest hesitated, not sure if he wanted to share his suspicion. Then he decided that his sons were old enough to handle it.

"I . . . can't be sure, but . . . I think it could be your mother."

The brothers immediately looked at each other and then the note. They recalled the letter that Father Pat had shared with them years before. They had read that letter several times and knew it by heart. This time, John was the first to speak.

"Father Pat . . . in the original letter, our mother said that she was unable to provide for us. Obviously, someone able to send you that kind of money could certainly provide for us. If it is her, why hasn't she tried to reach out and reunite with us?"

Father Pat had been considering the same point over the years that he had been receiving the money.

"I certainly don't know the answer, Johnny . . . I can only guess . . . that she . . . she still feels ashamed for abandoning you two boys. She may not be sure that you can ever forgive her."

James spoke up. "There were times in my life that I was very angry and felt hurt—especially when I would see other kids with their mothers. Then I started thinking of all the times I haven't followed the rules. I know that I got you angry and upset plenty of times, but you never stopped loving me—no matter what I did! I also remembered that you said something terrible . . . very terrible must have happened and that she still loved us. So, I forgave her a long time ago."

Father Pat's heart was filled with warmth and admiration at what his son had just said. He thought to himself, *Yes, in the end, Jimmy will do what's right!*

# 5

## Brother and Friend

**Archbishop John Donnelly**
**Saint Joseph's Cemetery | September 2016**

ARCHBISHOP JOHN DONNELLY smiled to himself, still staring at Father Pat's headstone. He was gratified by how well the local parishioners continued to maintain his father's gravesite. Except for in the winter months, there were always plenty of colorful flowers planted. Nevertheless, he instantly regretted not bringing any flowers today. He'd make sure to bring some on his next visit.

He'd never forget his wonderful upbringing with Father Pat. He looked up into the clear autumn sky and said, "Thank you, Father Pat, for being a wonderful priest, an outstanding father, and always . . . a good friend." Silence funneled into his pause between words, filled only by the sound of the birds chirping in the nearby trees. "How I wish you were traveling to Rome with me, but I do know that your spirit will always be with me. I love you, Father Pat."

With Father Pat officially visited, he proceeded to his next stop, only a few feet to the right, where another headstone—also well maintained with flowers—awaited him.

"Well, hello there," he said to his brother, studying the headstone's inscription:

> *James Donnelly*
> *"Jimmy"*
> *1961–1985*
> *Son Brother Friend*
> *Taken too soon, but always in our hearts.*

Even now, more than thirty years later, the archbishop still teared up when he thought about the brother and best friend that he'd lost on that fateful day. Almost autonomously, his hand rested on the polished face of the marble headstone. "I think about you all the time," he whispered, a very different kind of confession. "Every single day, I wonder what this world would look like if you were still in it—and that's what I try to replicate."

He paused. Autumn leaves, tousled by the wind, rustled softly.

Swallowing, he patted the headstone fondly, sitting back. "I know, *I know* . . . You're right, of course, that it doesn't serve to dwell. I just . . . I'm glad you're with Father Pat. I just wish you were both here with me instead. That's all."

He could practically hear his brother teasing him for being so sentimental. They'd always enjoyed ribbing each other.

The archbishop laughed, thinking about those times, and then silence funneled in once again. He allowed his mind to wander back to the inherent differences between him and his brother—which hadn't just been in terms of their spirit and temperament.

# PART TWO

# THE CROOK

# 6

# The College Years

## John Donnelly
## Boston College | 1979–1983

COLLEGE WAS DEFINITELY a major change for the two brothers. Living away from home and from each other seemed very strange. Each was assigned a roommate. John opened the door to his designated dorm room and was greeted by a smiling face and a mass of red hair.

"Well, hello there. I'm your new roommate." The young man held out his hand. "I'm Francis Roland. Please, call me Fran."

John had not known what to expect, so he was delighted by this warm welcome.

"Hi, Fran. It's a pleasure to meet you. I'm John Donnelly."

The two roommates began a lively conversation, sharing their backgrounds, and both were pleasantly surprised when John mentioned the name of his hometown in western Massachusetts.

"That's incredible! That is the same town where my dad grew up."

"You're joking."

"No, I'm serious. He said it was a fantastic place to live. I never got a chance to visit because my grandparents moved to the Midwest shortly before I was born."

"Wow, that is an amazing coincidence. I bet your dad would know my father."

"I'll ask him. What's his name?"

"Reverend Patrick Donnelly, but everyone knows him as Father Pat."

"Wait a minute. Your father is a priest? I've got to hear this story."

John always relished the reaction he got when he told people his father was a priest.

"My brother and I were left on his doorstep when we were infants, and he decided to adopt us."

"Wow! That's amazing. So, you have a brother?"

"Yeah." John smiled, anticipating the response when he shared the next piece of news. "We're identical twins."

John had the opportunity to meet Francis's parents—Christopher and Lauren. They were a lovely couple who had dated since they were in high school. Father Pat met them during the first parents' weekend and remembered them from years before.

"I recall when you two got married. The love you had for each other was very apparent. And I can see that it has grown even stronger over the years."

John was thoroughly amazed by his father's memory, but he was even more in awe of his ability to connect with people. He thought to himself, *I want to be the type of pastor who makes such a lasting connection with all of his parishioners.*

The two roommates developed a strong relationship. They were both serious students and would often study together. John thoroughly enjoyed his classes at Boston College. The theology classes were enlightening. One of the classes he found extremely interesting was comparative religion. *God in Search of Man* by Abraham Heschel was one of the required readings. The author was one of the most prominent Jewish theologians of the twentieth century. This course helped to broaden John's understanding of and appreciation for Judaism.

The business classes provided him with a solid foundational understanding of commerce and finance. His academic habits served him well, even with the most challenging classes. He spent several hours each day reading, studying, and completing his assignments. He was always well prepared for his exams. Consequently, he was on the dean's list each of his four years and graduated summa cum laude.

When the two roommates weren't focused on schoolwork, they would share a beer and talk about their future plans.

"So, you really want to become a priest?"

John reflected on his many long conversations with Father Jason. "Yes, I do. In fact, since I was about thirteen, I have felt the calling. I want to have a positive impact on people and bring them closer to God."

"That's great! You'll be an outstanding priest. I bet your father is excited that you will be following in his footsteps."

"You know . . . the funny thing is . . . he has never pushed me in that direction. I think that he'll be happy about it, but he has never insisted that either one of us follow a specific career path. He simply said to find something that you enjoy doing and do it extremely well."

"Actually, I also plan on following in my father's footsteps. Just like him, I'm majoring in accounting and economics at BC. I plan on pursuing a career in the insurance industry, too. I only hope that I'll do as well as he has done."

"I'm sure you will!"

They remained close friends and roommates for the entire four years of college. John proved himself to be an especially dear friend during their junior year.

John returned from a weekend visit home in early October. As he entered their room, he found Fran sitting on the edge of his bed. His eyes were red and swollen from crying.

John immediately went to his friend and asked, "What is it? What's wrong?"

"It's . . . it's my mom. She has cancer. It's really . . . really bad!"

Fran's mother—Lauren—had been diagnosed with a very aggressive form of breast cancer. The doctors in Connecticut suggested that she seek treatment in Boston.

"My uncle Tom arranged for her to meet with one of the top oncologists at the Dana-Farber Cancer Institute. An entire team of doctors evaluated her case. They said that the cancer has spread to other organs, and they are unable to operate until the tumor is shrunk."

John was shocked at this news. Mrs. Roland had always appeared to be so healthy and vibrant. He could actually feel Fran's anguish.

"Why is this happening to my mom?" Fran screamed angrily as tears rolled down his cheeks. "Why would God do this to such a wonderful person?" His whole body shook as he shouted these words.

John tried to think of how his father would respond to someone who was so distraught. "I wish I could give you an answer. I've heard Father Pat say that when a person gets a serious illness, it's not a punishment from God. He says that God loves and cares for all of his children and that he hurts when they hurt."

"I don't know how I could handle it if anything happened to her." Fran broke down and began crying again.

John held his friend in his arms and said in a soothing whisper, "I'm here for you, and I'll be with you every step of the way."

During the entire time of Lauren's illness, John provided invaluable support and empathy to his friend. While John realized that he couldn't take away his friend's pain, he did his best to help Fran deal with it. He also became aware of something else. This compassionate instinct was moving him more closely toward the priesthood.

The chemotherapy significantly weakened Fran's mother, but it was unable to slow the rapid spread of the cancer. Within six months, Lauren passed away.

# 7

## The College Years

**James Donnelly**
**University of Massachusetts | 1979–1983**

AS SOON AS James entered his freshman dorm room, he was struck by the tantalizing aroma of Italian food. He was greeted by a good-looking young man whose tight-fitting T-shirt accentuated his muscular frame. He handed James a dish overflowing with lasagna and meatballs. The lasagna had cheese oozing out from all sides, and the meatballs were the size of tennis balls.

"I hope you brought a healthy appetite with you," the young man said as he handed James the plate. I'm Anthony—Anthony Martoni—your new roommate."

"Wow, this looks amazing! Thanks, Anthony. I'm James Donnelly. It's definitely a pleasure to meet you." After taking his first bite, James exclaimed, "Oh my God, this is absolutely delicious! Did your mom cook all of this food?"

Anthony's dark-brown eyes twinkled as he laughed and then explained, "No, Mom didn't make this spread. It came from my pop's restaurant."

"Your father owns a restaurant?"

"Actually, he owns a bunch of restaurants in the North End."

"What's the North End?"

"What's the North End? Where are you from—outer space?"

"No, not quite that far out. I come from a small town near Stockbridge—about two and a half hours from here."

"Well, I see that I'll have to educate this country bumpkin about Boston," Anthony teased good-naturedly. "The North End is Boston's Little Italy. There are plenty of great Italian restaurants there, but the Martoni restaurants are the best. In fact, my father's places serve the best Italian food in all of Massachusetts."

"Well, if this lasagna is indicative of the quality of food that he serves, then I'm not surprised. So, your father is in the restaurant business?"

"That's one of his businesses. He's involved in some other businesses, too." James noticed that Anthony didn't elaborate but instead changed the subject. "I'm being groomed to take over the restaurant business. That's why my father wants me to get a college education. In fact, I'll be the first in my entire family to go to college." Then Anthony asked, "What about your old man—what's he do for a living?"

James thought to himself, *This is going to be fun.* "He runs a church and school."

"Oh, so is he some sort of administrator?"

"No, he's actually a priest—a Catholic priest." James got a kick out of the surprised look on Anthony's face.

"Are you shitting me? No way! How can your father be a priest? What'd he do—knock up some broad and then escape to the seminary?"

James roared with laughter at Anthony's question. "No, far from it. He actually adopted my brother and me after we were left on his doorstep." He went on to explain the details. As he saw Anthony get over his initial shock, James anticipated the next question.

"So, you have a brother—younger or older?"

"We're not quite sure."

"What do you mean you're not sure?"

"Well, we're twins—identical twins—and we don't know who was born first."

"Holy shit! Twins raised by a priest. That's got to be something for the record books!"

The two roommates talked well into the night, getting to know each other. Similar to his brother and Fran, James also developed a strong friendship with Anthony over the next few months.

Like James, Anthony had a wild streak, and college life gave each of them the freedom to test their limits—and test them, they did! There were late-night drinking parties, frequent poker games, and of course, there was always the pursuit of attractive coeds. Anthony and James frequently traveled to Boston for dinner at one of the Martonis' restaurants. Anthony's father—Mario—would occasionally join the two of them for dinner. James noticed how extremely respectful everyone was to Mr. Martoni. He assumed it was because Anthony's father owned the place. James also observed that the same two men—Frank and Sal—were always with Anthony's father. Each man was built like a linebacker.

James was curious and asked, "Anthony, what's the story with those two guys who are always with your father?"

"They're security for my father."

"Security? Why does your father need security?"

"Because he's a very important man!"

James could tell that his friend didn't want to discuss it any further.

A few weeks later, he learned why Anthony had been so terse with him. They were playing cards with their regular group, which consisted of Fred, Ralph, and Rocco. They usually played for nickels, dimes, and quarters, with a maximum bid of no more than one dollar. The card playing was accompanied by plenty of beer and pizza, as well as some good-natured teasing.

"So, Ralph, when are you going to stop rooting for those New York Yankees and start cheering for the Red Sox?"

Ralph, who grew up in the New York borough of Queens and was a diehard Yankees fan, had a quick retort, as usual.

"When your Red Sox start winning the World Series. Remind me again, how many years has it been since they last won a series?"

The card game had already been going on for a few hours. Rocco and Anthony were winning the majority of the hands. It was during a hand of five-card draw that the trouble started. Rocco had drawn three aces in the first round, and Anthony had drawn two pairs—kings and queens. When it was Anthony's turn to bid, he immediately put down one dollar. Rocco, who was up next, not only matched Anthony's bid but raised it by another dollar. James immediately folded since he had a terrible hand. Fred and Ralph did the same. So, it became a showdown between Anthony and Rocco.

Anthony tossed in one card. The new card was another king, giving him a powerful full house. James could tell from the animated look on his roommate's face that he had a terrific hand. Rocco asked for two cards. He had a mischievous smile on his face when he nodded for Anthony to bid again. James had seen that same grin on Rocco's face many times before when he had bluffed his way into winning. He assumed that Anthony was not going to let Rocco get away with it this time.

"So, Rocco, would you like to make it really interesting?"

"What did you have in mind?"

"How about changing the maximum bid on this hand to ten bucks?"

"You sure you don't want to make it a little higher?"

"So, what are you thinking, Rocco?"

"Look, I won about forty dollars so far tonight . . . so, let's say forty bucks!"

Fred, who had been relatively quiet most of the night, spoke up. "Hey guys, I think you're both getting way out of line here. This is supposed to be a friendly game."

The two players simply ignored Fred and stared at each other with smirks on their faces. As James watched the two of them, he was reminded of the old Westerns that Father Pat would allow him and John to watch on television. There was often a high-stakes poker game in these movies that would eventually end in a gun battle. He thought to himself, *Thank God there are no guns here!*

Anthony bid forty dollars, and James, who had been convinced Rocco was just bluffing again, was shocked when Rocco immediately matched the amount. He could see that everyone else was equally surprised.

"Okay, Anthony, show us what you've got!"

"Well, Rocco, I have these three beauties." Then he slowly laid down each king.

"Is that all that you have?"

"Oh no, my friend, I also have these two beautiful ladies!"

He then dropped the two queens onto the table.

"Wow . . . You really did have a great hand!" Rocco sounded disappointed. "You fooled me. I thought you were trying a Rocco-style bluff. Well done, my friend."

Just as Anthony reached for the pot, Rocco stopped him.

"Wait a minute, Anthony. I said that you had a great hand, but I didn't say that you beat me."

Then Rocco slowly and methodically laid down four aces. Everyone's jaw dropped, especially Anthony's. Rocco started laughing as he began scooping up the pot. James could see that his roommate was stunned and embarrassed.

Nevertheless, Anthony smiled and good-naturedly said, "Why, you bastard . . . you little bastard . . . you really played me for a fool. I'm going to get you for this!"

Rocco could not control his excitement at winning such a large pot at Anthony's expense. He jokingly said, "So, what are you going to do, send some of your old man's goons after me? Maybe they'll throw my body into the harbor. Ha ha!"

That's when it happened. Anthony's smile immediately disappeared. His face turned a deep red, his brown eyes became black as coal, and he lunged for Rocco.

"You fucking bastard! Don't you ever say that again! I'll rip your head off!"

By this time, Anthony had knocked Rocco to the floor and was ready to land a punch to his face. James grabbed Anthony's arm just in time. It took the three of them—James, Ralph, and Fred—to pull the muscular Anthony off Rocco, who was thoroughly stunned and frightened. He began apologizing profusely.

"I'm sorry, Anthony! I'm really sorry! I only meant it as a joke. It was dumb for me to say it."

James and Ralph were still holding Anthony back, who had not calmed down yet and seemed ready to charge again.

"Get the fuck out of here . . . and don't you ever come back here again. Get out now!"

Rocco, looking pitiful and shocked, grabbed his jacket and ran out the door, leaving his winnings behind. Fred and Ralph quietly followed soon afterward.

It took another half hour before Anthony calmed down. James had never seen his friend act this way. When he thought the time was right, he gathered the courage and asked, "Anthony, what the hell was that all about? I've never seen you get so angry before. You literally had fire in your eyes. We could barely pull you off him. What happened, man?"

Anthony stared at James for several seconds and then said, "You really don't know, do you, Jimmy?"

"Know . . . know what?"

"My father . . ."

"What about your father?"

"He's a crime boss, one of the most powerful bosses in the Northeast!"

Now it was James's turn to be stunned.

"You . . . you mean like in *The Godfather*?"

"Yeah, like in the movies—but for real, Jimmy!"

Now it all came together for James—the respect everyone always showed Mr. Martoni and the reason he had security. Nothing was said between the two friends for several minutes. During this time, James could only think of the extreme differences between his father and Anthony's. Father Pat was a warm, kind, and gentle person who lived his faith every single moment of his life. He wouldn't even kill a fly. Instead, he would try to catch it and take it outside the house. He would tell his sons that the fly was also one of God's creatures. James could only imagine what Mario Martoni had done.

As James was contemplating these differences, Anthony finally spoke. "That's my father, Jimmy. I'm not him! I love the man, but I hate what he does! I don't plan on following him into the crime business. That's why

I'm taking over the restaurant business. I don't want anything to do with the rest of his organization."

James put his hand on his friend's shoulder and said, "I really didn't know. I'm not sure what to say." Then, after thinking about what had happened earlier in the evening, he said, "What about Rocco? You scared the shit out of him. Don't you think you should do something about that?"

"You're right, Jimmy. I really lost it! I'll talk to him tomorrow and apologize. Maybe I'll even take him and the rest of you bums to one of our restaurants for a really nice dinner." Then Anthony looked directly into James's eyes and said, "Thanks for being my friend. You are a really good friend. I'll never forget that."

That was the last time the two of them discussed what Mario Martoni did for a living.

Every Sunday, James would take the train to Chestnut Hill and spend the entire day with his brother. Given the amount of partying the night before, he might not arrive until late morning, but John would insist that they attend mass at Saint Ignatius. During these visits, James got to know Fran, who would sometimes join them. He liked Fran and was glad that his brother also had a great roommate.

The two brothers maintained a strong bond, and the time they spent together was very important to both of them. The observation that Father Pat had made when the boys were young children was still very much apparent. They had a special connection with each other and always enjoyed each other's company. While there was naturally some good-natured teasing between the two of them, there was never a harsh word spoken.

"So, have you figured out where the library is yet at UMass?"

"I haven't even figured out where the classrooms are yet!"

Some days they would walk around the campus and then head to Newton Centre for a late lunch or an early dinner. As they passed the huge houses in Newton, James would comment on the homes.

"Can you imagine the money it takes to buy one of these mansions? What do you think these people do for a living?"

"They're probably doctors, lawyers, bankers, or corporate executives."

"I'd love to be friends with the owners of one of these mansions. Someday, I'll be welcomed inside one of these big houses."

"Yeah, sure, and I'll have a private audience with the pope!" John laughed and rolled his eyes.

At the end of his freshman year, James was placed on academic warning. He came to the realization that late-night partying and last-minute studying were not going to work in college. This was the angriest that James had ever seen Father Pat. When his father read the notice from UMass, his face turned a flaming crimson, and he scolded James.

"Jimmy, I am so . . . so disappointed with you. You are not even trying! If you're not going to make an effort, you might as well drop out of college right now. I'm not going to be around forever, Jimmy. It's time for you to shape up. You need to get serious about your future."

James was not sure what upset him more—Father Pat's disappointment or what he had said about not being around forever. Father Pat was his father, and he loved the man deeply. He realized that his father was getting older, and James did not want to think about a time when Father Pat would not be there. He also did not want to disappoint this wonderful man.

"You're right, Father Pat," James responded in a sincere and remorseful tone. "I really screwed up. I didn't take it seriously. This will never, ever happen again. I promise you!"

Then, with tears in his eyes, he hugged his father.

James kept his word. He left the partying to the weekends and rarely joined any of the poker games on weeknights. He attended his classes, took notes, and completed his assignments on a timely basis. His grades began to improve, and while there was some slippage at times, he generally maintained at least a B average throughout the remaining semesters of his college career. He even aced all of his remaining accounting classes.

# 8

# Real-World Advice

**John Donnelly**
**Rectory | 1983**

AS THEY ENTERED the last semester of their senior year, the brothers began to finalize their career plans. John was still leaning toward the priesthood and was surprised by the advice he received from Father Pat and Father Jason. It was a Sunday afternoon during the Christmas break when the two priests sat down with John. Father Pat was the first to speak.

"I don't think you should apply to the seminary right after college."

John felt puzzled and hurt. He asked, "But why not? Don't you think I can handle the seminary? Look at how well I've done in college. Or is it that you don't think I would be a good priest?"

"Just wait and let me explain. Of course I think you can handle it. You're extremely bright and have always been a hard worker. So, there is no doubt in my mind that you can handle the grind of six years as a seminarian. As far as being a priest, you have the ability to be an outstanding one! You've always been caring, and you are a natural leader. People look up to you. They respect you. Yes, yes, you definitely have all the essential qualities to be an amazing priest."

Now John was completely baffled and asked why his father didn't think he should apply to the seminary. It was Father Jason's turn to explain.

"Father Pat didn't say to *never* apply—he simply said not to apply *right after college*. There's a difference! We both think you would benefit from working for a year or two. With your grades and your second major in business management, you will have no problem landing a job with a good company. This will give you the opportunity to interact with many different types of people and circumstances in the real world. If and when you become a priest, you'll be an even more capable priest because you will have formed a better understanding of the challenges your parishioners face in their day-to-day lives. This experience will lead to a deeper empathy. In addition, the business experience will help you when you have to manage your own parish."

At this point, Father Pat took over. "Think of it as an extension of your education. And there's also another reason. Being in what Father Jason has described as the *real world* will give you the opportunity to decide if the priesthood is really what you want. Who knows . . . while working in Boston, you might meet an attractive young woman, fall in love, get married, and make me a grandfather. And that would be great, too! Look, if you are still committed to becoming a priest after being in the real world for a while, then you won't have any trouble getting the recommendations that you will need for Saint John's Seminary. Just trust that God will guide you wherever he wants you to go."

This was a lot for John to absorb. He said that he needed a few days to process everything. By the following Tuesday, he thoroughly grasped the logic of their advice and actually began to see it as a wonderful opportunity. His excellent grades, combined with the powerful BC network, landed John a management trainee job at the Gillette company in Boston. The famous razor company actually started in South Boston in the early twentieth century. John was enthusiastic about the training program because it would expose him to all aspects of the business, including sales, manufacturing, and finance. He felt that this program would definitely provide him with the real-world experience that Father Jason had described.

# 9

# The Offer

James Donnelly
University of Massachusetts | 1983

JAMES BEGAN THE interview process with the accounting companies that came to the campus to recruit. He was hoping to land a job with one of the Big Eight firms. He was able to get interviews with two of these firms: Price Waterhouse and Arthur Young. Each interview appeared to go extremely well, but he was not invited in for an office visit with either organization. He spoke to his accounting adviser about it and learned that there were limited openings that year. Therefore, the firms were using grades as the deciding factor. That first year of partying had significantly reduced his cumulative GPA.

James was extremely upset. He blamed himself for being so foolish during his freshman year. He realized that he was just as bright as the accounting students who were getting offers from the large firms. Ironically, he was getting straight As in most of his classes during his senior year. *Too little, too late,* he thought to himself. His adviser saw the potential in James and had a suggestion.

"James, you are a bright student! Yes, you screwed up during that first year, but I have seen how hard you've worked since then. I have a suggestion that you might want to consider. Keep up the hard work—continue getting high grades for the rest of your senior year. Then go on and get your master's degree. You can get it here or apply to one of the other fine universities. I would actually recommend my alma mater—Bentley. Maintain a high grade point average while getting your master's, and you will be sure to land a position at one of the big accounting firms."

James listened to what his adviser said. He was grateful that there still might be a way to achieve his career goals, but he wasn't sure that he wanted to spend more time in school. He felt like he was ready to start working and make some real money. He thanked his adviser and said that he would take some time to think about it. As he walked back to his room, James was feeling several different emotions—anger and frustration at one moment, hope and excitement the next. His head was spinning by the time he got back to his dorm. Anthony was already in the room when James arrived.

"Hey, Jimmy, how you doing?"

"Pretty shitty. I'm feeling like a real loser right about now."

James went on to explain that he had not been invited to any second interviews and that his adviser had suggested graduate school. Anthony thought the world of James and had an idea.

"So, what do they pay at these big accounting firms?"

"I've heard that they start you at around twenty grand plus bonus."

"That's all? You're worth more than that! Hell, you are one of the smartest guys I know."

"Yeah, thanks a lot, but my grades don't show it."

Anthony grabbed two bottles of beer from the refrigerator, handed one to James, and then said, "Fuck the grades. You have the smarts and plenty of common sense."

He thought that his friend was just trying to make him feel better, but the next thing Anthony said made James practically spit out the beer he had just sipped.

"How would you like to make twice as much?"

After wiping the beer from his chin, James laughed and replied, "Yeah, sure . . . in my dreams!"

"No . . . no, I'm dead serious, kiddo. You can come work for me in the restaurant business."

James continued laughing and said, "I don't know the first thing about the restaurant business. What do you want me to do, be your head waiter? You've got to be kidding, man. Thanks for trying to lift my spirits, but you can't be serious."

"I'm dead serious. And no, I don't want you to be the head waiter—although you'd probably look pretty good in a tux. Look, you want an accounting job, right? Our controller, Nick, needs an assistant. He's been with the business forever. My father says that Nick is the best. Pop says no one knows the numbers like Nick does. You could learn from the best, and someday you could take over for Nick. Just think, Jimmy, you'd be my controller—my numbers guy. You'd be making a lot more money than those pansies in the big accounting firms. And you would always eat at the best restaurants in Boston!"

James could not believe how quickly circumstances had changed for him. Less than an hour before, he'd been feeling like a victim, and now he felt as though he was on top of the world. He asked Anthony again, "Are you serious—forty thousand?"

"I'm absolutely serious! I'll call my father right now. He has always liked you, and Nick is going to love you."

# 10

## The Job

James Donnelly
Boston | 1983

"ARE YOU OUT of your fucking mind?"

James had come to his brother's apartment to share the good news about working for the Martonis. The reaction from John was not what James had expected. This was unusually strong language coming from his brother. James had never seen his brother so agitated. "What do you mean?"

"What do I mean? They're criminals!"

"Look, I know that Anthony's father is a criminal, but I won't be working for him. I'll be working for Anthony, and I won't be involved with any of that criminal stuff. I'll be in the restaurant business. It's completely legitimate!"

John stared at his brother and just shook his head in disbelief. His tone was filled with emotion. "You sound very naive, and I don't think you are naive. You know what I think . . . I think you are being blinded by the money. How do you think they acquired all of those fancy restaurants? Do you think they went to the bank and got a loan? No . . . no! They used the money from the drugs, extortion, and God knows whatever other crimes they commit to take over those restaurants."

By now, John was yelling at his brother. "It's not a legitimate business! It's just a front. It's all criminal! And you know what, if you work for a crook . . . then, dammit, you *are* a crook!"

James felt hurt by that last statement, but he understood that his brother was only concerned about him. So, he took a deep breath, placed his hand on his brother's shoulder, and then, in a voice filled with tenderness and love, reassured John. "How can you call me a crook? I'm no crook! You're overreacting. I'm telling you, Anthony wants no part of the criminal business. The restaurant business is really legitimate. It's going to be fine. Don't worry!" James could see from the expression on his brother's face that he wasn't convinced.

In a much calmer voice, John said, "I love you. You mean the world to me. I don't want to see you mixed up with anything bad. Imagine what it would do to Father Pat. Please . . . please at least promise me that if you see yourself getting involved with anything that doesn't seem right, you'll quit the job immediately. Promise me!"

John's voice broke over the word *promise*, and he fell silent. Looking away, he raked his fingers through his hair. *My God*, James thought to himself, *I've never seen him so upset.* He was unsure whether it was wise to say anything more.

He decided it wasn't. It would be better if he didn't say anything. So, he stepped forward and hugged his brother—who, thankfully, accepted the gesture, leaning into his embrace.

And for a few seconds, it felt as though they were kids again.

"I wish you could see how much I want to make you proud," James confessed, words soft against his brother's shoulder. "I wish you could see that everything I do is to make you proud, to somehow step out from behind your shadow and prove that I'm doing good, too."

John went rigid, standing a little straighter. "Jimmy . . ."

"I love you, too, Johnny," he added, stepping back to clap his brother on the shoulder, their eyes locked. "You're not just my brother—you're my best friend and always will be. I absolutely promise you—I *swear* to you—I will quit the job if I ever think or feel something is not right. I *promise*."

Anthony had told James to arrive for his first day of work by nine o'clock. The business office was upstairs from Sofia's—an upscale restaurant named after Mario Martoni's mother. Eager to make a good first impression, James arrived by eight thirty, dressed in his brand-new blue suit. When he arrived at the office, Nick Mancuso, the controller, was already there.

He smiled at James and, in a pleasant voice, introduced himself. "So, you must be Jimmy. I'm Nick . . . Nick Mancuso." He thrust a hand forward for a handshake, which James was happy to accept. Despite being in his late fifties, Nick had a bright, youthful smile. "Anthony can't stop talking about you. He says that you are one of the smartest guys he knows."

"It's a pleasure to meet you, Mr. Mancuso. I really appreciate the opportunity. Anthony said that you are an outstanding controller. I'm looking forward to working for you and learning from you."

Nick smiled at James and said, "First of all, the name is Nick, not *Mr. Mancuso*. And I am very happy to have you on board. I've been begging Mario for years to hire an assistant for me. I'm getting up there in age, and

I want to retire someday, so I need a backup. He's always been hesitant about getting someone else involved with our financials. It's a trust issue for him. When Anthony approached his father about hiring you, Mario finally agreed. He told me that he really likes you and that his son absolutely loves you. So, welcome aboard."

Just then, as if on cue, Anthony walked through the door with his father, raising his brows in an effort to look highly impressed. "Well, well, well," he said, glancing James over from head to toe, "look at the early bird trying to make a good first impression!"

James smiled and shook hands with both Mario and Anthony, then thanked Mario for the opportunity to work there. Mario gave James a pleasant smile, pointed to his son, and said, "Anthony is the one you have to thank, Jimmy. He wouldn't stop singing your praises to me. And Nick has been pestering me for years that he needs an assistant. So, you have a great opportunity. Just work hard and learn from Nick. He is the best, and I trust him with my life!"

James assured Mario that he could count on him. Just then, Anthony handed James a set of keys and said, "Here are the keys to your new company car. I bet none of those pansies at the big accounting firms got their own car . . . and certainly not a hot red Mustang GT."

James could not believe what he had just heard. The salary was more than he could imagine, and now a brand-new car? It was unbelievable! He was more committed than ever to not let Anthony down.

During the first few weeks, James impressed Nick with his hard work and ability to learn quickly. Nick continued to give James additional responsibilities and was never disappointed. He was thrilled with James's suggestions to improve the accounting processes and procedures. After six months on the job, James took charge of converting their manual accounting system to a computerized system. He also worked with a major payroll company to implement a new payroll system for the restaurants. By the end of the first year, Nick was telling Anthony what a great hire James had been.

James could not be happier or more grateful to Anthony. He thought back to that day when he realized that none of the big accounting firms were interested in him. At that moment, it had felt like one of the worst days of his life. Now he realized how wrong he had been. If he had been hired by one of those large firms, he would never have gotten this tremendous opportunity.

# 11

# The Announcement

**James Donnelly**
**Rectory | 1984**

JAMES PULLED UP in front of his brother's apartment, where John was sitting on the front steps, waiting for him. He saw his brother point to his watch and shake his head. They were going to drive home and visit Father Pat—which was rapidly becoming a weekend tradition.

As John got into the Mustang, James apologized, "I know . . . I know I was supposed to be here a half hour ago. The payables took longer than I had anticipated. I'm sorry!"

"No problem. I just like to give you a hard time. Besides, it gave me a chance to read the paper while I was waiting."

"I'm looking forward to seeing Father Pat. He seems a lot more rested since he turned all of the pastoral responsibilities over to Father Jason." Then James thought about their plans for the weekend. "So, where do you want to hike tomorrow morning?"

"How about our special place?"

Over the many years that they had been trekking through the mountains, they had found an exceptional area where very few hikers had ever gone. It was a beautiful open valley situated deep in the woods. From this spot, they would admire the beauty of the Berkshire Mountains.

"Perfect! We'll leave early so that we can be back by three o'clock. That will give us enough time to shower and get ready for the vigil mass. So, are you sure you can keep up with me?"

John laughed. "I think I can manage that. Hopefully, no one falls on his ass again."

"Do you remember when Father Pat took us on our first hike? What were we—about seven or eight?"

"We were eight. It felt like we were climbing straight up the mountain. We finally reached the top of the trail and sat down to have lunch, and he shared the story of the Transfiguration, when Jesus led Peter, James, and John to a high mountain. He taught us that Jesus's clothes became a brilliant white, and he began speaking with Moses and Elijah."

James smiled at the memory, then shared an intimate thought. "You're going to think this is corny, coming from me, but when I am up in the Berkshires, absorbing the magnificent beauty . . . I really feel close to God."

John gently hit his brother's arm with his fist. "Well, well, well, there may be hope for you after all. Maybe some of the Holy Spirit finally reached you."

"All right, wiseass, I knew I shouldn't have shared that with you."

"Don't get mad, Jimmy. I'm just teasing you. In fact, I know exactly what you mean. I feel the same way when I'm surrounded by all that beauty in the mountains."

---

Father Pat got up early the next morning to cook his sons a hearty breakfast. As they were leaving, he confided in them, "I really miss not being able to hike anymore, but I will enjoy it vicariously through you. So, have a wonderful time today, and tell me all about it tonight." Then, hugging both sons, he reminded them to be back in time for mass.

They made it to their special place in record time and sat down for lunch. James had noticed that his brother had been unusually quiet during their hike to the valley and asked, "Is everything okay? You seem like you are in another world."

"I've got some things on my mind that I'm still trying to sort out."

"Do you want to talk about it?"

"No . . . not right now . . . but I will later."

James thought to himself, *I wonder what it is? Could it be my job at the restaurant, and he's just trying to figure out the best way to bring it up? I know he's still not happy with my decision.*

They got back to the rectory by two thirty. After mass, they enjoyed one of Father Jason's gourmet meals rather than going to a local restaurant. Drawing from his Italian heritage, Father Jason had become a superb cook.

"Father Jason, that meal was fantastic! If you ever decide to give up being a priest, I can probably get you a job at one of the Martonis' restaurants," James joked.

"I don't think I'll take you up on that offer."

Father Pat laughed. "Well, that's a relief. I'm getting used to being retired, and I don't want to have to train another priest. So, on that note, what do you say we move into the living room for our two fingers?"

Father Pat poured scotch for everyone. They would usually talk until nearly midnight. James watched as his brother took a sip of the scotch and let it go down slowly. He could tell that his brother was processing something in his head.

John announced, "I have something I want to share with all of you."

They looked at John. Aside from the clink of melting ice cubes in their drinks, the room was silent. James sat a little straighter, alarmed by the shift in his brother's voice—the slightly higher octave, the gravel to it. Whatever this was about, it was going to be serious. He guessed he would soon find out the reason his brother had been so quiet earlier in the day.

"It's been about a year since I started working at Gillette, and it's been a truly outstanding experience. I have completely enjoyed it. I've met some great people and learned a lot. I now realize that it's one thing to learn about business from books but an entirely different experience in the real world. I've even dated some very nice young ladies."

John smiled at his brother and continued, "I also did a lot of praying during this time. I asked God to guide me." He took another sip of his scotch, aware that he had their full attention. "And after many prayerful thoughts, I still feel a strong calling to the priesthood. So, I have decided to apply to Saint John's Seminary. I will need recommendations from the clergy. I think I know of at least two fine priests who might write a recommendation for me."

Both priests smiled and nodded their agreement.

"If all goes well, I hope to start the seminary next fall. That will give me almost another year of that real-world experience."

As he ended his announcement, John took his last sip of scotch. Father Pat was the first to respond. He grabbed the bottle of scotch and poured another finger into everyone's glasses. Then, with tears of joy in his eyes, he raised his glass and offered a toast.

"Johnny, I couldn't be any happier than I am tonight. I pray that God will continue to bless you and guide you on this wonderful journey. It's been nearly fifty years since I became a priest, and I've enjoyed every single moment of it. While I made plenty of mistakes along the way, I realized that each mistake was really an opportunity to learn and grow. It is so rewarding, so very rewarding, to bring the word of God to people . . . to be a shepherd of his flock! And I know in my heart—in fact, I've always known—that you are going to be an outstanding priest."

At that point, Father Pat became very emotional and could not utter another word. So, with tears running down his cheeks, he put down his glass and simply hugged his son. James looked at his brother with loving admiration, knowing that their father was absolutely right.

# 12

## The Family Business

**James Donnelly**
**Boston | 1984**

THE FOLLOWING MONDAY, James was at his desk, reconciling the bank accounts, when Nick and Anthony walked in together with smiles on their faces. Nick was the first one to speak.

"Jimmy, you've done a great job during your first year working here. I couldn't be more pleased. No matter what I ask you to do, you always get it done and usually find a better way of doing it than me. You have definitely made my life so much easier!"

"And so, Jimmy, my man," Anthony said, "we decided that you earned yourself a bonus."

James was handed a check. When he looked at the amount, he couldn't believe it.

*Ten thousand dollars?*

His jaw dropped. His shock and amazement were apparent as he exclaimed, "I . . . I don't know what to say! I never even expected a bonus, and now to receive this much money is unbelievable. Thank you! Thank you so much!"

James shook hands with both men and continued thanking them.

Anthony laughed and said, "Jimmy, you are part of the family now. And we always take care of our family."

James was on an amazing high for the rest of the day. He was even more committed to his job. He promised himself that he would accomplish much more during his second year.

Over the next few weeks, James noticed that Anthony was spending much less time at the office. When he asked Nick about Anthony's absence, he was told that Mario was getting Anthony involved with other parts of the business. James was confused, since he thought Anthony was only going to be involved with the restaurant aspect. When he mentioned this to Nick, he got an interesting and insightful response.

"Mario has been grooming Anthony since the kid was in diapers. Anthony will run more than just the restaurant business someday."

James did not ask any more questions—but later, back in his apartment, he felt uneasy. He thought about the night in college when Anthony had said that he was not his father and did not plan on following him into the crime business. He also remembered John telling him that he was being naive. He tried blocking it all out of his mind, but he couldn't shake the uncomfortable feeling.

# 13

# The Audit

| James Donnelly
| Boston | 1984

NICK CONTINUED TO give James more responsibilities and seemed to be thoroughly impressed with his work ethic and performance. He gave James plenty of freedom and didn't micromanage him. So efficient was James that even with his additional responsibilities, he still had extra time on his hands—so, he decided to proactively take on a project that he was certain would impress Nick.

What was it his auditing professor had said once? *"You should pretend to be a crook."*

The teacher had gone on to explain that a good auditor determines how to steal from the company and then puts controls in place to catch this potential theft. "You would be amazed at the number of people who rob their companies," he'd said. He gave examples of sweet little old ladies or mild-mannered clerks who had stolen thousands from their employers.

James thought that the restaurants were extremely ripe for this type of theft because of the numerous cash transactions. Although the employees seemed very loyal, you just never knew if someone might succumb to temptation.

So, he pulled out his auditing textbook and began developing audit procedures to test the cash receipts at each of the restaurants. He was confident that Nick would be pleased with this initiative and decided that he would perform the tests over a three-month period so that the audit would cover a fiscal quarter. At the end of the test period, James could not believe the results. He went back several times to check his calculations. It made no sense to him.

Not only was there no stealing taking place, but it seemed that the receipts were inflated. Several times, he added up the customers' bills and compared them with the cash deposits. The weekly deposits were always significantly higher. At first, he assumed that some of the customer checks had been misplaced. So, he actually visited restaurants on different nights and observed the number of customers throughout the entire evening. He then used some realistic averages to estimate the nightly deposits. Once again, the actual deposits were significantly higher.

After he compiled his audit work, James decided it was time to share the results with Nick. He explained what he had done and the confusing results.

"Nick, it doesn't make any sense! The weekly deposits for each restaurant are at least ten thousand dollars higher than they should be. A few times, they were nearly twenty-five thousand higher than the corresponding customer checks."

Nick listened with what appeared to be a high degree of interest. James noticed that the more he described the situation, the redder Nick's face became. When James finished explaining everything, Nick got up from his desk and shut his office door. Next, he pulled up a chair and sat right next to James. He hunched over in the chair and then began to rub his forehead with both hands. James could actually see perspiration beading on Nick's forehead. He looked James directly in the eyes and spoke in a very low and serious voice—almost a whisper. "Listen, Jimmy, you should not have done that without asking me first. I know that you were just trying to be helpful, but there are certain lines you should never cross in this business."

James listened closely to what Nick was saying. It was almost as if the controller was frightened of something. He also picked up on the fact that Nick had said "this business" and not "the restaurant business." Several seconds of silence went by, and then Nick put his hand on James's shoulder and said, "Look, kid, I like you a lot. You're hardworking and very bright. I don't want you to get into any trouble! So just forget about this receipt stuff. Forget about it! And don't you ever tell anyone—and I mean *anyone*—about what you did or what you found! And don't ever start a project like this one again without running it by me first! Do you understand me?"

At this point, James felt like his head was spinning.

"Yes . . . yes, I understand. I'm . . . I'm really sorry . . ."

Nick simply stared at James. "Good! Now go back to work. And remember—this never happened!"

That evening, back at his apartment, James kept replaying the conversation with Nick in his head. The more he thought about it, the tighter the knot in his stomach got. He eventually realized what was really happening at the restaurants. *My God! This is classic money laundering! The Martonis are filtering the money from their illegal businesses through the restaurants to make the cash appear clean.* He remembered his conversation with his brother before starting this job. He could still recall his brother pleading with him. *It's not a legitimate business. It's just a front. It's all criminal.*

And now John's warning came back to haunt him.

*If you work for a crook, you* are *a crook.*

James remembered the promise he'd made his brother about quitting the job if he ever thought something was wrong.

The next morning, James's mattress was soaked from his sweat—which wasn't very much of a surprise, really, considering how little he'd slept the night before. He dragged himself out of his half-sodden bedsheets and into a piping-hot shower, unable to do much of anything—outside of lean miserably against the white tile wall, chasing his thoughts in circles—until the hot water ran cold, spurring him back into motion.

He knew the smart choice was to quit the job. That was obvious. But every time he thought about quitting, he also thought about that $10,000 bonus check and the Mustang GT. Would he ever have this sort of income again? Wouldn't it be easier to simply forget about all of this and pretend like it never happened, the way Nick suggested?

He picked up a cup of coffee at the local deli on his way to work, but he had no appetite for any breakfast. It was the end of the month, which meant the closing of the books. He buried himself in the month-end process and tried to block everything else from his mind, and for the time being, that was all he could bring himself to do.

During the next several weeks, he did everything possible to simply focus on his accounting work. He wasn't *personally* involved in anything illegal, after all, but actually believing that was another story. He remembered that when he was a kid, Father Pat would talk to him about "your good and bad angels." These two angels seemed to be having an intense battle in his head right now. He wasn't sleeping or eating well. He lost weight and had dark circles under his eyes.

One afternoon, when the two brothers were together, John raised the issue.

"Jimmy, you look like shit. What's the matter? You feeling all right?"

James desperately wanted to share what had happened with his brother, but at the same time, he was embarrassed about how foolish and naive he had been. He realized that at some point, he would confide in his brother, but he was not yet ready.

"Everything is fine. I've just been working some crazy hours, and I had some kind of stomach bug earlier in the week."

John studied his face for a moment, his silence speaking volumes. James felt his face heat up, and he looked away, bracing for his brother's reprimand, but he only got, "You probably caught something bad at one of your restaurants."

He nodded quietly, chest tight. *You don't know how right you are, Johnny!*

# 14

## The Favor

**James Donnelly**
**Boston | 1984**

JAMES WAS IN his office reviewing some invoices a month later when Anthony walked in, looking very much like he had just stepped out of *GQ* magazine. He wore an impeccably tailored blue pinstripe suit, and not a single hair was out of place. James stood up to greet him.

Anthony walked around the desk, gave James a friendly hug, and said, "Jimmy, I haven't seen you in ages, and I've missed you. Nick tells me that you are doing a terrific job. He says you're so good, he'll be able to retire early. And remember what I told you, Jimmy—someday, you're going to be my controller. See? I wasn't kidding you!"

Being Anthony's controller was the *last* thing in the world that James wanted. He concealed his true feelings, smiled at Anthony, and quickly changed the subject. "You look fantastic, Anthony. I've missed seeing you, too. Nick has been an outstanding teacher, and I've learned a lot from him."

Anthony smiled and reminded him, "I told you that my father said Nick was the very best!"

Then it was Anthony's turn to change the subject.

"Hey, Jimmy, I have a favor to ask of you."

James's heart began to beat rapidly. He was afraid that Anthony's request would entrench him even further into "the business," but once again, he masked these thoughts, the knot in his stomach getting even tighter.

"Sure, Anthony, anything for you. What is it?"

Anthony had a huge grin on his face. "I'm dating a gorgeous woman. Her name is Andrea. Wait until you see her. She's an absolute knockout! Well, her sister, Shari, is visiting from Miami this weekend. Andrea doesn't want her sister to feel like a third wheel. I told her not to worry because I knew just the guy for Shari. I want you to join us for drinks and dinner downstairs at Sofia's."

"That sounds great, Anthony," James said, expelling a sigh of relief. "It's been a long time since we've been on a double date. I can't wait to meet Andrea and her sister."

Anthony playfully put his arm around James's neck and said, "Perfect, Jimmy. I knew I could count on you. I told Pasquale to reserve a very special table for the four of us. We'll meet at six o'clock on Friday night. Who knows, maybe you'll fall in love with Andrea's sister. We might even become brothers-in-law! Well, I gotta go. The old man wants me to take care of something. I'll see you on Friday, Jimmy."

Anthony left, and for a moment, it almost felt like those wonderful times in college when they would hang out together. The feeling quickly evaporated once James saw that Frank and Sal were now accompanying Anthony, as they once had his father. He was reminded of what Nick had said. *Mario has been grooming Anthony since the kid was in diapers.*

Once again, James attempted to block the negative thoughts.

James left the office earlier than normal on Friday. He wanted to go for a run and still have plenty of time to shower and get ready for the dinner date. He thought that the exercise would help remove the stress and anxiety he was feeling. He was correct. By the end of the four-mile run, the endorphins had kicked in, and he was feeling much better. In fact, he was looking forward to a relaxing evening.

James was waiting at the bar and speaking with Pasquale, the general manager of the restaurant, when Anthony and the two women arrived. Anthony had not been exaggerating about Andrea being an absolute knockout. Her hair, the color of dark chocolate, was cropped in a short bob, which accentuated her almond-shaped eyes and high cheekbones. A peony-white dress hugged her hourglass figure in a way that made him wonder if she'd had it made specifically for her.

Andrea's sister was equally attractive. There was a definite resemblance between the two sisters, but Shari was slightly shorter, with hair that tumbled over her shoulders and cascaded down her back.

James prayed that all of Anthony's favors would be this easy.

Anthony smiled as soon as he saw James and introduced his two guests.

"Jimmy, this is the wonderful and magnificent woman that I told you about. Please meet Andrea Wagoner and her lovely sister, Shari. And ladies, I want you to meet one of my closest and dearest friends, James Donnelly. Jimmy and I were roommates through all four years of college. And can you believe he always used to cheat off me?"

James smiled as he shook hands with each woman and gave it back to Anthony.

"Actually, it was the other way around. In fact, even after four years, I'm not sure Anthony ever knew where the library was," he quipped, winking. That got a laugh out of Anthony, who gave James a playful headlock.

Pasquale escorted the group to a reserved table. Their waiter for the evening, Danny O'Brien, was already at the table, waiting to greet them. Danny resembled a young Paul Newman with long blond hair. He had a warm, enticing smile and was always quick with a pleasant compliment or friendly wisecrack. Danny had been working at Sofia's for the past five years and was well-liked by everyone. Pasquale considered him one of the most talented waiters at the restaurant. That was the reason he assigned Danny to "the boss" for the entire evening.

James had gotten to know Danny well because he often brought meals from the restaurant up to the office. The young waiter frequently pulled up a chair and chatted with James. He learned that Danny, who was a few years younger than him, was supporting a widowed mother and a kid brother. That was the reason Danny worked as many shifts as Pasquale requested. He often bragged about his younger brother, Eric.

"The kid is a genius! He'll graduate at the top of his class in high school and then go to one of the best colleges. I love that kid. I'd work ten jobs for him. He's going to have a great future!"

James was impressed with Danny's sense of responsibility and his love of family. He looked forward to their friendly conversations.

Danny's good looks did not go unnoticed by Andrea and her sister. After Danny had taken their drink orders and left the table, Andrea was the first to comment. "Wow, that Danny looks like a movie star. Are all your waiters that handsome?"

That comment simply got a forced smile from Anthony. The young waiter returned with their drinks. Andrea and Shari had both ordered vodka martinis. Anthony ordered his usual bourbon on the rocks, and James had his regular, too—scotch, neat.

"So, Andrea, how did you and Anthony meet?"

"I'm an interior designer, and he hired me when he purchased his condo in the Back Bay. It was a terrific challenge because it looked like nothing had been done since the late fifties. We completely gutted the place and renovated the whole thing. I guess he liked my work, so he asked me out."

"Liked it—I love what she did." Anthony put his arm around her and exclaimed, "This beautiful lady is an absolute artist."

"That sounds great. And what about you, Shari—are you also an interior designer?"

"No, I work with a real estate developer in Miami. We're in the middle of building a luxury apartment complex right by the marina. It's going to be amazing!"

James observed the way his friend was looking at Andrea, barely taking his eyes off her and focusing on her every word. James had never seen Anthony behave this way with anyone else. He thought, *He is really hooked on her. Seeing as how she is eyeing other guys in this place—especially Danny—my gut tells me the feeling isn't mutual. She may be enjoying Anthony's company for now, but I doubt that she is looking for anything permanent.*

When Danny brought the appetizers, Andrea gave him a sensual smile and asked, "How long have you been working at Sofia's, Danny?"

James could tell that Danny was oblivious to her flirtations and responded in his normal friendly manner. "It'll be five years in September. This is a fantastic place to work, and we have the best food in town!" Then he pointed to Anthony and joked, "The only problem is the big boss. He's not the nicest guy to work for."

She laughed. "Yeah, I know what you mean. He was a real bear to work with when we did his condo."

Everyone laughed—except Anthony. James knew he never liked being the butt of anyone's jokes, and he certainly did not appreciate this waiter upstaging him in front of Andrea. James, who knew Anthony well, could tell from the look in his eyes that his friend was getting upset, so he tried to change the subject.

"Danny, tell us about the specials tonight."

Danny rattled off the specials without glancing at his notepad. His description of each dish was tantalizing. Andrea, who had not taken her eyes off Danny, said, "That was amazing, Danny. It was almost like you were describing works of art. And you did it all from memory. I am so impressed! Tell me what you would recommend."

"If you prefer a meat dish, I highly recommend our veal osso buco. The meat simply slides off the bone and melts in your mouth. It comes with our excellent saffron risotto and sautéed spinach. On the other hand, if you feel like seafood tonight, our fish stew is outstanding. It includes lobster, shrimp, swordfish, calamari, clams, and mussels. It's like feasting at the ocean."

"You sold me on both of them. That's not fair!"

"Then order both! The big guy can afford it, and if not, we'll make him do the dishes."

This got another huge laugh from Andrea and her sister, but this time, Anthony did not even bother forcing a smile.

During dinner, Andrea seemed to be interested in James's background.

"Anthony tells me that you and your brother are identical twins and were raised by a Catholic priest. You must have had an interesting upbringing."

"Ah, Father Pat was an amazing parent. I could not have asked for a better father. Unfortunately, I probably gave him more gray hair than he deserved."

"And what about your twin? Did he also give Father Pat grief?"

James shook his head. "Johnny? No way, he's the good son. He always follows the rules! In fact, that's how I think Father Pat was able to tell us apart."

Andrea cocked a brow, resting her chin in her hand. "So, what's your brother do now?"

"He's decided to follow in Father Pat's footsteps. He's entering the seminary next year."

Shari gasped, eyes wide, and exclaimed, "Wow! That is amazing! Sounds like you two are very close."

"Oh yeah, Johnny is my best friend!"

"So, do you think you'll be going into the priesthood, too?" asked Andrea.

Anthony almost spit out his wine when he heard that question.

"First of all," James said, "I don't think they would take me. Second, I don't think I could ever live under those strict conditions."

Shari winked and asked, "You mean the one about celibacy?"

"Yeah, that one for sure!"

Danny was back with the dessert tray. Everything looked incredibly delicious. Andrea continued flirting with Danny.

"Danny, since your suggestions for the entrées were excellent, I think I'm going to leave it to you to choose my dessert. But I do have a question...a smart, good-looking guy like you should be in the movies. When am I going to see you on the big screen?"

"Well, I keep telling my agent to find me the right role. I've been turning down several offers, and this guy...what's his name...Harrison Ford...has been their second choice."

Andrea told Danny that he must invite her to the premiere of his first movie. He assured her that she would have a front-row seat.

By this time, Anthony had heard about enough and abruptly said, "Wrap up a mixture of desserts to go. We'll have them with after-dinner drinks at my place."

The others appeared taken aback by Anthony's decision, which he seemed to pick up on, and in an effort to diffuse the tension, he put his arm around Andrea and said, "This way, Shari and Jimmy can see the marvelous job you did with my condo."

Anthony had a car take them to his place.

He was correct—his new home looked marvelous. He gave them a tour of the condo, and it was clear that he was very proud of it. They sat down in the dining room for dessert and drinks. The conversation was friendly and enjoyable, until Andrea mentioned Danny.

"That Danny was fantastic, wasn't he, Shari?"

That was when Anthony exploded. His face turned a deep red, and he shouted, "I've heard enough fucking shit about Danny to last me a lifetime! Don't you realize that you are with me? He's nothing but a pretty-boy waiter! Do you think that fucking asshole has any future? Do you think he could take you out to fancy restaurants and classy night-clubs? The jerk still lives with his mother!"

James was reminded of Anthony's outburst years ago, when Rocco had teased him about his father. Before he could say something to calm the situation down, Andrea raised her voice.

"Hey, don't you *ever* talk to me that way, mister! You don't own me! I can say whatever I want, and I don't appreciate your yelling at me. Who do you think you are, anyway? Come on, Shari, let's go!"

"I'm sorry," Anthony said immediately, clearly aware that he'd crossed a line. He lunged after her, catching her by the arm. "Andrea, I'm really sorry. You're right—I absolutely do not own you. I guess I got a little jealous. I'm really, really sorry! Please sit down. Don't leave."

Andrea did eventually sit down, but the rest of the evening had a distinctly tense air, and the pair would stop seeing each other shortly after that evening.

# 15

## Danny

**James Donnelly**
**Boston | 1984**

A FEW MORE weeks went by, and James was still struggling with his stressful thoughts about the money laundering. As soon as he decided he should quit and get an accounting job elsewhere, he began to wonder if the Martonis would ever allow him to leave. Would Nick tell them about the audit he conducted? Had he told them already?

James also considered going to the police, but that felt like he would be betraying a friend. He could still recall Anthony's words. *Thanks for being my friend, Jimmy. You are a really good friend.*

But the longer he waited, the more he felt like a criminal. He continued to work diligently and maintained a positive facade, but the stress was tearing him up inside. One day, he walked downstairs to grab lunch for Nick and himself. He realized that he had not seen Danny since the double date with Anthony.

"Hey, Pasquale, where have you been hiding Danny? I haven't seen him in a few weeks."

Pasquale's smile evaporated, and it seemed like the blood drained from his face. He stared at James for an uncomfortable amount of time and then responded in a somber tone, "Danny doesn't work here anymore. He quit."

James could not believe what he'd just heard. He knew how much Danny had enjoyed working at the restaurant.

"Quit? What do you mean he quit? He's your best waiter! Why did he quit? Where did he go? Why didn't he at least say goodbye?"

James could see Pasquale take a deep breath and fight back tears.

"I don't have any answers, Jimmy. I'm confused and upset. I loved that kid. He didn't even have the decency to come and talk to me about leaving."

Now James was truly puzzled. "What do you mean?"

"Anthony told me that Danny spoke to him and said he was leaving to pursue other opportunities—but he didn't give us his two weeks, let alone a goodbye. That's all I know."

James's chest tightened with a deep sense of dread. It was bad enough that he'd discovered the restaurant was involved in money laundering—and even worse, that Anthony not only had to know about it but was likely sanctioning it on a daily basis—but now, he was forced to consider something no "really good friend" ever should—was Anthony behind this?

He wanted to say no, of course not—*never*—but all he could think about was Anthony's eyes going red when he yelled at Andrea for speaking fondly of Danny, and he had to be realistic about what he was looking at here.

Was it possible he wasn't looking at his friend anymore? Was it possible he was looking at a born-and-bred mob boss in the flesh?

"Hey, Jimmy."

James felt his whole body go cold. He jerked his head around, along with Pasquale, to see none other than Anthony approaching them from behind.

"What're you boys up to?" Anthony asked innocently, readjusting the new Rolex he had sparkling on his wrist. Sal and Frank flanked his sides like two shadows.

Pasquale opened his mouth to say something James was sure wouldn't be the truth—but frankly, he'd had quite enough of that.

"Anthony," James interjected calmly, "what happened to Danny?"

Anthony glanced at Sal and Frank. A few seconds of silence slipped by, the tension rising with every single one. Anthony cleared his throat and asked, "What do you mean?"

James's jaw felt tight. "Pasquale said that he quit."

"Oh...yeah." Anthony laughed, but James knew good and well it was a farce. "He said he wanted to, uh...try something different."

"Different?" James pressed, despite Pasquale's warning glance. "What's he going to do?"

"I don't know what the fuck he's going to do," Anthony replied curtly, that red flashing in his eyes once again. "Maybe he's going to Hollywood to be in the movies. Don't ask so many stupid questions, Jimmy."

With that, Anthony began walking away—with Frank and Sal following suit. James watched as they approached the door and thought to himself, *Or else what?* He finally acknowledged the gut feeling he'd tried to shove away for weeks, ever since the audit. Something was wrong here—*very* wrong.

The next day was Saturday, and James went for a long run before breakfast. On his way back, he picked up the *Boston Globe* at the newsstand near his apartment. He poured his coffee, sat down at the kitchen table, and unrolled the day's paper.

The first thing he saw was Danny's face looking back at him.

His blood ran cold.

Next to the picture, the headline read:

### Body Found in Fens Identified

*Police found a partially decomposed body in the Fens area of the Back Bay on Thursday evening. It appears the body was the victim of foul play. The individual, a young man, was badly beaten and then shot in the head. The police have since identified the victim as Daniel (Danny) O'Brien.*

James immediately felt his stomach roil, cold chills rolling in waves over his body like a reverse fever. He ran to the bathroom and vomited. It felt like the whole world was crashing down on him. He sat on the edge of the tub for several minutes in a stupor, then took a shower. As the hot water splashed down on his body, he began to cry harder than he could ever remember. In his heart, he knew exactly what had happened, and at that very moment, he decided to talk to the one person he trusted the most.

When John saw the expression on his brother's face, he immediately asked, "Jimmy, what's wrong? What's happened?"

"I need to talk to you! It's bad . . . really bad!"

They sat down on John's couch, and James, in a halting voice filled with pain, embarrassment, and anger, began to tell his brother everything. He explained how he had uncovered the money laundering and then been warned not to say anything. James confessed that he had been struggling with what to do.

"And then, this morning, I read this in the *Globe*."

He threw the paper down on the coffee table and pointed to the article about the body being found. James shared with his brother how jealous Anthony had become when Andrea flirted with Danny. He explained how Anthony had told him that Danny had quit.

"In my heart . . . in my gut . . . I know exactly what happened to Danny. That jealous bastard had him killed for no reason at all. You were so right, Johnny. I was naïve . . . and I was blinded by my friendship with Anthony . . . and by the big bucks. You warned me that if I worked for a crook, I would become a crook. I feel so foolish . . . so fucking foolish and so, so dirty."

James began to sob uncontrollably; his whole body seemed to be convulsing. John reached over and held his brother.

James eventually settled down. John got up, grabbed a wet washcloth from the bathroom, and handed it to his brother. As James wiped his face, John poured a glass of scotch for both of them. Although it was barely noon, he knew that they both needed a drink. James slowly sipped the scotch. John could tell that his brother's mind was racing.

"Aren't you going to say *I told you so?*"

"I love you and would never say that to you! You are full of enough pain and remorse. You don't need me to kick you while you are down. Besides, I know that you have a good heart and will always do what is right."

After several minutes of silence, James said, "They have to pay for what they've done! The only way that I'll ever feel clean again is to do everything in my power to bring them to justice!"

"How do you plan on doing that?"

"I'll go to the police . . . no, not the police . . . the FBI. They're the ones who investigate organized crime. I'll tell them about the money laundering and the murder of Danny."

"Jimmy, these are really bad people," John said, picking his words carefully. "You're going to have to be extremely cautious. If they killed that young man for something as innocent as flirting, what do you think they'll do to you if they find out you've gone to the cops?"

James no longer appeared to feel like a victim and instead looked more like a fighter, an avenger who wanted to right a terrible wrong.

"Johnny, I can't let this go. If I do—if I simply *ignore* it—then they win, and worse yet, I become as bad as them! I couldn't live with myself if I did nothing."

James seemed to think of something, smiled, and said, "You remember when we would go to confession with Father Jason, and instead of giving us prayers for our penance, he would give us assignments that were somehow connected to our sin?"

"Yeah, I remember. I always hated it."

James laughed and replied, "Me too! I'd say, 'Come on, Father Jason, give me some Our Fathers and Hail Marys to say instead.' He would ignore my pleas. The strange thing is that after I had completed whatever task it was, I always felt much better. Well, this is my penance! This is my assignment!"

Then, James asked his brother for the phone book. He opened it up and looked under *F* for the Federal Bureau of Investigation. He located the number and saw that the office was in Chelsea. He grabbed the phone and dialed the number.

# 16

# The FBI Agent

**Joe Atkins**
**Boston | 1984**

"GOOD MORNING, THIS is Miss Lyons. How may I help you?"

"I . . . I want to speak to someone about the Martoni crime family."

"May I ask what this is about?"

"I have information about their money-laundering activities."

"Would you mind repeating that?"

"I have proof that they are filtering their crime money through their restaurant business."

"One moment, please. I'm going to connect you with one of our agents."

Each day, the FBI office in Chelsea would assign a different agent to handle the tip line. Their responsibility was to listen carefully to each caller and determine whether the information sounded legitimate. On this particular day, the agent on duty was Joe Atkins. It was a fortunate coincidence that Joe's regular assignment was with the organized crime unit.

"Good afternoon, this is Agent Joseph Atkins. To whom am I speaking?"

"This is James."

"James who?"

"Let's just stick with James for now, okay?"

"Sure, that's all right, James. You can call me Joe. Now, Miss Lyons said that you have information regarding the Martonis and money laundering. Is that correct?"

"Yes, that's right."

"How did you obtain this information?"

"I . . . I'm the accountant for the Martonis' restaurants."

When Joe Atkins heard this, his eyes lit up. The FBI suspected that the Martoni family was using the restaurant business to launder cash from their illegal activities but had no hard evidence to support this suspicion. Through surveillance operations and coordination with other agencies, the FBI had accumulated a significant amount of information about this crime family but not enough to obtain indictments. US attorneys rarely sought an indictment unless they had an overwhelming amount of evidence that would result in an open-and-shut case. Consequently, their success rate was over 90 percent.

Joe was elated because now he actually had someone who worked in the restaurant business and was willing to volunteer information. He recalled that earlier that morning, he had been upset when told he would be the agent assigned to the tip line. He disliked working on Saturdays because it took him away from his family. Then, to be listening to all types of crank calls was like pouring salt into the wound. After hearing what James was offering, Joe recalled his mother often saying to him, *Now, Joseph, remember that everything happens for a reason. You just have to trust in God.*

He smiled at the wise advice from his saintly mother and continued his questioning.

"James, are you personally involved in laundering the money?"

"No . . . absolutely not! I've only worked there for less than two years. I . . . I took the job because I was assured that the restaurant business was completely legitimate. Now I realize that I was extremely naive. A few months ago, I decided on my own to audit the cash receipts. I wanted to make sure that no one was stealing from the restaurant. To my surprise, it seemed that just the opposite was happening. After checking and double-checking, I found that the actual cash receipts were significantly higher than they should be."

"How much higher?"

"Each of the restaurants averaged at least ten thousand dollars more than expected on a weekly basis. Sometimes, it was as much as twenty-five thousand more. When I raised the issue with my boss, Nick, he warned me to forget it and never to mention it to anyone else."

"Nick? Would that be Nick Mancuso, the controller?"

"Yes, yes! Do you know Nick?"

"Let's say we know of him. We know that he has worked for the Martoni family for a very long time. He is extremely bright and highly trusted by Mario Martoni. But no . . . no, I don't know him personally. Our paths have never crossed."

Joe Atkins did some quick mental math and realized that the figures James provided could easily account for five to ten million of illegal cash being laundered on an annual basis. This amount was consistent with the FBI's estimate of the Martoni family's proceeds from their illegal activities. It appeared that James's information was credible. The agent was curious as to what would drive someone to risk coming to the FBI and so asked, "James, tell me why you're bringing this information to the FBI."

"My brother!"

"Your brother? What do you mean by that?"

"My brother warned me against taking this job. He said that if I worked for a crook, then I was a crook. And I do not want to be a crook!" After a few moments of silence, James said, "There is something else."

He then told the agent about Danny O'Brien, choking up when he described reading about Danny's body being found. Atkins listened attentively to everything James said. His intuition told him that this caller was being completely honest. It was obvious he got caught up with the wrong people and not only wanted out but also wanted to do something about the wrong.

Joe wanted to meet James in person, so he asked, "Would you be willing to meet me privately . . . someplace away from the FBI office?"

"Sure . . . I guess so. When?"

"Tomorrow is Sunday. How's tomorrow morning work for you?"

"My brother and I usually attend mass at Saint Ignatius Church."

"You mean near Boston College?"

"Yeah, that's right."

"I'm very familiar with it. I got my undergraduate degree at BC. What time is mass?"

"Ten o'clock."

"Okay, I'll meet you at Alumni Stadium a little after eleven. I'm in my early forties, slightly over six feet, with a slim build and dark-brown hair. I'll be wearing a Red Sox cap and a yellow Boston Eagles T-shirt. I'll be carrying two cups of coffee. How do you like your coffee?"

"Just black. Thanks."

"Good. I'll see you in the morning. And James . . ."

"Yes?"

"You are doing the right thing."

"Thanks, Joe. I'll see you in the morning."

—∞∘⦿∘∞—

As discussed, James and John attended mass the next morning. Ironically, the first reading was from chapter 28 of Ezekiel: "But if the wicked, turning from the wickedness he has committed, does what is right and just, he shall preserve his life . . ."

Upon hearing these words, the two brothers turned to each other and smiled.

After mass, James headed for his meeting with Agent Atkins. John walked to Newton Centre, where he planned to wait for his brother.

It was a short walk from the church to the stadium. Atkins was easy to spot, and James walked straight toward him.

"Hello, Joe, I'm James."

Joe smiled, handed James a coffee cup, and said, "It's a pleasure to meet you, James. Let's walk to the other side of the stadium and find a quiet, shady spot to sit."

After they sat down, Joe asked James if he had gone to BC.

"No, my brother attended Boston College while I attended UMass. And now he's off to the seminary."

"No kidding? He's going to become a priest? So, is he older or younger than you?"

"He's the same age as me. We're twins . . . identical twins."

"Wow! Identical twins! That must've been something growing up."

They spent the next half hour getting to know each other personally, an approach Joe used to help build trust and rapport with witnesses. James learned that after undergraduate school, Joe attended law school. He applied to the FBI in his final year of law school and was accepted upon graduation. Joe was married with two children—a son and a daughter—and lived in Waltham.

Then they got down to business.

"Now, James, I want you to tell me exactly how you determined that the cash receipts were higher than they should be."

James explained the specific audit procedures he had used in his investigation. Joe listened carefully and was impressed with the thoroughness of the audit work.

"That is amazing. Where did you learn to perform such substantive audit procedures?"

"Our auditing professor at college had worked for one of the Big Eight accounting firms. He brought a lot of his knowledge and experience to the classroom. In fact, I can honestly say that his audit class was probably one of my favorite courses."

"Well, he certainly taught you well. I have a very important question for you. Do you actually have access to these audit work papers?"

"Yes, I brought them to my apartment. Once I saw Nick's reaction to my findings, I decided to remove any trace of my work from the office."

"Good thinking. Would you be willing to hand those work papers over to me?"

Without hesitating, James said, "Well, of course! I want to do whatever I can!"

"Outstanding! Can you meet me one night this week?"

"Sure. Just tell me where and when."

They established a time and place for the next meeting. Then Joe asked his next question.

"James, what I'm going to ask you next is very risky. If you should get caught, you'll be in extreme danger. These are bad people. I want you to really think before answering me. Are you willing to take the risk?"

"I am certain that Anthony had Danny killed out of jealousy. I can only imagine what Anthony or Mario would do to someone who betrayed them, but I am committed. Like I said, I want to do whatever I can to make things right. I'm willing to take the risk."

Joe explained that it would entail getting into Nick's office without being seen. Then, after describing the types of documents he wanted, he said, "I will provide you with a miniature camera to take pictures of any documents you're able to find."

"There is a separate file cabinet in Nick's office. It's always locked, but I know where Nick keeps the keys. The documents you described would most likely be in that cabinet."

Joe was intrigued when he heard about this file cabinet. He knew it could contain a treasure trove of information. He modified his instructions for James.

"In addition to the types of documents I described, take pictures of anything else you think would be of interest. Just remember everything your auditing professor taught you."

Then Joe became very serious and warned James, "This is a great opportunity, but under no circumstances—absolutely no circumstances whatsoever—are you to take any of these actions until I tell you it's all right to do so. This is extremely important! Do you understand me?"

Joe was being especially firm on this last point of not proceeding without permission. Joe's adamancy was because he needed to request authority from the US attorney for these actions. Without this authority, an FBI agent was forbidden from asking anyone to commit what could be construed as a crime, such as breaking into a locked file cabinet.

"I understand the assignment, but I have one important question. Is there anything you can do about the murder of Danny O'Brien?"

Joe thought about the question before answering. He realized how much this meant to James.

"James, we will definitely look into it, but I don't want to lie to you. I think your suspicion about who killed Danny is absolutely correct. However, it's all circumstantial. People like Mario and Anthony rarely do the dirty work themselves. They have their most trusted associates handle the killings. And these killers are absolutely loyal—loyal to the end! They rarely give up their bosses. As far as the gun is concerned, it's probably sitting at the bottom of the Boston Harbor. We will investigate it, but I'm not confident we will be able to prove anything."

"That's a big disappointment . . . but . . . I appreciate your honesty."

The agent then gave James his emergency pager number and said, "You can call this number anytime, day or night. Don't hesitate to use it, especially if you feel threatened. And one more thing: if I think you're in danger, I'll call you with a code word or phrase. It will essentially mean for you to get out of there immediately. So, what do you think is a good phrase for me to use?"

"Let's use the phrase 'Sons of Thunder.'"

Joe smiled at James. Having been raised in a devout Catholic family, he knew where that name had come from.

"Sons of Thunder, huh? So, I take it your brother's name is John."

James smiled back in acknowledgment.

They shook hands and confirmed that they would meet the following Wednesday night at nine. Joe left feeling that his task force was on the verge of crippling a major crime family thanks to the efforts of a courageous young man. At the same time, he worried about keeping James from any harm.

# 17

## The Decision

**James Donnelly**
**Boston | 1984**

DURING THE NEXT three days at work, James did his best to disguise his true feelings. Agent Atkins advised him to continue acting as if nothing had happened; the last thing they wanted to do was raise any suspicions. Maintaining this facade was extremely stressful. James tried to ease the internal tension by focusing on how he would feel once this was all behind him.

After work on Wednesday, he went on his usual run, showered, and then ate dinner before gathering his work papers and stuffing them into an old briefcase. He and Agent Atkins had agreed to meet at a quiet coffee shop in Watertown.

Joe was already sitting in a corner booth when James entered the shop. There were only a few other customers in the café, and they seemed to be caught up in their own conversations. James shook hands with Joe, sat down, and placed the briefcase between them. The waitress poured each of them coffee. Atkins was the first to speak.

"It's good to see you again, James. How are you holding up?"

"To be honest with you . . ." James paused, cupping his hot mug of black coffee. They had only known each other for a few days, but he knew that he either had to trust this man completely or not at all. *Honesty is key.* "These past few days have been stressful. I'm just glad that Anthony hasn't dropped by the office; I'm not sure that I would've been able to hide my contempt for him."

Joe sighed, shaking his head slightly. James thought for a moment that he might even reach forward and pat his arm comfortingly, but he didn't. "That's completely normal, James. Under the circumstances, it would be difficult for anyone to hide their true feelings, but I'm warning you—it's *essential* that you do. You don't want them to start questioning your loyalty; you already know that they play for keeps."

James nodded and promised to remain vigilant of his emotions.

The agent told James that he could now proceed with gathering the information from Nick's file cabinet because the US attorney had provided the proper authorization. Joe handed the miniature camera to James and then instructed him on how to use it. Once again, they discussed the documents of interest. Joe seemed genuinely concerned for him. "I want you to be extremely careful, James. When do you think you can safely get into Nick's locked files?"

James had been thinking about it and had a plan. "Nick usually leaves the office early at least once or twice each month to visit his daughter's family in New Hampshire. He hasn't gone up yet this month, so I suspect he'll be going within the next two weeks. When he leaves, I'm the only other person in the office. That's when I plan to get into his file cabinet."

"And you're not worried about someone walking in on you?" asked Joe.

He'd actually thought about the possibility of someone coming upstairs from the restaurant.

"It's not likely, but just to play it safe, I plan on locking the door before going into Nick's office. It's a dead-bolt lock, so if someone should decide to come up from the restaurant, they'll have to knock first. This will give me plenty of warning to get out of Nick's office."

Joe nodded slowly, taking a sip of his coffee in a way that seemed indicative of his approval. "Sounds like you thought of everything. That's good . . . very good. I want you to call my emergency pager number from your apartment once you have taken the pictures. I'll call you back immediately, and we'll schedule another meeting. All right?"

"I understand . . . but I want to ask you something."

"What is it, James?"

"After you have all this information—my work papers and pictures of the documents—how long will it be before you can arrest them?"

"Our task force has been working with the US attorney's office for years. If your audit work and the documents you obtain are as good as I suspect they are, the US attorney will go to the secret grand jury to seek indictments. Then we'll get clearance to make the arrests. So, we are probably talking about a few weeks from the time you turn over the information to me."

"So, what happens to me? Will I have to testify to this secret grand jury?"

"No, that won't be necessary for the grand jury. I'll be the only person testifying." Joe was quiet for several moments after that, as though envisioning his testimony. "James, I know that you are a good person who simply got caught up with the wrong people. I also know that you have an extremely close relationship with your family. Before we go any further, I want you to consider something very, very carefully . . ." Joe looked directly into James's eyes. "While you won't testify before the grand jury, you will be required to testify at the actual criminal trial. From the time of the arrest until the trial, you will be kept in a series of safe houses. Even though the indictments will be sealed, it won't take them long to figure out that you are the informant. Then, once you actually testify, you'll be placed in a witness protection program with a completely new identity. You will receive financial assistance and be established in a new job in an entirely different part of the country. James Donnelly . . . will no longer exist."

James stared back at Agent Atkins, slack-jawed. "That's temporary, right?" he asked, only for the man sitting across from him to stare silently in response. Heart beating faster, James leaned across the table and whispered, "That's *temporary*, right, Joe?"

Joe didn't so much as blink when he answered, "You will never, ever be able to see your family again."

James swallowed hard and then asked, "If I don't testify, what does that do to your case?"

"We probably won't go forward with the indictment. Your testimony is critical to our case. We would have to wait until we found another crack in their organization. It could literally be years before that happens."

"Years? So, they would go on stealing, selling drugs, and killing for years?"

Joe nodded and then reiterated, "It's essential that you understand what you will be giving up."

"I really appreciate your honesty. Can I . . . discuss this with my family before I make a final decision?"

"Of course! That's exactly what you should do. They need to know the ramifications of your decision as well."

"My brother and I are going to visit our father this coming weekend. That's when I'll talk to them."

In the meantime, James was left to ponder a future without his brother, without Father Pat or Father Jason, without anybody he'd come to love and hold dear. It was bad enough that he'd already lost a close friend in Anthony, but now *this* . . .

He pulled out his wallet to pay for his coffee, only for Agent Atkins to beat him to it and take the bill, insisting it was on him. With a numb and wordless nod, James stood from the table, making his way to go.

"James," the agent said as he grabbed the briefcase. "I know this is hard. Hell, *hard* is a massive understatement. You'd be giving up everything, but . . . think of the lives you'll save."

*Think of the lives you'll save.*

James nodded dully once again, then left, pushing his way through the café's exit and into a rainy evening. *Think of the lives you'll save.* The words echoed in his brain, an encore that he had no interest in hearing, but it was true.

*Think of the lives you'll save . . . in exchange for sacrificing your own.*

John offered to drive that weekend—even though that was typically his brother's job, given the simple fact that he drove a Mustang GT while John drove an ancient Honda Civic. He suspected that his brother would have a lot on his mind, and based on his silence throughout the drive, John's assumption was spot-on. At first, he figured it was best not to bring it up, but something told him James needed his guidance. Call it a brother's intuition.

"Jimmy, you've been awfully quiet," he began, keeping his eyes trained on the road ahead of them and his voice as neutral as possible. "I'm guessing you've got a lot on your mind. I want you to know that I think what you are doing is amazing. Nevertheless, I'm sure it's gotta be pretty difficult and stressful. I'm always here for you."

James stayed silent for a moment before actively fighting back tears. John wasn't sure what the appropriate move was—consoling his brother or not making a big deal out of it. He decided to compromise by clapping his brother on the shoulder and saying, "Better out than in, man. Tell me what's on your mind."

"Thanks, Johnny. I know I can always count on you."

"Of course you can," John replied, glancing sidelong just in time to catch his brother see the sign for the next rest stop on the Massachusetts Turnpike.

"Let's stop there," James said earnestly. "I really need to talk to you."

After finding a parking spot, John shut off the engine, turned to his brother, and saw the tears welling up in his eyes.

"If... I agree to testify... then..." James broke down before he could finish the sentence. He buried his face in his hands and began to bawl.

John reached out and placed his hand on James's shoulder in a way that showed both concern and support. When his brother finally stopped crying, John asked, "What is it? If you testify, then what?"

"I'll never see you again!"

John was stunned by what he'd just heard. James explained, "If I testify against this crime family . . . then I'll be a target. The FBI will place me in the witness protection program. They'll move me to a different part of the country . . . give me a different name . . . and . . . and we will never, ever be able to see each other again!"

John now understood why his brother had been so reticent and pensive. "My God, Jimmy, that's a tremendous burden you are carrying. It's an unbelievably tough decision. What are you going to do?"

"I honestly don't know. I just don't know! I'm so torn inside. If I don't testify, then those miserable bastards will go on committing crimes for many more years. If I do testify, then I'm forced to say goodbye to you and Father Pat forever. And Father Jason, too . . . He's been like a big brother to us. I can't even begin to imagine my life without the three of you in it. Even if I decide not to testify, I know there is no way I can continue to work for the Martonis, but I'm not sure they'll ever let me go. They're ruthless!"

James paused for a moment and then continued, "I realize that if I had only listened to you, I wouldn't be in this terrible mess. You warned me about going to work for these criminals. You can't begin to imagine how many times I've cursed myself for not listening to you."

John was not sure how to respond, so he simply reached out and hugged his brother. James immediately wrapped his arms around him, and it seemed neither wanted to let go. After several minutes, they resumed their trip in complete silence.

As soon as they pulled into the driveway, a smiling Father Pat came out of the rectory to greet his sons. They were escorted inside, where Father Pat announced Father Jason's special seafood dish for the night— *baccalà alla polenta*. Father Pat provided an excellent Italian wine to complement the dish. There was plenty of laughter and playful teasing throughout the meal.

The next morning, Father Pat cooked omelets and Canadian bacon for breakfast. As his father placed the three-egg, spinach omelet, which was oozing with cheese, on his plate, James said, "This meal looks fantastic. Between Father Jason's delicious seafood dinner last night and this morning's feast, you are going to fatten the two of us up!"

"That's nonsense, Jimmy. You need your energy if you are going to hike those mountains today. I even made some lunch for you boys." After a few moments, Father Pat added, "How I wish I was young enough to join you! Just be prepared to tell me all about it when you return."

Placing his arm around his father, John reassured him, "You can count on it!"

Afterward, the two brothers left for their trek in the Berkshires. The cloudless deep-blue sky enhanced the rich green foliage of the mountains. The rain earlier in the week had intensified the flow of the waterfalls.

After standing at the ridgeline and silently looking out, James finally said what was on his mind. "It's going to be difficult not experiencing the beauty of these mountains with you." Then, after letting that statement linger for a while, he changed the subject. "Doesn't Father Pat look great? It's hard to believe he is in his late seventies!"

"He does look fantastic. He seemed full of energy. And he hasn't stopped smiling since we arrived last night. We were truly blessed that our mother chose to leave us on his doorstep." Then after a brief silence, John asked, "Do you think she ever expected that he would adopt us?"

"I'm not sure . . . but I'm definitely glad he did. We have had an amazing life—Father Pat, Father Jason, the nuns . . ." James's voice began to crack, and he looked up into the sky and shook his head. "You know . . . I was hoping that someday we would have a chance to meet our mother. If I go into this witness protection program . . . that's never going to happen . . . for me. I'm hoping it happens for you, Johnny. And if . . . when it does . . . tell her that . . . that I love her." James was clearly agonizing over his decision.

John reached out, placed his hand on his brother's shoulder, and rubbed it gently. After a few moments, he said, "I'm guessing you're going to bring it up tonight after dinner."

James took a deep breath and slowly nodded. "Yeah . . . yeah . . . and I'll need plenty of Father Pat's scotch to discuss it. Hell, I think we'll all need it!"

———∞o∘👁∘o∞———

James's mind was racing during the vigil mass on Saturday evening. One moment, he was praying for guidance. The next, he was mentally rehearsing what he was going to say to his family. After mass, the four of them left for one of their favorite local restaurants. The chef's special that night was a reverse-seared T-bone steak. They all decided to order the special and agreed that it was the best steak they had ever tasted. On the drive home, Father Jason entertained them with his wonderful singing voice.

Back in the living room of the rectory, Father Pat poured two fingers for everyone. After they had toasted and taken their first sips, James decided it was time to share his difficult decision with his family. He took another swallow of his scotch and said, "I have something to share with all of you."

Clearly not realizing what was coming and recalling a similar opening statement from John, Father Jason joked, "Don't tell us that you are entering the seminary too, Jimmy?"

James pursed his lips and swallowed hard, wishing very much that was what he was about to say. *Anything* was better than what he was going to share. "I wish it was that, Father Jason. Unfortunately, it's much . . . much more serious than that."

The room went silent.

Father Pat glanced instinctively at John, who deliberately wouldn't meet his eyes. He set down his glass and asked, "How serious, my boy?"

James looked sorrowfully at Father Pat and decided to start from the beginning.

He explained how he took the accounting job at the restaurant even though John had tried to convince him against it. He acknowledged that he had been blinded by his close friendship with Anthony, as well as the money. He professed that he truly enjoyed the job and had learned a great deal. He explained how he was given increased responsibilities and challenging projects. Next came the details of his audit and how he uncovered the money-laundering activities. He told them that he felt extremely stressed and experienced a tremendous amount of internal conflict when he realized the Martonis were using the restaurants to launder their ill-gotten gains.

By this time, Father Pat had poured more scotch for all of them. This is when James told them about Danny's murder and how this tragic event was the final straw for him. He discussed meeting with the FBI agent and becoming an informant. Then he got to the toughest part. He took another long sip of his scotch and then shared his latest conversation with Joe Atkins. When he finished, the room was completely silent.

Father Pat took several minutes to seemingly gather his thoughts. James knew his father wasn't one to speak without thinking, and when he did speak, he always had something valuable to share. A childlike part of him hoped that, somehow, Father Pat would have a way to solve this problem, to get him out of this. But based on the way the old priest's expression seemed to deflate, his eyes downturned with unspoken grief, James knew there wasn't a way out—for if there was, Father Pat would've discovered it already.

"Jimmy, you have been carrying a terrible . . . a *horrible* burden, my son. I can't even begin to imagine how you must be feeling. I heard you say that you wished you'd never taken the job and how you are beating yourself up for being foolish and naive. And quite honestly, I don't even want to think about spending the last few years of my life without seeing or speaking to you. I'm sure that Johnny and Father Jason feel the same way."

He paused and took another drink of his scotch. Throughout their entire lives, Father Pat had always taught his sons to look at issues from all perspectives before making a final decision, and now, to James, it seemed he was about to do it again.

"But before you continue berating yourself, I want you to think of another possibility. Maybe . . . just maybe . . . as bad as this all seems . . .

God has a plan for you. These are clearly evil people. They do terrible things. It's possible that God is using you to put an end to this evil. And yes, the four people in this room will pay a very personal and painful price, but just imagine how many lives will be positively affected if this evil is destroyed. Think of how many fewer victims there will be when these gangsters are put away."

James had never been as fully devoted to his faith in God as Father Pat or his brother, but in that moment, he could've sworn he felt something. A shift in the air, in the light—in the very energy of the room—that felt very much like God's message to him. As though, perhaps, God *was* listening. That all along, he'd been listening.

Father Pat finished his drink, put down his glass, and looked James in the eyes with all the sincerity of a man speaking not to a boy, not to his son, but to another man capable of making the hard decisions dished out by life.

"Jimmy, I love you with all of my heart and soul. I thank God every day for blessing my life with you and Johnny. But I think everybody in this room is aware that this is bigger than any of us. If you, my son, have the chance to do something that will save the lives of others," he said, pausing to smile, despite it all, "then what a privilege and a gift that is, no matter the personal sacrifice."

James looked at his father with loving admiration. "You're right," he said, and Father Pat's hand found his, gripping it tight. "You've given me a lot to think about. I'm going to sleep on it and make my decision tomorrow."

But James didn't wait until the following day to make his decision. In his heart, it was very much already made. And so that night, before bed, James called Joe and told the FBI agent that he had decided to testify at the criminal trial.

"My father gave me the guidance to view my decision from a different perspective," he told Agent Atkins when asked. "Essentially, while it will be a significant personal sacrifice for my family and me, it will be for the greater good of society to put these criminals away."

Joe was quiet over the phone for a few moments before expressing that he was thoroughly impressed by what he'd just heard and told James that his father must be a very wise and wonderful person. James insisted he was so much more than that.

"I've been blessed to have him as a father, mentor, and friend throughout my entire life. He not only preaches his faith, he lives it to the fullest extent each and every day. I will always love him . . . and even though we're sleeping under the same roof right now, I already miss him."

# 18

# The Evidence

**James Donnelly**
**Boston | 1984**

JAMES ARRIVED AT the office just before eight o'clock. *This is the day,* he thought to himself. Nick was taking a three-day weekend to visit his daughter, and James would be completely alone. He hadn't slept much the night before—rehearsing every step of the plan, wondering what would happen if he were caught. The fear and anxiety were real, but so was his commitment. He kept remembering Father Pat's words. *God is using you to put an end to this evil.*

James focused on completing all of the work that Nick had left for him and was finished by two thirty. Then, at long last, it was time to obtain the information from Nick's office. He couldn't avoid it any longer, even if he wanted to—which he didn't. At this point, he was ready to rip off the Band-Aid that was this gigantic source of anxiety. And so, he went about his plan. With shaking hands, he secured the dead-bolt lock on the office door. Then he went to the controller's office and pulled out the bottom desk drawer where Nick always kept his keys. The drawer contained several manila folders. But—

The keys weren't there.

James swore under his breath, panicking. If he didn't find the keys, then his plan was botched, and he'd have to wait another month for Nick to leave again. But he took a deep breath and moved the files around. Sure enough, the keys had fallen underneath one of them. He reminded himself that he needed to place the keys back exactly where he had found them.

Then he walked to the locked file cabinet. It took a few tries before he found the correct key. He opened the top drawer and began looking through the contents. It contained ledgers that he'd never seen before. He opened one of them, and it appeared to track receipts from several different businesses unrelated to the restaurants. As James examined each page more closely, he realized that it was a detailed analysis of the illegal activities of the crime family. There was even a legend at the back of the ledger that provided an explanation of each source. Joe Atkins had informed James that most organized crime families kept a comprehensive second set of books to track all of their activities. In reviewing the monthly totals and doing some quick mental calculations, James realized that these figures closely approximated the excess receipts that he had found during his audit. He took out the miniature camera and began taking pictures of each page exactly the way Joe had instructed. The ledgers were separated by years and included revenue, expenditures, receivables, and payables. Nearly two hours had passed by the time James finished taking pictures of all the ledgers.

There were no ledgers in the next drawer. Instead, there were approximately a dozen hanging files. James pulled out the first file and realized it contained bank statements. He looked at the name and location of the bank and immediately realized it was an offshore account. He reviewed the rest of the files and determined that each represented a different off-shore bank account. He also noticed that the names of the depositors were unfamiliar companies. He took pictures of each of the bank statements.

The third and final drawer appeared to contain legal documents. The names of the companies on the bank statements were on these documents as well. He theorized that these might be the shell companies Joe Atkins had mentioned when discussing the various documents. James took pictures of each page. It was nearly six o'clock when James finished putting the last documents back into the file drawer.

At that very moment, he heard loud knocking on the office door, and his heart began to pound rapidly. Next, he heard Anthony's voice. "Hey, Jimmy, what are you doing up there? Are you sleeping?"

James could not think of a worse time for Anthony to show up. He quickly slammed the drawer shut, locked the cabinet, pulled out the keys, and placed them in the desk drawer exactly where he had found them. He shouted down the hallway, "I'll be right there! Hold on a minute."

"What the hell are you doing up here with the damn door locked, Jimmy?"

James had practiced his answer several times, although he never expected to be using it with Anthony. He opened the door and said, "I had to use the john, so I locked the door. Nick isn't here, and I didn't want anyone from the restaurant coming into the office area. We have a lot of confidential information that the restaurant employees shouldn't see."

Anthony seemed to consider the point, then, nodding approvingly, said, "Smart thinking, Jimmy . . . but why are you working so late on a Friday night?"

"There were quite a few items that Nick asked me to get done. Then I also started working on our accounts payable to get a little head start for next week. I kind of lost track of time."

"You work too hard, Jimmy! I'm going to tell Nick to give you a raise. Look, grab your jacket and come downstairs. I've already told Pasquale to set a table aside for us. We'll have some drinks and a nice dinner together. Just like old times! Come on—let's go!"

James realized that Anthony would not take no for an answer, so he said, "Sure, Anthony, that sounds great. Go on down, and I'll be there in five minutes. I just want to clear a few things off my desk."

Anthony laughed, pointed to his Rolex, and said, "All right, you've got exactly *five* minutes. If you're not downstairs by then, I'm sending Sal and Frank up here to get you!"

James had felt the adrenaline rushing through his body as he was talking to Anthony. Now he *really* needed to use the bathroom. He wet his face with cold water and took several deep breaths to calm himself down. He also remembered Joe's counsel to hide his true feelings about Anthony, so joining him for drinks was definitely a smart idea, but what about the camera? He couldn't keep it on his person; that was just asking for trouble. He decided that it would be safer to leave the camera in the locked drawer of his desk and then retrieve it after dinner.

Anthony had already ordered drinks for both of them when James got to the table. Anthony was in an especially good mood. He appeared warm and friendly to all of the waitstaff. When Pasquale came by to personally take their dinner order, Anthony was extremely complimentary of the restaurant. James thought to himself, *Is this the same guy who had a young man murdered for no reason other than jealousy? Is this the future head of one of the most notorious crime families in the Northeast?* And for a split second, he started to second-guess himself. Anthony was a friend of his, arguably one of his closest friends. It was one thing for his father to be involved with money laundering, but was he seriously convinced Anthony had *murdered* somebody?

Then he remembered something Father Pat had said to him years before. *Beware, Jimmy, beware! The devil comes in many shapes and forms. He will seduce you with his warm and friendly personality and at the same time be plotting to steal your eternal soul.*

Never had those words rung truer than at that moment.

As usual, the appetizers and entrées were excellent. During dinner, Anthony explained that he had not been around much because his father was getting him involved in the other businesses. He spoke of how busy he was and how much he was enjoying it all. It was as if he had totally forgotten his statement to James that night in their college dorm room. *I don't plan on following him into the crime business . . . I don't want anything to do with the rest of his organization.*

After finishing his espresso, Anthony got up to leave, smiled at James, and said, "I really enjoyed tonight, Jimmy. You are a really good friend. And remember . . . someday, *you're* going to be my numbers guy."

Knowing the contempt that he held for Anthony and that he was about to bring down this entire crime family, James had to draw from his deepest resources before smiling and responding, "I'd really like that, Anthony. I agree this has been an outstanding evening! Thank you so much."

They parted company, and James hurried back upstairs to get the camera. He placed it at the bottom of his briefcase and then put some miscellaneous files on top of it before locking the briefcase. The adrenaline was still pumping through James's body when he arrived at his apartment. He immediately set the briefcase down and called Joe Atkins. "Joe, I have it! I have the evidence!" The excitement in his voice was evident.

"That's wonderful, James. I couldn't stop thinking about you for the entire day."

"I want to get the camera to you as soon as possible. Should we meet tonight?"

"No...let's meet early tomorrow morning—say, eight o'clock—at BC."

"Same spot?"

"Yes. And James..."

"Yes, Joe?"

"You've done the right thing! Thank you!

It was a bright, sunny day when James arrived at the campus. Joe smiled when he saw James, and then they found a quiet spot on the other side of the stadium. As soon as they sat down, James took the camera from his pocket and handed it to Joe. Then he described everything he had seen in the file cabinet. James also told Joe about the unexpected visit from Anthony.

"James, you've done an amazing job! You were extremely thorough, and your ability to recall so much detail is quite impressive. We will develop the pictures immediately and then begin to compare them with all of our other information. Based on what you've told me, I'm extremely confident that the US attorney will move forward with requesting the indictments from the secret grand jury."

Before James could even ask his next question, Joe continued, "As I told you, I suspect that it will take a few weeks...possibly a month before we can get the indictments. The US attorney wants to make absolutely certain our case is airtight. And to ensure that you don't give off any vibes, I won't warn you before we make the arrests. If you know the exact day, you might inadvertently say something that alerts them. Your body language could also give them an unintentional warning. I want you to be as surprised as everyone else. In the meantime, just keep doing your work. You will also be taken into custody on the day of the arrests. This will give the appearance that you are being charged as well. In reality, you will be taken to a safe house. However, it won't be long before they begin to suspect that you are our informant. As we discussed before, you may be moved to a variety of safe houses. The Martonis will use any means possible to track you down and prevent you from testifying. It will be six to twelve months from the time of the arrests to the conclusion of the trial. Once the trial is over, you'll be put into the witness protection program. Even with a conviction, there will be a target on your back. The Martonis will want their revenge. They'll have their people watching your family very closely in hopes that you try to reach out to them. That is why it is absolutely necessary for you to be in this program."

James listened to everything and wondered what he would do to occupy his time during those months in a safe house. He also considered how difficult it would be to never see his family again, but he didn't allow his mind to linger there for long, as that wouldn't do him any good. His focus right now had to be on doing whatever it took to complete the next step in this process until it was all said and done.

"I have to ask you again, James," Agent Atkins said, looking at the campus's rolling greens for a few seconds before turning to fix his gaze on James. "Are you really up for this? It's not too late to back out now—"

"In my eyes, it's already too late," James replied bluntly. "It's too late for Danny. I won't wait for it to be too late for somebody else."

Agent Atkins nodded slowly, pressing his lips into a fine line before saying, "You're a good man, James. You're a good man."

James left to pick up John and drive to western Massachusetts for another visit with Father Pat. The brothers had agreed they would spend as much quality family time together as possible during the remaining weekends prior to the arrests. Each time James said goodbye to his father, he hugged him tightly and did not want to let go. He realized that it might be their last time together. There were plenty of tears during these goodbyes. It had been three weeks since his last meeting with Joe Atkins, and each day, James wondered, *Will today be the day the FBI makes the arrests?*

It was taking longer than a month due to all of the valuable information James had provided. The accounting documents, combined with the information they had previously gathered, enabled the FBI to build a solid criminal case. The information about shell companies and offshore bank accounts permitted them to follow the money and identify several accomplices. This process would result in a multiple-person indictment.

It took six weeks to finalize the data and schedule the secret grand jury. Joe was the only witness to testify, and during several hours of testimony, he was able to lay out the evidence in a clear and concise manner. The US attorney obtained an eighteen-person indictment against the top echelon of the Martoni crime family. He actually brought a RICO— Racketeer Influenced and Corrupt Organizations—charge against each of these individuals. Before this law was enacted by Congress, prosecutors had found it difficult to convict the higher-ranking members of crime organizations because they were rarely the ones who actually committed the crimes. With this law, prosecutors simply had to prove the individual owned or managed a business that committed these illegal activities.

The indictment included multiple counts of money laundering, tax evasion, and extortion. The grand jury approved the indictments late on Friday afternoon. It was decided that the FBI task force would make the arrests on the following Monday.

# 19

# The Final Visit

**James Donnelly**
**Rectory | 1984**

SO, JAMES WAS able to spend another weekend with his family, not knowing that it would be his last. Fortunately, James had convinced his brother to take Friday off so that they would have a three-day weekend with their father. They drove out on Thursday evening and arrived at the rectory around nine thirty. James had not told his father that they would be arriving a day earlier because he wanted to surprise him. He got his wish when Father Pat opened the door. At first, the old priest tilted his head with a quizzical look on his face, and then he quickly smiled with uncontrolled excitement. Father Jason brought out the bottle of scotch, and the four of them stayed up past midnight, talking and enjoying each other's company. It was as if James had a premonition that this might be their last weekend together and wanted to hold on to each precious moment.

It was a glorious three days. After Friday morning mass, the four of them walked over to the convent for breakfast with the wonderful sisters, whom both brothers always considered their foster mothers. Sister Annette had not lost her sense of humor and was soon teasing James about finding a nice girl and getting married. That night, Father Jason cooked another wonderful Italian dinner. The two brothers went off for a hike to their special place early Saturday morning. After the vigil mass, they had an outstanding gourmet dinner at a local inn. And naturally, the scotch came out when they returned to the rectory. It was not long before Father Jason was leading them in a medley of Sinatra songs. The next day, he confessed that he'd struggled through the early Sunday morning mass.

When James said goodbye to his father, he could not control the tears. As he wrapped his arms around Father Pat, he said in a soft, gentle voice, "I love you so much. I can never express to you how much you mean to me . . . how grateful I am to have you in my life. I'm going to miss you so very much. You will always, *always* be in my heart."

Father Pat was so choked up that he could not speak. Instead, he gave James a big smile and kissed his son's cheek.

James parked the car when they reached John's apartment. Realizing that this could be their last time together, he turned to his brother and said, "It was an amazing weekend. You know . . . I'm not ready to let it end. What do you say I come in and have a beer with you?"

"Sounds like a perfect idea to me."

John took two bottles of beer from the refrigerator, and they sat down. After taking a sip of his beer, James turned to his brother and shared what he was thinking. "Do you remember that movie that Father Pat loved to watch every Christmas . . . the one with Jimmy Stewart?"

"You mean *It's a Wonderful Life?*"

"Yeah, that's it. Well, I was thinking, this has been a wonderful life! Being raised by the kindest, gentlest man in the universe...having Father Jason as a big brother...and those nuns..."

"You're right—it has been pretty special."

"And I was able to share it with you—my twin brother...and most importantly, my best friend! Sometimes you don't realize how good you have it until it's too late. So, I want to make sure you know how much I love you."

"I know that, Jimmy. I have always known that...and you should know how grateful I am for having you in my life."

They spent the next few hours reminiscing. Recalling the various events in their lives brought both tears and laughter. When they finally said their goodbyes, James hugged his brother as if he would never let go.

# 20

## The Arrest

**James Donnelly**
**Boston | 1984**

JAMES ARRIVED AT the office before eight o'clock the next morning.
Since he had taken Friday off, he wanted to get an early start on his work.
Nick walked in about a half hour later. He smiled at James and asked,
"How was the time with your family?"

"Good morning, Nick. We had a wonderful time together, and you
know, I really didn't want it to end."

"Yeah, I know exactly what you mean. When we visit my daughter, I
don't want it to ever end, either. Family is so important!" Before heading
to his office, Nick said, "Stop by my office in about a half hour. There are
some invoices I want to review with you."

James was in Nick's office reviewing the invoices when there was a
loud banging on the office door, and then James heard the words that he
had been anxiously anticipating.

"FBI! OPEN UP!"

Nick's eyes widened in alarm, and his face turned ashen. Their eyes met, and James thought to himself, *Will he know it was me?* His heart began beating rapidly, and beads of perspiration covered his forehead.

Before either of them could get up from their desks, the FBI agents burst through the door. It made a thunderous noise as it fell off its hinges and hit the floor. Next, eight agents—four representing the arrest team and four representing the search team—marched into the office area with their weapons drawn. James had not expected such a forceful entrance and immediately thought of several questions. *Why did they knock down the door? Do they really need to have their guns out? And where is Joe?*

The agent who appeared to be in charge shouted, "Stand up and put your hands where we can see them. We have federal arrest warrants!" James and Nick immediately complied with their requests. James's hands were shaking as another agent frisked both of them for any concealed weapons. This same agent then placed handcuffs on both men and asked, "Are there any weapons on the premises?"

"No . . . there are . . . no weapons," a shaken Nick responded.

Now that the area was safely secured, James noticed that the FBI agents took a calmer, more considerate approach. "You gentlemen can sit back down. Do either of you require medication?"

"I-I've got high blood pressure," Nick stammered. "My prescription bottle is in my desk."

The agent who had cuffed them took out the bottle of medication and examined it, and as he handed it to Nick, he asked, "Do you need to take any pills now?"

"Yeah . . . I think . . . I could use one now . . . thanks."

James would later learn that this step was to avoid a potential medical emergency, as well as to build some degree of trust that might be leveraged into future cooperation.

The agent with the search warrant explained to Nick that it covered the entire office, including filing cabinets and desks.

"Are any of the drawers locked?" one agent asked, and Nick nodded to the filing cabinet in his office, which James had rifled through several weeks before. "Are there keys to that cabinet?"

To James's dismay, Nick hesitated to answer.

"We'll be gaining access to that cabinet with or without the keys," the agent said bluntly, and Nick's face went pale. "Your cooperation in making this access easier would be appreciated, however—and duly noted."

Nick appeared to think about what the agent had just said before telling him exactly where the keys were.

The arresting agents led both handcuffed men out of the office area. Pasquale, along with the early restaurant crew, stood in stunned silence as the FBI agents walked Nick and James through the restaurant. Nick turned and looked at James as they were being led out of the building. The expression on Nick's face seemed to be a combination of shock, pain, and anger. It was the last time James would see Nick until the trial.

James had very mixed emotions about Nick. On the one hand, he liked his boss as a person. Nick had always been kind and supportive of James. On the other hand, James knew that Nick was clearly aware of and involved in the multiple crimes being committed—and now he and his family would suffer for that.

Later, James would learn that at the same time the FBI entered the accounting offices, similar arrests were being made throughout the state. Mario was having a breakfast meeting with four of his associates when the feds arrested all five of them. Anthony was leaving his apartment in the

Back Bay when the agents took him into custody. By noon, all eighteen had been jailed, all of the bank accounts had been frozen, and the shell companies were shut down. Essentially, the Martoni organized crime family was dealt a critical blow.

# 21

# The Safe House

**James Donnelly**
**New Hampshire | 1984**

JAMES WAS ESCORTED to a separate car from Nick. As he saw the driver take the ramp for 93 North, he realized that they were headed to New Hampshire. The agents remained silent until they crossed the state line. Then the agent on the passenger side turned around and spoke to James.

"You can relax now, James. I'm Agent George Olson, and this is Agent Mark Willis. Here—give me your hands so I can remove those cuffs. We are taking you to a safe house in New Hampshire, and Joe Atkins will be joining us this afternoon. He led the team that arrested Mario. How are you feeling?"

James thought about the question. How *was* he feeling? How could he even begin to explain the tangle of emotions in his chest—the sense of relief weighed down by the despair of having to betray somebody who was once a close friend and the anxiety of coming face-to-face with him in court in the near future? And of course, most of all, the reality that he'd never see his family again, the sheer agony of it dulled only by the reassurance of knowing this chapter was coming to a close.

"I have a lot of mixed emotions right now," James settled on, rubbing his wrists from where the cuffs had chafed. "I'm glad the waiting is over, but I'm sad I'll no longer be able to see my family. I'm anxious about the unknown of the next few months and nervous about the actual trial."

George, who seemed slightly older than Mark, acknowledged what James had just said.

"What you are feeling is absolutely normal. Your actions took a tremendous amount of courage, and the sacrifice you are making is immense. We couldn't have made these arrests today without your valiant efforts. We are all extremely grateful for what you have done, and we will do everything within our power to make this time as comfortable as possible for you."

James thought about the way the arrest had taken place and inquired, "Why did you come in with such force this morning? I was really surprised when you broke down the door and had your guns drawn."

"Good question. Our background information on Nick indicated that he isn't a violent person. Nevertheless, he has been part of this crime family for many years. When someone has so much to lose, we are not always sure how they'll react. He may have immediately suspected you and tried to kill you; he could have shot at us or even tried to harm himself. Agents have been killed in the past when conducting what was considered a relatively safe arrest. We don't like to take any chances. And aside from safety, we didn't want him attempting to destroy any evidence."

James felt a cold shiver run up his spine when he considered the possibility that Nick might have tried to kill him, but he forced himself to remain calm. "Well, that explains a lot. I don't mind admitting that you scared the hell out of me!"

They drove for another forty minutes before exiting the highway. Then they traveled on remote country roads. Finally, they turned into a private, unpaved driveway. At the end of the gravel road was a red farmhouse with a large barn behind it. Mark Willis pressed a remote-control button that was on the car's sun visor, and an oversize garage door began to open on the side of the barn. The garage area, which was exceptionally neat and clean, was large enough to accommodate four vehicles. At the front of the garage was a painted cinder-block wall with a large steel door.

George opened the door and said, "Welcome to your new home, James. Come on in. We'll give you the grand tour."

Upon entering, James saw a large open area with a desk and several monitors. George introduced James to the agent who was sitting at the desk and explained that he was part of the surveillance team. "We have placed cameras, along with sound and motion detectors, throughout the entire area to make sure we have no unwanted visitors. An agent will be monitoring these devices around the clock." The phrase *unwanted visitors* struck James like a ton of bricks. He immediately recalled Joe telling him there would be a target on his back. The reality of his new life was becoming uncomfortably clear.

There was a room to the left of the open area, and George motioned for James to enter. It was a well-equipped fitness room that included a weight machine, treadmill, and exercise bike.

"The days can get very long and sometimes extremely stressful when you are staying in a safe house," George explained. "This will help you to burn off some energy and stay in shape, both physically and mentally. You look like someone who keeps himself in good shape." James thought, *I'll certainly need the mental part!*

They left the fitness room, and George pointed out two more large rooms and a full bathroom. The two rooms were bedrooms for the FBI agents who would be protecting James. Next, they walked through a narrow hallway, which took them to an enclosed walkway that led to the back door of the farmhouse. This door opened into the kitchen, which had been upgraded with modern appliances, including an oversize refrigerator, a six-burner gas stove, and a microwave oven. George opened the refrigerator to show James that it had already been fully stocked. Then he walked James to a pantry that was also filled with all types of nonperishable foods.

"We'll keep you well-fed while you're here, James. And if there's anything else you want, just let one of us know. We all tend to pitch in with the cooking. We find that it's a nice distraction and helps to pass the time. And it really beats eating takeout every day!"

The room next to the kitchen was a dining room with a long table and eight chairs. James noticed that there were sandwiches and sodas on the table.

"Once our tour is complete, we'll enjoy lunch—and like I said earlier, Joe's going to join us for all that," George said, escorting James to the living room, where there was a long couch on one side with large stuffed chairs on either side of it. There was a television opposite the couch, and one of the walls had a huge built-in bookshelf that was filled with many different books.

George must've noticed James eying the bookshelf because he said, "You'll have plenty of reading time here. There are some great books, and we just added a new novel by Tom Clancy."

They walked across the hallway, which led to the front door, and passed a room that looked like an office. There was a desk and several chairs in the room. George explained that this was where the US attorney would be preparing James for trial. Then they proceeded upstairs, where there were three bedrooms and two full bathrooms. George pointed to the bedroom that James would be using. It contained a full-size bed with night tables on each side and a large dresser. The furniture was a dark mahogany with carved engravings. The style of the furniture reminded James of Father Pat's bedroom—particularly the dresser he'd dinged up as a child while roughhousing with Johnny instead of doing their homework. The memory was so fresh, it was as though it'd only taken place yesterday. He could still see Father Pat's anger, could still hear the laughter creep into his voice, despite it all. Father Pat had never been a good disciplinarian, but he'd never needed to be, really—not when James and John were so eager to make him proud. He was the sort of good parent whose trust and affection were a better reward than rebellion and rule breaking, even though James had certainly had his share of the latter.

He immediately got a lump in his throat. He'd never see Father Pat again. Ever! The idea of losing not only his father but also his brother had been too terrible to conceptualize, but as he stood before his new bedroom—with its empty shelves and drawers—he was realizing in full measure exactly how much he'd agreed to give up.

There was a large empty closet in the bedroom, and James immediately wondered what he would do for clothes. As though reading his thoughts, George said, "James, if you give us the keys to your apartment, we will get your clothes and any other personal items you may want. We'll also let your landlord know that you will not be coming back."

*Will not be coming back.*

It hit him all over again, the finality of it all, and as George escorted him downstairs, he followed in a numb daze. Just as they entered the dining room for lunch, Joe Atkins walked in. He immediately smiled at James and shook hands with all three of them.

"Has George been treating you well, James?"

He was surprised by how good it felt to see Joe's familiar face. "George has been an excellent host."

Joe winked at George and said, "I'm not surprised. He is definitely one of our finest agents. Let's sit down and have some lunch. You must be starving by now. The local deli is not as fancy as Sofia's, but they make outstanding sandwiches."

During lunch, Joe updated James and the others about everything that had taken place that morning. Then he described what the next few months would be like for James.

"During the months leading up to the trial, you'll have lots of down-time. So, you'll have plenty of time to read, watch television, and work out. There will be a team of four agents with you at all times. Two agents will be with you in the house, and the other two agents will be conducting surveillance of the property. One will monitor the screens while the other patrols the area. There will actually be three teams—each working an eight-hour shift. George and Mark will be on one of those teams. Depending on how long it is before we go to trial, we may move you to at least one or two other safe houses. Each location will have a setup similar to this one."

"Okay." James hoped they couldn't tell that he was completely over-whelmed. Clearing his throat and injecting as much confidence as he could into his voice, he then asked, "So, what's the trial going to look like? How do we prepare?"

Agent Atkins nodded, resting his elbows on the table. "The US attorney will come here to prepare you for trial. His name is Robert Manion, and he is *the best*. He will bring one of the other attorneys from his office. This will be a very intense time for you. He'll go over every single question and answer with you thoroughly. They'll discuss your words, as well as your body language—especially your facial expressions. The other attorney will play the role of the defense lawyer, and he'll be extremely tough on you so that you are well prepared for the Martonis' legal team. This preparation time will be extensive and exhausting, but understand that Robert does this in order to be absolutely certain of a conviction. He doesn't leave anything to chance. He wants the evidence to be over-whelming and the testimony to be ironclad."

James listened thoughtfully to everything Joe said. His mind was racing, and he was still feeling many conflicting emotions. However, he clung to his certainty that he had made the right decision to proceed, and he was fully committed to doing whatever it took to ensure these criminals went to prison for a very long time.

And besides, there was no turning back now.

James adapted to his new environment during the first few weeks at the safe house. He began to develop a routine. Each morning, he would get up by seven o'clock and immediately head to the fitness room. He worked out for approximately an hour, alternating between running on the treadmill and lifting weights. Some mornings, one of the agents would join him in the gym. After his workout, it was time for breakfast, which usually consisted of coffee and cereal with fresh fruit. At least once or twice each week, James helped prepare a heartier breakfast for the entire team. Then it was time for a hot shower. He devoted the next few hours to writing down everything he could remember about his time working for the Martonis. This had been Joe's suggestion. He said it would help James prepare for his work with Robert Manion. James also began reading books that were on the living room's bookshelf. He hadn't been much of a reader in the past but was now finding it an enjoyable escape. He fluctuated between fiction and nonfiction. There were several history books, and he started off with one on the Civil War. Knowing the strong bond between himself and John, he was amazed that brothers could actually fight against each other during this terrible chapter in the nation's history. After he finished the first book, he began reading a spy novel. One evening, with a hot mug of tea in hand, he wandered to the bookshelf in search of more reading material but found a Bible instead.

James paused for a minute, staring at its dusty leather spine, its uncreased pages. It looked like it had never been touched—perhaps, even, as though it'd been waiting for him and him alone to pick it up. He'd never been particularly interested in studying the Bible. That was John's thing. Maybe Father Pat was right—maybe, just maybe, this whole informant deal was God's plan for him. All of this.

Wetting his lips, he picked up the Bible and decided that going forward, he would dedicate his Sundays to reading scripture, since he wouldn't be able to attend mass. If only Father Pat could see him now.

Every day around noon, he'd taken to grabbing a sandwich or salad for lunch and walking the grounds with one of the agents. The property consisted of about fifty acres surrounded by trees and a few hilly areas. The fresh air felt good and reminded him of hiking in the Berkshires. James watched very little television other than the news and one or two prime-time programs. This was a result of growing up with Father Pat. Television was generally not allowed on school nights, unless it was the news or an educational program.

Occasionally, he would play poker with a few of the agents, and he recalled the card games with Anthony at college. George Olson taught James how to play chess. He got to know all of the agents who were on his security team. With the exception of George, who was in his early fifties, most of the agents were in their late thirties or early forties. While each of them acted very professionally and took James's protection seriously, they were personable and made him feel comfortable. As George had indicated, the agents and James shared in preparing some of the dinners. James impressed the agents with a few of Father Jason's Italian recipes.

Joe Atkins stopped by unannounced about once a week. He and James would usually spend an hour or so together. The two of them had made a strong connection, and James looked forward to these visits. It was during one of these visits that Joe informed James that Robert

Manion, the US attorney, would be coming to the safe house the following day. Joe said that Robert would be accompanied by Brian Gordon, one of his assistants. Joe explained that this would be the first of many sessions preparing James for his testimony.

The next day, Robert Manion and his associate arrived at the safe house shortly after nine o'clock. James was nervous—there was no doubt about it—but he'd prepared as much as humanly possible, and it was time to get started with this next phase.

He met Robert Manion at the front door, along with the other agents, and was immediately presented with a man in his midforties who was shockingly handsome. "James," he said with an easy smile, holding out his hand for a handshake, "I'm Robert Manion, and this is my associate, Brian Gordon."

James shook Robert's hand and proceeded to Brian, who looked younger—perhaps only in his late thirties, despite the age implied by his receding hairline and narrow face.

Robert began bustling around the room, carrying himself with intention and authority, sort of like somebody in the military. James later found out that Manion had been a member of the JAG—Judge Advocate General's—Corps prior to joining the US attorney's office.

"I'm very happy to finally meet you," Robert went on. "Joe has spoken highly of you. You have been a tremendous help to us in inflicting major damage to organized crime in New England." He paused, looked directly into James's eyes, and added with empathy, "And we all appreciate the tremendous personal sacrifice you've made."

James felt a lump in his throat at the words *tremendous personal sacrifice*. It was still very difficult for him to accept that he would never see his family again. He took a deep breath as he recalled Father Pat's guidance. *If you, my son, have the chance to do something that will save the lives of others, then what a privilege and a gift that is, no matter the personal sacrifice."*

Remembering these words of wisdom gave James renewed fortitude. "I'm glad I have been able to help . . . and I am committed to doing everything—absolutely everything—in my power to help you finish the job!"

Then Robert got down to business.

"The evidence you helped us to uncover is significant. And your testimony will be critical to a successful conviction. That's why we are here today and will be coming back several more times. We will be preparing you for trial."

James asked, "When do you think the trial will take place?"

Brian answered that question. "We are at least two to three months away from the trial. So, you'll have plenty of time to get to know us and probably get tired of us."

Then they proceeded to the office and began working. They started by having James read from the notes he had been compiling over the past few weeks. Manion and Gordon listened attentively and were clearly impressed by James's thoroughness. They worked straight until one o'clock, when Brian finally smiled at his boss, tapped his watch, and said, "Hey, Bob, don't you think it's time for a lunch break?"

The three of them walked to the dining room, where the agents had laid out sandwiches from the local deli. While it felt good to relax after an intense morning, James realized that he was exhilarated by actually working and making a meaningful contribution. After lunch, they returned to the office for another three hours. Both attorneys were excellent listeners and asked probing questions for clarity and understanding. James was awed by their professional skill and wondered if he might attend law school in his new life.

When the afternoon session ended, Manion thanked James for his efforts. He complimented him on the solid notes and gave him homework for their next session. Brian said that they would probably meet at least once each week for the next month, and then, as they got closer to the trial date, they would meet several times each week.

He smiled at James and said, "That's when you'll probably start disliking me. I'll be playing the defense attorney and will purposely be extremely tough on you." Then he put his arm around James's shoulders and added, "But don't take it personally—I'll only be doing it because I care about you and want you to be completely prepared for whatever those bastards throw at you."

At the end of the day, James recalled Joe telling him that working with the US attorney would be exhausting. It certainly had been, but James did not feel drained. In fact, it reminded him of how great he felt after an intense workout.

# 22

# The Attempt

**James Donnelly**
**New Hampshire | 1985**

OVER THE FOLLOWING six weeks, James trained with Robert and Brian—who was just as tough and insufferable as he'd warned. A few times, James was ready to physically throw Brian out of the safe house's nearest and highest window. Everything was going according to plan, or so it seemed.

James was walking on a warm, sunny day with Mark Willis—the FBI agent who had driven him to the safe house. They were enjoying a lively conversation about the Red Sox when they heard shouting over the walkie-talkie that Mark was carrying.

"Breach . . . I repeat . . . there's been a breach! Take cover!"

Mark immediately pulled out his service revolver and pointed James to a clump of trees where they both would be shielded. James nearly tripped over himself getting to those trees, every thud of his heart heavy enough to clog up his throat. "Where might they—"

Mark shushed him sternly, bypassing the trees in favor of scoping out the area, his revolver held steadily out in front of him. As James watched this experienced professional in action, his heart was racing so fast that it felt as if his chest would burst. Perspiration began to cover his entire body. He could not remember another time in his life when he'd been so shaken. He immediately thought of Father Pat and John. In the next instant, he heard several gunshots in the distance. After what seemed like an eternity, they received an all clear message and were told to return to the house immediately.

Within an hour, Joe Atkins—along with several other FBI agents—converged at the safe house. After speaking with the agents on duty, Joe walked into the living room, where James was sitting. By now, the adrenaline rush had passed, and he was feeling totally drained and shaken. James felt a certain amount of relief when he saw Joe walk into the room. The FBI agent pulled up a chair and sat down.

"How are you doing, James?"

James let out a deep breath and shook his head. "Still a little shaken... but very, *very* thankful for the protection of your agents." He hesitated before asking, "What happened? How did they find me?"

Joe's face conveyed both worry and frustration; his cheeks seemed somehow hollower, and his nostrils flared. "We're not sure how they were able to track you down. We've taken every precaution to ensure nothing like this would happen. Whenever Robert and Brian have come to meet you, we've taken several steps to prevent anyone from following them. We are reviewing everything now to determine where we might have failed."

Joe paused for a moment, stretched out his long arm, and placed his hand on James's shoulder before saying, "James, I'm truly sorry for what happened today. You've given up so much and have been a real trooper during this whole process. We let you down! I'm going to do everything in my power to make sure this doesn't occur again. As far as what actually happened . . . an assassin was attempting to kill you. Fortunately, the surveillance team spotted him on one of our cameras. He was carrying a semiautomatic rifle with a scope. It appeared he was trying to find a position that would give him clear visibility to the entrance of the farmhouse. When the agents converged on him, they demanded that he drop his weapon. He complied and put the rifle on the ground, but as he was straightening back up, he pulled a handgun from his back. He got off one shot before our agents opened fire. He's in critical condition and has been rushed to the hospital. Based on his wounds, it's doubtful he'll survive. The first bullet grazed one of the agents, but he's doing fine. We took the would-be assassin's fingerprints, and I suspect he is not part of the Martoni crime organization. He's probably someone from out of town that they hired to do their dirty work."

Joe seemed to realize that he had just laid a lot on James, so he stopped for a moment to let it sink in.

James closed his eyes and absorbed everything Joe had just said, especially, *an assassin was attempting to kill you.* Several thoughts raced through his mind. *How could they have found me? Will they try again? What if they had succeeded? What would that do to Father Pat . . . and to John? What would have happened to the case against the Martonis? These are really evil people . . . and they must be stopped!* After a long silence, he looked straight at the FBI agent and said, "I won't lie to you. I was more scared than I have ever been in my life. And I'm very concerned as to how they were able to find me. But if these bastards thought they were going to stop me from testifying . . . then they were completely mistaken. I didn't think I could be any more committed to bringing them down, but after this attempt, I am even more intent on ending this evil!"

"You had every right to be scared, and I am so grateful for your unwavering resolve." Then Joe explained the next steps. "James, we're going to move you to another safe house. We've chosen a location in southern Vermont. We are also going to increase the size of your team. We'll be leaving tonight after dark. One of the agents will help you pack up your clothes and personal belongings."

Joe's reassuring presence and his sincere concern gave James a calmness he had not felt since earlier in the day.

"I completely understand the need to move . . . and really appreciate the extra protection!"

Later that night, they drove nearly three hours to a small town just north of Manchester, Vermont. The safe house was a large log cabin on wooded property. The house was actually situated on top of a hill, which provided the surveillance team with excellent views. The next morning, James and Joe grabbed a cup of coffee and walked around the property. James glanced in the distance and thought he recognized a mountain.

He turned to Joe and asked, "Is that Bromley Mountain?"

"Yeah . . . how did you know that?"

James smiled as he remembered his previous visits to this part of Vermont.

"This is less than two hours from where we grew up in western Massachusetts. When we were boys, Father Pat would bring John and me up to this area. We would stay at the Equinox Resort and go hiking in the mountains." Then he thought to himself, *I am going to miss hiking with my brother for the rest of my life!*

Although the realization that his life might end at any moment was always lurking in the back of his mind, James attempted to block it by forcing himself into a routine again. It helped that Robert Manion and

Brian Gordon began making more frequent trips to the new safe house, and the sessions were even more intense. The lawyers explained that the trial date had been set and that there were only a few more weeks left for preparation. James was relieved that the waiting was over. After the attempt on his life, he was even more focused on putting these criminals away. At the same time, he was anxious to begin a new life—whatever that might mean.

# 23

# The Trial

| James Donnelly
| Boston | 1985

ABOUT ONE MONTH later, Joe Atkins arrived unexpectedly and found James sitting on the front porch of the cabin, reading. As he approached, James sensed that this wasn't a normal visit.

"Well, the day is finally here! All of your hard work and preparation is over. You will be the first witness called tomorrow morning."

In that moment, James felt a sense of relief that the waiting was over. Then, in the next instant, he became anxious, wondering how he would handle himself at the trial. *What if I screw up and jeopardize the case?* His wrinkled forehead and tight lips clearly telegraphed his concern.

Joe broke this train of thought by reassuring James, "I've never seen any witness prepare as well as you have. Between the evidence you un-covered for us and your excellent testimony, you are going to ensure the Martonis are put away for a very long time!"

"Thanks for the vote of confidence. I pray that you're right!"

"Look, we all believe in you. So, relax and get to bed early tonight because we are leaving before dawn. The drive to the federal courthouse in Boston will take over three hours."

James went to bed early that evening, intending on getting a solid night's rest, but he had a difficult time getting to sleep. The nervousness and apprehension he'd felt earlier in the day persisted despite Joe's reassurance. He tried to focus on his testimony, but then a whirlwind of thoughts broke his concentration. *Oh God, am I fully prepared for what their attorney is going to throw at me? What's it going to feel like seeing Anthony and Nick in the courtroom? How will they react to me? How I wish I had never gotten involved with these criminals!*

It seemed like he had finally fallen asleep when the alarm clock went off. James had perspired so heavily during the night that the mattress felt as if someone had poured water on it. He showered, got dressed, and went downstairs. Joe poured him a cup of coffee and asked, "How did you sleep last night?"

James laughed mirthlessly and responded, "I barely slept at all. I was tossing and turning all night, thinking about the trial."

Putting his hand on James's shoulder, Joe assured him, "I'm not surprised. That's perfectly normal. After today is behind you, you'll be sleeping a lot more soundly."

The caravan left the cabin at five thirty. James sat in the back seat with the folder containing his trial notes on his lap. He spent the majority of the long drive reviewing the notes and making the final preparations for his testimony. They arrived at the courthouse shortly before nine o'clock. The FBI agents surrounded James and walked him into the waiting room, which was on the lower level of the courthouse. When he entered the room, he was greeted by Robert Manion and Brian Gordon. Manion was the first to speak.

"Well, James, this is the big day! How are you feeling?"

"Honestly, I've got mixed feelings. There's a part of me that's ready to get this over with and send those bastards away. At the same time, there's another part of me that's worried I'll screw up and ruin this case for you."

"Look, James, I've been at this for many years now, and I've never seen any witness who has worked as hard as you have to prepare for trial. All of that crap you took from Brian is going to make you ready for anything that the other side can possibly throw at you."

Brian smiled, patted James on the back, and reassured him, "Bob is right, James. I was pretty tough on you, kid, but it was only for your own good. You'll do great on the stand today."

James appreciated their support. They shook hands and told him that they would see him upstairs when he was called to the witness stand. He found a worn-down chair—the sort of generic chair you'd find in a doctor's office—and tried to get comfortable, but his heart threw itself against his chest with all of the ferocity of a caged animal.

*Today is the day. Today is the day it'll all be worth it, or it'll all be for naught.*

Before he was ready, there was a knock on the door. Joe gave him a sideways glance before standing up and answering it. James's palms immediately broke into a cold sweat. Joe spoke briefly to the court officer, then turned to James.

"It's showtime, James."

James immediately forgot everything he'd rehearsed.

He took a deep breath and slowly exhaled. He put on his suit jacket, and as they walked up to the courtroom, he said a silent prayer. *Dear Lord, I know that I haven't always been the best, but please . . . please help me through this trial. I promise you that I will be much better in the new life you have planned for me!*

As he entered the courtroom, James felt a sense of peace and confidence, knowing that God had listened to his prayer. He saw several heads turn as he walked down the aisle. And, as though through some act of divinity, the first person he saw was Anthony.

The whole room stilled. Time slowed to a crawl. Anthony looked back with venom in his eyes, and as much as James told himself to look away, he just couldn't. How had they gotten here, after all these years? He wanted to get in Anthony's face and cry, *Why? Why did you have to turn out just like your father? You promised me you wouldn't—and now we're here!*

Eventually, James dragged his eyes from Anthony and onto Nick, who seemed to be much thinner and paler than he remembered him. The look on Nick's face was one of sad resignation. Mario simply looked straight ahead, as if James did not exist.

James was sworn in, and when he finished the oath with "so help me God," he was reminded once again of what Father Pat had said to him several months before. *It's possible that God is using you to put an end to this evil.*

Robert Manion began the questioning. Given all of their time together, James was able to answer each question in a clear, thorough, and professional manner. Manion methodically and chronologically covered everything from when James met Anthony in college and developed a close friendship to when he was hired to work in the controller's office, uncovered the irregularities with the cash receipts, and finally, how he provided the FBI with the incriminating evidence.

When Manion finished, it was time for the defense attorney's cross-examination. James took a deep breath and remembered all of the brutal sessions with Brian. The attorney for the Martoni family was a powerful defense attorney from New York. He started off with some softball questions, then quickly transitioned to an extremely tough interrogation. He was forceful and relentless in his efforts to impinge James's credibility and testimony. James was now extremely grateful to Brian for those grueling practice sessions. Although the questioning was intense, he handled each probe in a calm, respectful, and effective manner. After nearly two hours of rapid-fire questioning, the defense attorney told the judge that he had no further questions.

The judge excused James, and as he passed by the prosecutor's table, Brian smiled and gave him a thumbs-up. James felt as if a tremendous weight had been lifted from his shoulders. He was both exhausted and exhilarated. It reminded him of how he would feel after winning a challenging high school football game. Joe escorted James out of the courtroom and to a group of other FBI agents. They surrounded James and walked him back to the waiting room, where he once again sat in that faded old chair—he looked at it very differently now, though. Joe explained that Robert would meet James there to provide his observations of how the testimony went.

There was a knock on the door about five minutes later. James was surprised that Manion was there so soon. Joe stood up to answer the door and looked at James, who noticed that the agent had a mischievous smile on his face. James thought, *That's strange; I wonder why Joe is smiling that way.* He would soon find out.

Joe opened the door wide to let someone enter. James could not believe his eyes when his father, followed by his brother, walked into the conference room. James shot out of his chair as if he had been propelled by a rocket booster.

"Father Pat . . . Johnny . . . oh my God . . . I can't believe it!" He wrapped his arms around both of them as tears streamed down his cheeks. "I . . . I thought I would never see you again!" Then he held his father's face in his hands and planted several kisses on the old priest's shiny bald head. Next, he turned to John, and the two brothers hugged each other as if neither would ever let go, reminding James of the last time they had seen each other so many months ago. After several moments, he turned to Joe and, bursting with the most joy he'd felt in a long time, said, "Joe, thank you . . . thank you so, so much! You cannot believe how happy you've made me."

"I can see how thrilled you are, but I can't take all of the credit. Robert came up with the idea and asked me if we could safely pull it off. I promised him that we would make it happen for you!"

At that moment, Robert and Brian entered the room. After brief introductions, Manion asked everyone to take a seat. He then looked directly at Father Pat and said, "You should be very proud of this brave young man. You've done a superb job in raising him. He has worked tirelessly, and his testimony this morning was impeccable! I'm extremely confident that we will put these criminals away for a very long time. We could not have done it without the courageous efforts of your son." He paused for a moment, took a deep breath, and then continued in a more somber tone, "I'm very sorry that we have to take him away from you. I can only imagine how difficult it will be for the three of you. Please, please understand that it is for his own safety. We wanted to at least give the three of you some precious time together before James is placed in the witness protection program."

After that, the attorneys and the FBI agents left the room and gave Father Pat and his sons some time alone. Lunch was brought in, and the three of them talked about everything. They each wanted to catch up on the past several months and cover as much as possible during the short time remaining. There was even some friendly teasing between the two brothers. James learned that his brother would be entering the seminary the following week and joked with his father, "So, now we will have two Father Donnellys in the family. What do you think about that, Father Pat?"

"Well, naturally, I'm very proud of Johnny. I know he will make an exceptional priest." Then Father Pat paused for a moment, and his face turned serious. "I want you to know how very proud I am of you, Jimmy. You may not have noticed it, but when Mr. Manion was praising you for your courage and hard work, this old chest of mine expanded a few inches. I am so, so very proud of you, son!"

James got up from his chair, bent down, and embraced his father.

"You taught us well, Father Pat. I only wish I had listened as well as Johnny did. I know I gave you plenty of grief over the years." He stopped, thinking all of a sudden about the dusty Bible he'd found on the bookshelf in the safe house, about how he picked it up and used it for his own Sunday devotions. He'd prayed, even, before court that day, and he felt God's presence in response, fortifying him throughout his cross-examination. "This morning, before I testified, I asked God to give me the strength to get through it, and I promised him that I would do much better in the future."

Father Pat froze, eyes welling with tears he didn't blink away.

James cleared his throat. "I make the same promise to you, Father Pat," he said, and in his peripheral vision, he saw Johnny smiling. "I'll do everything . . . *everything* in my power to become that person you always wanted me to be."

Father Pat smiled, tears dripping free, and said, "You've already done that, Jimmy . . . You have already done that!"

At that moment, Joe Atkins knocked on the door and opened it. "James," he said softly, clearly sorry to have interrupted what was obviously an emotional moment. "We've gotta go. We're leaving in ten minutes."

James immediately felt a tightness in his chest, as if his heart were being torn in two. He stared at the two most important people in his life and thought to himself, *I will never see them again.* Then, as if reading his mind, Father Pat provided words of wisdom and comfort.

"Jimmy, remember, this isn't goodbye! You will always be with us—in our hearts . . . our thoughts . . . our prayers. And someday . . . some wonderful day . . . we will all be together again in that special place that God has set aside for us."

James knew his father was correct, but that couldn't stop the pain he was feeling at the moment. Once again, he wrapped his arms around Father Pat and John. The tears flowed freely from all three of them as they said their final goodbyes.

# 24

# The Request

James Donnelly
Vermont | 1985

IT WAS LATE afternoon, two weeks later, when Joe Atkins arrived at the cabin with Robert Manion and Brian Gordon. James had been sitting on the front porch, reading a book. When he saw them pull up, he put the book down and walked toward the car to greet them. Manion was dressed in casual clothes and seemed more relaxed than he had during any of their previous meetings. He smiled and told James the good news.

"The trial is over, and all eighteen of them were found guilty of each count. They are going away for a very long time! We wanted to personally come up here and give you the good news."

Although Joe had assured him that Manion never lost a case, James was always nervous that somehow, the Martonis would get off. "That is fantastic! I am so happy . . . and relieved to hear that they will pay for their crimes." Then he remembered the horrible event that pushed him to come forward. "Well . . . for most of their crimes anyway. How I wish you would have been able to convict them for the murder of Danny O'Brien!" Then, looking up to the sky, he smiled as he imagined Danny saying, *Hey, don't worry about it! The important thing is that you've put those bums away, so they can't hurt anyone else. And besides, I'm having a great time up here.*

Brian started walking toward the house and then remembered something. He went back to the car and took out a small ice chest from the back seat. Then he opened it up, reached in, and pulled out a large bottle of champagne. He held it high over his head as if he were holding a trophy and said, "It must be five o'clock somewhere. Let's celebrate!"

In addition to the champagne, they ordered dinner from a nearby restaurant. There was plenty of friendly conversation throughout the meal. The three of them praised James for his courage in coming forward and providing the crucial evidence. They made it clear that he played a critical role in the successful prosecution of their case. It was during one of these congratulatory moments that James decided to make his special request. The idea had been formulating in his head ever since he arrived at the safe house in Vermont and realized he was less than two hours from the Berkshires. He knew it was a long shot, but he decided to ask anyway.

"It's been a pleasure working with all of you, although at times, it didn't seem so pleasant, especially when I was getting beaten up by someone's tough cross-examinations." He winked at Brian and then added, "I also appreciate the opportunity you are giving me to start a new life and a new career." He paused, considering his words carefully. "But . . . there is one more *request* that I'd like from you. It would mean a lot—an awful lot—to me." He felt the mood in the room change as all three of them leaned forward and focused on what he was about to say.

"I would like to spend a weekend in the Berkshires with my brother before I begin my new life. There's a beautiful open valley situated deep in the forest where very few hikers ever go. It's our special place. My brother John is also beginning a new life. He recently entered the seminary and . . . I just want one more memorable time with him before . . . we never see each other again."

James finished and waited for their response, fully expecting them to say it was impossible. There was complete silence as the three of them looked at each other, and then Manion spoke. "Well, James, my knee-jerk reaction is to say it is way too dangerous. They've already tried to assassinate you once before, and we still don't know how they got the information about the first safe house."

James had expected that type of response and had resigned himself to the fact that they wouldn't allow it, but then he was blown away by what the US attorney said next.

"However, as I said, we could never have won this case without you. And I can only imagine how difficult it will be for you to never see your brother again." He turned to Atkins and asked, "Joe, do you think that you and your agents can provide James and his brother with protection while they're camping in the Berkshires?"

Still in shock, James watched as the FBI agent rubbed his forehead with both hands and gazed down at the table in intense thought. James held his breath, waiting for Joe to say something.

Then, after several seconds, Joe looked up and responded, "Well, Bob, it will be easier to protect him deep in the woods as opposed to a more open area. Like you, I'm concerned about the previous leak and our failure to find the source, so we will need to keep our circle of protection extremely tight. Only a very small group of people can know about it. This information in the wrong hands would be . . ." He didn't finish his thought, but everyone knew what he meant. "I'll have to study the area to ensure that our agents will have adequate coverage." He turned to James and asked, "Can you draw me a detailed map that will get me to this place? I'll go out to the area with a few agents to scope it out."

"Draw you a map? I'll paint you a picture . . . I'll give you a blow-by-blow description of the entire area . . . anything you need!" James could not believe his good fortune. Although he had wished for this one last opportunity to be with John in the place that they both loved, he hadn't expected it to happen. God had truly answered his prayers.

# 25

## The Final Weekend

| John Donnelly
| Berkshires | 1985

TWO WEEKS LATER, John and the other seminarians attended a special morning mass at the cathedral. It was the cardinal's way of welcoming them. All of these young men were dressed in their black cassocks. The selected Gospel reading was from Matthew, chapter 9: "The harvest is plentiful, but the workers are few. Therefore, ask the Lord of the harvest to send out workers into his harvest."

The cardinal gave a powerfully motivational homily based on this Gospel verse. John felt inspired by every word. It reinforced for him that he had made the right decision about the priesthood.

By the time he was leaving the service, John was already imagining his life as one of the "harvesters." He was so focused on this vision that he failed to notice the gentleman at the back of the church. All of a sudden, he felt a large hand on his shoulder. John turned and recognized the FBI agent he had met at the courthouse. He felt his blood run cold, draining out of his face.

"Jimmy . . ." He gasped, staggering toward the FBI agent. "Is it Jimmy? Has he been hurt?"

Joe Atkins quickly reassured him, "You can relax, John. James is perfectly all right, but he had a special request, so you'll be coming with us."

They left through a side door and got into an unmarked car. As they drove away from the cathedral, Joe said, "Your brother wants to spend one more weekend with you before he begins his new life. He chose your special place in the Berkshires. He's already there and has set up camp for the two of you. There's a change of clothes in the back seat—"

"Wait, hold on," John interjected, feeling as though he were in a dream. "Are you telling me that I get to see Jimmy again?"

"I am," Joe replied with a grin. "It's a special exception." A second later, more somber this time, he added, "I can't promise this opportunity will ever arise again, John. That's why we're taking you straight there. Like I said, there are clothes in the back seat—I'm sure you'll find them an exact fit since we used James's measurements. I'm still amazed I cannot tell the two of you apart. I've met twins before but have always noticed differences, even if they were slight. I've spent an enormous amount of time with James, but if I didn't know better, I'd swear he was sitting next to me right now."

John laughed. "Even Father Pat struggled to tell us apart. He said that it was our personalities that helped him to keep us straight. I was usually calmer and quieter. Jimmy was more animated and exuberant. Father Pat would say that I was blessed with the Holy Spirit, whereas Jimmy was filled with the *wild* spirit."

They both laughed at the last comment and spent the rest of the drive getting to know each other. Having grown up Catholic and being naturally inquisitive, Joe had several questions about the seminary. John was equally interested in the FBI. He wondered how similar it really was to what he had seen in the movies and on television.

They arrived at the Berkshires midafternoon and parked the car in a secluded spot. John changed into the hiking clothes Joe had brought. He carefully folded his cassock and placed it in the backpack that Joe had provided. Then they began the hike. Joe explained that he would accompany John to his brother and then leave the two of them alone. He would join the rest of the agents who were responsible for guarding the area.

It was a gorgeous late-summer day, and the hike was invigorating for both of them. After nearly three hours, they arrived at the campsite. As soon as John's eyes met his brother's, he felt a surge of happiness penetrate every part of his body. John could tell from the glow on James's face that his brother was feeling the same way. As they hugged each other, John confessed, "I can't believe it. After our goodbyes at the courthouse, I thought we would never see each other again. Then to meet here in our special place—it feels like a dream." John's eyes welled up with tears of joy.

"More than a dream! It's a miracle . . . the answer to a lot of prayers. Honestly, I was floored when Joe and Robert agreed to my request. It's so good to see you, brother! I love you!"

Before excusing himself to join the protection detail, Joe reiterated the precautions that he and James had previously discussed. He also ensured that the two-way radio was working properly. The two brothers were to remain in the valley. The FBI agents had created a protective perimeter. There were agents in permanent positions, as well as rotating agents who would cover the area between each permanent station. Joe and his team had spent several hours investigating the area and developing the security plan. He had reviewed it with Robert Manion and provided him with a detailed copy of the plan, including the location in the Berkshires.

John was impressed with the campsite. There was a brand-new tent from L.L. Bean that could easily accommodate six people. It even had a self-closing door with magnets. Inside, there were two sleeping bags. Each bag was atop an air mattress. There was one cooler filled with food and a second one that contained beer and soda. John also noticed the bottle of scotch next to one of the mattresses. Outside was a Coleman two-burner stove with plenty of shiny pots, pans, and dishes. There was even a table with chairs.

John smiled at his brother and exclaimed, "Well, this is what I call luxury camping, Jimmy. It's a lot different from any of our past camping trips. Can you imagine what Father Pat would say?"

James laughed. "You're absolutely right—he wouldn't exactly consider this roughing it, but I think he would have enjoyed it . . . especially the scotch. You'll have to describe it all to him the next time the two of you are together."

Tears welled up in James's eyes—and call it a twin's intuition, but John immediately knew that it had to do with his brother realizing he'd never see Father Pat again. James quickly regained his composure, however, and told John to grab a couple of beers for them as he got the stove ready for the steaks and baked potatoes.

After dinner, James brought out the bottle of scotch and poured each of them their usual two fingers. After the first sip, it became clear to them both, once again, that this would be the last time they would see each other.

"You know, Johnny, I often replay in my head that day when you warned me about going to work for the Martonis. I'd never seen you so angry. If only I had listened to you! I really fucked up! And now, I'll never see you or Father Pat again. I won't even be James Donnelly anymore. I'll be a stranger with a fake past. Oh . . . how I wish I had listened to you that day!"

John saw how much his brother was hurting. But now that time had passed and he'd grown a little older—and definitely wiser—he could see the past for what it really was and, by proxy, Jimmy for who he really was.

"Jimmy, stop beating yourself up. Yes, you made a bad choice—a very bad choice—but you were young and naive, and you chose to give Anthony the benefit of the doubt. You had faith in him as a person. That's a *good* quality. Remember what Father Pat said the night you broke the news to him? He said that God was actually using you to end something evil. And you certainly ended it! Just think—all eighteen of them have been sent to prison for a very long time. I heard the US attorney say that none of this could've happened without you. I remember serving at all of those funerals with Father Pat, and he would always say, 'I know how much you are going to miss your loved one's presence in your life. I also know how much you loved each other. Remember—love never dies!'

"Jimmy, I'll miss you every single day of my life, but the love we have for each other will last forever. So, you will always be in my heart, and I know I will always be in yours. And now—just think—you have a clean slate to start all over again. You can do anything you choose to do. I heard a quote recently. I'm not sure who said it, but it goes something like this: 'Every saint has a past, and every sinner has a future.'"[1] John placed his hand on his brother's shoulder. "So, brother, take the future that God is giving you and do the very best you can with it!"

James seemed to reflect on everything his brother had just said, nodding quietly while staring blankly at the grass underfoot. Then he stood up, poured each of them some more scotch, smiled, and said, "You are going to be one hell of a preacher, Father John!"

John laughed for a moment. It still felt so strange being called *Father John.*

"So," James went on, "tell me about the seminary. Are they teaching you to say mass yet?"

---

[1] From *A Woman of No Importance* by Oscar Wilde.

John laughed at the question and corrected his brother. "Jimmy, they don't teach us to celebrate mass until our final year. These first two years are strictly philosophy and language. We don't even begin to study theology until the third year."

James seemed confused and asked, "Philosophy? You mean like Aristotle? Why do they have you study philosophy?"

"Yes, like Aristotle, Socrates, and Plato. Philosophy is the love of wisdom. Before we can have a relationship with God, we have to think about who we are as humans. So, philosophy helps us to understand how we think, how we relate to others, and most importantly, how we relate to God."

John was in his element now. He mentioned a Monsignor Mike, who was the dean of men. "Monsignor Mike is the disciplinarian whose role is to keep all of us in line. He acts like a drill sergeant, but he really has a heart of gold. He's tough but also very supportive." Then, laughing, he described the monsignor. "He looks and acts just like the movie star John Wayne. In fact, some of the older seminarians even call him Monsignor Wayne behind his back." John went on to describe his classes, his weekly schedule, and some of the new friends he had made at the seminary.

Finally, he turned to his brother and said, "Enough about me! What about you? Have you thought about what you might do with this clean slate?"

James took another sip of scotch and jokingly said, "Yeah, I think I'm going into the seminary, too, so I can be just like you and Father Pat. We'll be the 'Three Father Donnellys.'"

John started laughing and gave it right back to his brother. "That's great! Then we will have the father, son, and *wild* spirit! Now, stop being such a wiseass and tell me what you *really* think you might do."

James's smile faded, a sober expression taking over. "Well, Johnny, you're not going to believe this, but I'm thinking about going back to school. Actually, I'm considering law school. I was really impressed with Robert and Brian. We spent a tremendous amount of time together preparing for the case. When we would take breaks, I'd pick their brains about law school and the criminal justice system. The government is willing to foot the entire bill and arrange for me to get into a very good law school. And I know that I'll be a much better student this time around."

John could tell that his brother had given this decision a lot of thought. He was confident that his brother was actually going to do his very best with the future that God had given him.

"That's great, Jimmy! You will make an outstanding lawyer. I know you'll do wonderful things with your life."

The brothers finished their scotch and headed to the tent. As he was getting comfortable in his sleeping bag, John turned to his brother and said, "Tonight was really special. I'll remember it for the rest of my life. Thanks for making this possible."

"We'll make tomorrow even more memorable! Love you, brother."

The next morning, John woke up first. He put on the coffee, sat back, and admired the natural beauty. After about a half hour, he heard James waking up. *Wow! He's going to law school. He'll be an amazing lawyer. I wonder what type of law he will ultimately practice. No matter which direction he chooses, he'll always do the right thing!* John felt pride burgeoning in his chest, and while it devastated him to face a future without his brother, it was comforting to know that at least Jimmy would be doing a lot of good in the world—as God intended.

He poured a cup of coffee for James—black, as he'd always liked it—and looked forward to their day together.

Robert Manion heard loud banging on his front door. *Who could it be this early on a Saturday morning?* When he opened the door, he was surprised to see Brian Gordon.

"Brian, what's the—" He stopped short. Brian's face was ashen, and he looked shaken. Manion had never seen his associate like this before, and he felt his body break out in a cold sweat. "Brian, what's wrong? What's happened?"

In a voice that exuded anger, shame, and embarrassment, Brian exclaimed, "I . . . I found the leak. It's me. I'm the leak!"

Manion stared at him, confused. "You? What do you mean?"

"Shortly after we arrested the Martonis, I met a woman. Her name— at least the name she gave me—was Jessica . . . Jessica Vaughn." He wet his lips, face absolutely pallid. Manion gestured for him to sit down, but he refused, insisting on standing. "She was extremely attractive. She told me that she worked for a high-end real estate company in Boston. We hit it off immediately . . . or so I thought. I had not dated much since my divorce. I couldn't believe that someone this perfect would be attracted to me . . . I should've known it was too good to be true!"

"What happened, Brian?" Manion asked—more firmly this time. With every word of his colleague's story, he felt worse and worse.

"She seemed very impressed by the fact that I worked in the US attorney's office. We started off slow but quickly progressed to something more serious. Do you remember when the attempt was made on James's life?"

Manion nodded. "Of course."

"We met with James the day before and worked into the early evening. It was a Wednesday. That Tuesday, Jessica told me that she had tickets for the Sox game on the following night. She said the seats were right near the dugout. I told her that I couldn't go on Wednesday because I had an important meeting with my boss and wouldn't get back to Boston until very late."

Manion stopped his associate right there. "Brian, what makes you think that resulted in the attempted assassination? It could just be a coincidence."

"That's what I told myself at the time, but after what happened last night, I'm certain that it was no coincidence!"

"What do you mean, Brian? What happened last night?"

"When Joe met with us early yesterday morning to review the security plans for James and his brother, he gave us a detailed diagram of the location, which also had information on where each agent would be located . . ."

Manion looked Brian in the eyes. "Don't tell me . . ."

"After our meeting," Brian pressed on, "I folded my copy and put it inside my jacket pocket. I had intended to put it in my file cabinet, but then I got distracted by another case and forgot about it. Jessica and I met for an early dinner. When I reached into my jacket pocket to take out my wallet, I pulled out the diagram—"

"Brian . . ." Manion interjected, voice rising.

"I guess she could tell by my reaction that I wasn't pleased with myself," he went on, talking rapidly now. "She asked me what was the matter, and I explained that it was an important document that should have been left locked in my office. I foolishly said, 'People would literally kill to get their hands on this document.'"

"*Brian.*" Manion spoke his friend's name like a groan this time, and Brian shook his head, clearly furious with himself.

"We left the restaurant and went back to my place. We barely got through the door before she became very passionate. We quickly removed our clothes and began making love—I won't go into the details, but it was a lot wilder than it had ever been before. Afterward, we just stayed in bed and fell asleep . . . at least, I did. I woke up about an hour later, and she was gone. I was surprised that she left without saying anything. I tried calling her apartment, but there was no answer. I figured she might still be on her way there, so I started gathering up my clothes. When I grabbed my jacket, I realized that the diagram was missing. I immediately drove to her apartment, and the bellman told me that he hadn't seen her in several weeks. Next, I called the president of the real estate company where she told me she worked. He said that no one named Jessica Vaughn had ever worked for his company. That's when I came here."

"We'll deal with it," Manion said, lying to himself as much as Brian. "We'll handle this, and nothing will come of it, all right? I'm going to call Joe."

"Okay," Brian said, breathing heavily. "I'll get us a drink."

Manion turned away, already calling their colleague. When Joe picked up, he said, "We've got a problem—a serious problem," and told him everything.

Joe didn't waste any time. "Stay on the line. I'm going to radio our FBI units." A few long moments passed, and just when Manion started to hope that everything was all right, Joe got back on the line and said, "One unit failed to respond. I've ordered several of the agents to double-time it to that specific spot, but—"

"The area has been breached," Manion finished for him, slamming a fist into the wall.

"I'm taking two agents with me to personally investigate. I'll call James via the two-way radio right now. I'll keep you posted," Joe said.

"No! Keep me on the line . . . I have to know that he is safe!" Manion's head began to throb, and he felt a tightening in his stomach. He turned around, facing Brian, who handed him a shot of bourbon. He gulped it down in one swallow. The burning sensation of the liquor matched the blazing feeling throughout his body. "After all that kid has gone through, we can't let him . . ."

Before he could finish, he overheard Joe speaking with James via radio. James's tone of voice seemed to indicate he was completely oblivious to the danger he was in—and Manion could have sworn he overheard James say, "We're just enjoying some breakfast," when all of a sudden, three gunshots rang out.

He went perfectly still. He brought the phone to his lips. "Joe," he barked. "What the hell was that?"

But Joe didn't answer. There was rustling and frantic conversation on the other line before the phone call ended, leaving Manion in silence. But somehow, he knew—and so did Brian—what had just taken place.

James had been shot.

# PART THREE
# THE SEMINARIAN

# 26

# The Funeral

**John Donnelly**
**Church | 1985**

THE FUNERAL WAS three days later. John insisted on being a pallbearer. As he entered the church, carrying the casket of his brother and best friend, he wished it was all just a bad dream—a horrible nightmare—but he knew it was real. He could still feel his dying brother in his arms, still hear his last words. Then, an anguished thought struck him. *Memorable— it was going to be a memorable day. It will be a terrible memory that I'll live with each and every day of my life!*

John saw that the church was completely full—just like for Christmas or Easter, but this was no joyful holiday. The entire town was there to honor James. They loved Father Pat and wanted to support him during this sorrowful time, just like he had supported them so many times in the past. They wanted to show respect to the courageous young man who had been brutally murdered.

A somber and heartbroken Father Jason celebrated the funeral mass, and Father Pat delivered the eulogy. Although the old priest was visibly shaken by the loss of his son, he was able to give a touching and inspirational tribute while affirming an uncompromising faith in eternal life. He shared several "Jimmy stories"—including the vinegar-for-altar-wine switch—that had the congregation laughing uncontrollably. He finished by declaring how proud he was of the son who had sacrificed his life to destroy an evil. There was not a dry eye in the church.

John sat frozen in the pew. The entire funeral mass was a blur to him. He was still in shock at seeing his brother slain before his eyes. Beyond the shock, he felt guilt. *Why my brother and not me?* He was also furious at the gullible attorney who had leaked their location. And finally, he felt hatred toward those who had murdered his brother.

It was after seven o'clock by the time the last of the guests left the church hall. The three of them—Father Pat, Father Jason, and John—slowly walked back to the rectory in silence. They sat in the living room, and Father Jason poured each of them a glass of scotch. John thought of the countless times the four of them had enjoyed their two fingers together and knew it would never be the same again.

After several moments of silence, Father Pat turned to his son and said, "Johnny, I know you are hurting, son. You have barely spoken since Saturday. I can see how much you have bottled up inside of you right now. It's completely understandable, but you have to let it out; otherwise, you're going to implode. You know you can always talk to me or Father Jason. It might even feel better speaking to one of the priests at the seminary."

John turned to his father and said, "You're right, Father Pat. There's a lot going on inside me right now. Different thoughts . . . different emotions . . ." In some ways, he felt nothing—a gaping abyss of nothing. Maybe this was what shock felt like. Maybe it simply hadn't settled in yet.

But he'd seen it with his own eyes, and . . .

"I'm not ready to talk about it right now," he said, his voice a croak. "I . . . I need some time to sort it all out."

Father Pat gave his son a sympathetic glance, put his hand on John's shoulder, and said, "I'm always here for you . . . always!"

Then the old priest suggested, "I think the best thing you can do right now is to return to the seminary and continue on your path to the priesthood."

The young man stared at his father for a few moments, then slowly nodded in apparent agreement, but in his heart, he was not sure that this would be his path.

# 27

## The Older Brother

Archbishop John Donnelly
Western Massachusetts | 2016

ARCHBISHOP DONNELLY WIPED the tears from his eyes, looked up to the sky, and repeated the words from their last night together. "I'll miss you every single day of my life, but the love we have for each other will last forever. So, you will always be in my heart..." He gave a solemn nod to Father Pat's headstone, adding, "Take care of him up there, will you? Make sure he's not getting into any trouble. I pray that you both continue to rest in heavenly peace. And don't forget to watch me be named a cardinal. I would have never been able to do it without the two of you!" Then he turned to walk slowly toward the car.

Paul saw the archbishop approaching, put down his book, and started the vehicle. They had made this visit to the cemetery numerous times over the years, so he knew that the archbishop would be quiet for the next several minutes. John appreciated the fact that, in a way, Paul could understand his pain; having been a street cop in Boston, he'd seen his share of violence and heartbreak. He understood that the pain of brutally losing a loved one never goes away.

After leaving the cemetery, they drove to the retirement home where Father Jason was now living. The priest, who had been like an older brother to the Donnelly twins, was elated to see the archbishop. Father Jason was in his eighties now, and while he suffered from severe arthritis, which required him to use a cane, his mind was as sharp as ever. Occasionally, he would still assist the younger pastor at the church, just as Father Pat had assisted him many years ago. They drove to a local Mediterranean restaurant for lunch, a hole-in-the-wall called the Hummus House, which had existed for three decades in the same ramshackle cobblestone building. Jimmy used to rave about their falafel, claiming it was better than anywhere in the world—even Greece itself, which always made John laugh.

Father Jason and John, however, had always favored the gyro. Paul ordered the pita wrap. After placing their order, they found a table out front. The trees swayed in the autumn breeze, shedding multicolored leaves in a confetti-like burst, and to this day, it still saddened the archbishop, knowing that his brother wasn't there to see the world trip from one season into the next.

"How were Father Pat and Jimmy?" Father Jason asked, resting his cane against the table.

The archbishop chuckled. Father Jason always asked after Father Pat and James in a way that felt like they were still alive. It was . . . comforting. "They are great. I reminded Father Pat to keep my brother in line."

"Always a good thing." They paused as their server delivered their meals and water with lemon, which Father Jason sipped at meaningfully before saying, "You know, I am extremely proud to say that my 'younger brother' is being named a cardinal. If it weren't for *this* blasted thing"—he swatted at his cane, leaning innocently against the table— "then I'd be there in person, but I'll be watching every second of the ceremony on TV, trust me."

"You'll be there in spirit, Father Jason, and that's all that matters," the archbishop replied with a genuine smile—not because he knew Father Jason would be watching him on TV but rather because he'd just referred to him as his younger brother. It made him feel less alone.

It was nearly three o'clock when they dropped Father Jason off and headed back to Boston.

Later that week, the archbishop visited Saint John's Seminary in Brighton. He made it a point to visit the seminary on a regular basis. It was enjoyable, meeting with the young seminarians and hearing about their backgrounds and reasons for pursuing the priesthood. Everyone was anticipating his visit on this particular day. The rector had even planned a special dinner to celebrate Archbishop John's elevation to cardinal. As he exited the car, he thought back on his life as a seminarian over thirty years before.

# 28

# The Seminary

**John Donnelly**

**Saint John's Seminary | 1985-1989**

JOHN RETURNED TO the seminary with a heavy heart, extremely uncertain about his future. The seminarians and faculty warmly welcomed him back. They were sensitive because none of them could imagine the pain that he was experiencing. Over the following weeks, it became clear to most of them that the trauma of losing his brother had changed John. He'd become withdrawn and detached. His eyes and body language sent an unsettling message. He seemed to have a lot of emotion bubbling right under the surface, like the rumbling felt before a volcano erupts. At times, he seemed very distracted—almost to the point of confusion. He rarely engaged in conversations, and his schoolwork also suffered. He was unprepared for classes and failed to remember previously covered material.

Initially, his instructors had been understanding and tolerant. They knew he needed time to mourn and then move forward, but after more than a month, they'd become concerned enough to raise the issue with Monsignor Mike. The monsignor had also observed the changes in John, but he had chosen not to say or do anything sooner. Now he knew that it was time to take action.

Two days later, John was told to report to the monsignor's office. He wasn't sure what to expect when he knocked on the door. The monsignor had decided it was time for some tough love. So, when he heard John's knock, he got up from his desk, opened the door, and told John to have a seat. Rather than sitting down himself, the monsignor stood over John, placed his hands on his hips, and simply stared at him for what seemed like several minutes. And then he spoke to John in a serious and brutal tone. "So . . . you think you are good enough to be a priest, huh?" John wasn't sure where this was going, and the monsignor did not give him a chance to respond. "Well, I certainly don't think so! You are completely behind in your studies. I've watched you at services, and you don't even know what you're doing. You're never going to make it! What a waste . . . a terrible waste! You might as well quit now because you're never going to be a priest."

That's when the volcano finally erupted. All of the emotion he had been holding inside since that tragic morning exploded to the surface. John sprung up from the chair with such force that it fell backward, and he shouted at the monsignor, "Why, you miserable son of a bitch! You heartless bastard . . . You can't even imagine what I've been through, what I'm feeling!"

All the anger, pain, and emotion of being a victim finally rushed out of him. He seriously considered grabbing the monsignor by the throat and throwing him up against the wall. At that very moment, two things happened. First, an image of his brother flashed in his mind. His twin was smirking and giving him one of those looks that implied, *Relax . . . Calm down . . . It's going to be all right.* Second, rather than responding in anger, this towering figure—who actually did look and sound like John Wayne—spoke in a mild and soothing voice.

"Well, it's about time, John. Let it out, son. Let it all out. If you don't let that emotion out of your system, it will kill you! It's like a poison that destroys you from within. It's an anchor that is just going to weigh you down and prevent you from moving forward. You have to let it go!"

The monsignor looked at John with obvious empathy and concern before continuing, "You are absolutely correct—I can't even begin to imagine how difficult, how gut-wrenching it was for you to lose your brother in such a violent and senseless way. You have every right to be angry, upset, hurt . . . It's normal to feel the way you're feeling, but you have to make a choice! No one can make this choice except you. You can either remain stuck in this sorrowful state, or you can move forward with your life. John, the choice is up to you. Losing your brother, especially under such tragic circumstances, was horrible. You loved your brother with all your heart, and I'm sure he loved you as well. That love will never die! It lasts forever! He will always be alive in your heart. Think of what he would want you to do with the rest of your life."

Tears were streaming down his face as John listened to what Monsignor Mike said. They were practically the same words from the last night with his brother. At that moment, the young man fell to his knees and began crying uncontrollably. The monsignor reached down and pulled him up. He wrapped his broad arms around John and let him just cry it all out.

From that moment on, John was committed to moving forward. He realized that the pain of losing his brother would always be with him—but more importantly, the love that they had for each other would keep his brother alive in his heart. Rather than letting the pain be an anchor that held him back, he decided to let the love for his brother be the sail that moved him forward.

John devoted himself to his studies with a passion, and he quickly caught up on all of his work. He was focused and attentive in class as well as friendly, outgoing, and fully engaged with the other seminarians. Monsignor Mike kept up the tough persona, but he always made himself available to John for support and guidance. Since the night of the eruption, the two had developed a close bond. At the end of the pre-theology program, the monsignor pulled John aside, looked him in the eyes, and, uttering the same words from two years before, said, "So . . . you think you are good enough to be a priest, huh?"

Then, with a huge laugh and supportive smile, he put his arm around John and said, "Well, maybe . . . maybe so!"

The next three years of study at the seminary consisted of theological training. The courses covered the Bible, doctrines of faith, fundamental theology, morality, and church history. John found some of the classes challenging, but he enjoyed the vast majority of them and continued to do well academically. In addition to academics, there were two other pillars of formation: spiritual and pastoral.

To assist in his spiritual development, each seminarian was assigned to a spiritual director or adviser. John met with his adviser—Father James Flint—every other week. Father Jim had been a parish priest and college counselor for several years. He had a relaxed manner and made each person feel extremely comfortable and special. He was an outstanding listener, and he helped to guide John into a deeper and more meaningful spiritual understanding of his faith.

One day a week was devoted to the pastoral pillar of development. During his seminarian years, John worked at homeless shelters, nursing homes, hospitals, and various parishes. He found the work in the homeless shelters to be especially enlightening. He met men and women who were battling drug and alcohol addiction. Each of them had a deeply personal story. Many of the men were veterans of the Vietnam War; the trauma that they had seen on the battlefield led them to drugs or alcohol to erase the memories that still haunted them. Others had experienced some terrible tragedy in their personal lives that led them down this path of decline. It was through this work that John developed a strong social consciousness and learned not to judge others.

Whenever he had a long weekend, John would drive out to spend time with Fathers Pat and Jason. He attempted to follow the same routine that he and his brother had so many times—a brisk hike on Saturday morning, vigil mass in the late afternoon, a delicious dinner (either prepared by Father Jason or a local restaurant), and then the traditional two fingers of scotch, along with warm, friendly conversation. They would always make a toast to the one who was no longer with them. That invariably led to a funny story about raising the "Sons of Thunder." There was plenty of laughter, along with a few tears.

It was during one of these visits that Father Jason and John arranged a surprise eightieth birthday party for Father Pat. The church hall was filled with parishioners. The food and desserts, which were provided by the local restaurants and bakeries, were plentiful and delicious. Naturally, Father Jason was encouraged to sing a few songs with his impressive voice. John gave a warm and emotional toast. He raised his glass of wine and said, "Here's to you, Father Pat! You have been an outstanding shepherd of God's people, a kind and caring parent, an insightful and wise mentor, and a patient and knowledgeable teacher—but more than all these things, you have been the embodiment of total and unconditional love! It's the kind of love that Saint Paul speaks of in his letter to the Corinthians. And everyone in this room has felt your love in countless ways. May God continue to bless you now and forever! Happy eighty years young, Father Pat."

There was not a dry eye in the entire hall after this moving tribute.

# 29

# The Cousins

**John Donnelly**
**Braintree | 1989**

ONE AFTERNOON, JOHN received a message from someone he had not seen since college—Francis Roland. Upon graduation from BC, John's roommate had taken a job with an insurance company on the West Coast. Other than a very touching sympathy card and flowers when his brother died, John had not heard from Francis. He was not sure what they would talk about after nearly six years. John held on to the message for a few days but eventually overcame his hesitancy and made the call.

"Hello, Fran, this is John . . . John Donnelly."

There was a brief silence on the other end, and then John heard the friendly voice.

"Johnny, I'm so glad you called back. I was getting worried that you hadn't received the message. How are you? How's the seminary?"

"I'm doing fine, and the seminary is even better than I had expected. What about you?"

"I'm doing great! In fact, I just moved back to Boston."

"Boston? You're back here? You left the job in San Francisco?"

"Well, actually, I left it a few years ago and enrolled in a graduate program at Stanford. I just accepted a job at an investment banking firm in Boston."

"Investment banking? That sounds pretty interesting. I guess you decided not to pursue the insurance business like your dad."

"Yeah, in fact, it was my stepmother who suggested I get into investment banking. She's had a very successful career doing it."

"Stepmother? Sounds like a lot has changed in these past six years."

"It has, John." Fran's tone changed. "And I am sorry that I wasn't there for you when . . . James died, the way you were there for me when my mom passed."

There was an uncomfortable silence before John assured Fran, "There is no need to apologize. You were over three thousand miles away. You couldn't be here for me."

"Thanks, John. You were always so sensitive and understanding. That's why I knew you'd become a great priest."

"Well, I'm not quite there yet, but thanks for the vote of confidence."

"Hey, I'd like you to join me and a couple of friends for drinks this weekend. There's a small, quiet tavern in Braintree. It will feel great to reconnect after all these years."

John surprised himself by quickly agreeing to meet Fran and his friends.

As soon as John walked into the cozy Irish bar, he spotted Fran and his two companions at a corner table. When Fran caught sight of John, he jumped up from his seat, rushed to him, gave him a big hug, and exclaimed, "Johnny, I'm so happy to see you. It's been way, *way* too long. You look fantastic! I guess that they're treating you well at the seminary."

This warm welcome felt good and brought back fond memories for John. They walked to the table, where Fran handled the introductions.

"Guys, I'd like you to meet my good friend John Donnelly. And Johnny, I'd like you to meet Michael Berillo and Stephen Ruffo."

Michael, who appeared to be slightly older than the rest of them, greeted John first. "Hello, John. It's great to meet you. I've got to warn you, though . . . Fran has spoken so highly of you, you've got some great expectations to meet."

Stephen smiled, poured a glass of beer for John, and said, "I'm sure he'll live up to everything our cousin has said."

"Cousins? You guys are cousins?"

Fran explained. "They're my *step*cousins. I told you that my dad remarried a few years ago—I ended up with two great cousins in the deal."

John sat down, took a sip of his beer, and said, "That's excellent news about your dad. Did he marry someone from work?"

"No. Ronnie is someone he has known for thirty years. She attended college with my aunt Stephanie and would often visit with my grandparents when they lived in Massachusetts. She has remained close friends with Aunt Steph and was invited to my grandparents' fiftieth wedding anniversary party. That's when she and my father reconnected. I'm really happy for him. She is a great lady and very bright."

"Yeah, you mentioned on the phone that she's the one who convinced you to pursue investment banking."

"I hope that I'm half as successful as she has been in her career." Fran changed the subject. "So, how are Father Pat and Father Jason doing?"

"Father Pat is in his eighties now, but he's still as sharp as ever. Father Jason has taken over all of the administrative duties for the church and school. The two of them are doing really well." John turned to the other two and asked, "So, how are you guys related?"

Stephen responded first. "My dad is Aunt Ronnie's older brother, Joe. He made a career in the military. When he retired from the army, he took a job with a defense contractor, and we moved from Texas to Massachusetts."

"Wow, that was quite a move. How are you liking these New England winters?"

"Still getting used to them."

"So, I'm guessing you didn't choose a career in the army?"

"I'm really proud of my dad being a war hero and all, but I chose to follow in my mom's footsteps. She's a successful lawyer. I just finished law school and am working in the district attorney's office."

John felt a stab to his heart as he recalled the discussion about law school with his brother on their last night together. He quickly took another sip of the beer to calm himself.

"And my mom is Aunt Ronnie's older sister, Tonia," Michael explained. "She was a nurse, and it must have rubbed off on me because I decided to go to medical school."

"Wow, I'm in great company—a doctor, a lawyer, and an investment banker!"

Stephen grinned and joked, "No, I think we're in even better company! You've got a connection with the big guy upstairs." He laughed and then said, "Tell us what it was like being raised by a priest."

Fran already knew the story about Father Pat, but his cousins were intrigued to learn what life was like for John. They were also curious about the seminary. The four of them talked for hours and agreed to meet again. John thoroughly enjoyed himself and was glad that he had overcome his initial uncertainty about returning Fran's call. It felt good to reconnect with Fran, and although he had just met Stephen and Michael, he felt a strong connection with them. From that night on, they saw each other regularly and developed lasting friendships.

# 30

## Danielle

**John Donnelly**
**Berkshires | 1989**

IT WAS COLUMBUS Day weekend, and John was hiking in the Berkshires. He had driven from the seminary right after classes the previous afternoon. Although it had rained heavily early in the week, it was a beautiful, sunny day. He approached a small stream and began to slowly navigate his way across by stepping on the rocks. It reminded him of a similar time when he was hiking with his brother and, after slipping on the rocks, had fallen right into the water—into a stream very much like this one. His brother, who had already easily made it across, started laughing uncontrollably. He smiled at the memory, treading carefully over a fallen log to cross the water, when—lo and behold—he slipped and fell into it all over again.

It was October, so the water was definitely cold, and John yelped while hobbling out of the water as fast as possible. He could practically hear his brother laughing his head off—

Wait. That was *real* laughter he was hearing.

He turned around and spotted a young woman a few yards behind him. She had long blonde hair that was tied back in a ponytail and the large, round eyes of a doe that were an intense and breathtaking hazel. After she finally stopped chuckling, she teasingly said, "I'm really sorry. I know I shouldn't be laughing at someone else's misfortune, but your fall was classic."

John shook the water out of his boots, forced a smile, and bowed before proceeding to the other side. "I'm pleased that I was able to bring you such entertainment."

To add insult to injury, the young lady simply skipped across the rocks as she crossed the stream, deciding she didn't even need the log he'd tried to use. When she reached John, she smiled, held out her hand, and introduced herself. "Hi, I'm Danielle . . . Danielle Harrison."

He reached forward, took her hand, and instantly fell captive to her wholesome beauty. Her eyes sparkled over high cheekbones, and her skin was somehow tan and glowing, even though they were a month into autumn. She was at least five and a half feet tall, with an attractive, athletic figure. John realized he was staring and quickly shook her hand as he introduced himself.

"It's a pleasure to meet you, Danielle. My name is John . . . John Donnelly."

Now that they were up close, he realized he wasn't the only one who was staring. Danielle's eyes darted over his face, as though noting his wavy black hair and his blue eyes. He raked a hand through his hair nervously, desperately trying to make himself look a little more handsome—which was an impulse that surprised him, given his status as a seminarian.

She smiled back at John and said, "Well, it is nice to meet you, John Donnelly. And I am sorry for laughing at your misfortune. That was very cruel of me. I hope you didn't hurt yourself."

John grinned, brushed off his backside, and said, "Only my pride, Danielle . . . but then, a little humility is always a good thing."

"Well, do you mind if I hike along with you? This way, I can catch you before you fall again," she said with a grin.

John laughed. "I would be most grateful, Danielle."

After they had quietly gone a few hundred yards, John decided to break the silence. "I grew up not far from here and have hiked in the Berkshires all my life."

Danielle laughed. "Hiked here all of your life, and you still can't cross a little stream without falling in?"

"Boy, you're tough!"

"I'm sorry—I couldn't resist. That's the last time I'll tease you about it . . . maybe!" She gave John a mischievous smile before telling him about herself. "I teach English literature at Amherst. I'm staying at a bed-and-breakfast in Stockbridge for the holiday weekend. The innkeeper recommended hiking in the Berkshires. Since I had never been before, I decided to give it a try."

"Wait a minute—you've never been hiking before?"

"No . . . no, I didn't mean that I've never hiked. I've never been to the Berkshires. I grew up in New Hampshire and hiked the White Mountains. My fiancé . . . uh . . . ex-fiancé and I used to hike all the time."

John sensed a change in Danielle's mood as she mentioned her ex-fiancé. Before he could say anything, she explained.

"We recently broke up, and I'm still getting used to it. That's why I wanted to spend time away this weekend."

John could tell that this was a tender subject for Danielle. He thought of how Father Pat would respond and tried his best to emulate him. "It must have been very painful to end the relationship. Would you like to talk about it?"

"Normally, I wouldn't," she said honestly. They kept their eyes on the leaf-littered path in front of them, walking in tandem. "But I feel like I can open up to you. Maybe it's because you're a stranger . . . It's weird how that is, isn't it?" At this, she glanced sideways at John, and he felt his whole body lock up at the sight of her hazel eyes. She was *beautiful*. "Weird how sometimes it's easier to open up to a stranger than friends or family . . . Have you ever noticed that?"

John, frankly, hadn't heard a word she'd just said and frantically nodded.

*What had gotten into him?*

"Anyway, you've got kind eyes. I can tell you're a good person, and . . ." She sighed, arms swinging wide to gesture to the nature around them. "What better time to get something off one's chest than now, right?"

"Absolutely," John replied.

"Russell and I have known each other since elementary school. We started off as competitors—each vying to get the highest grade in the class. The competition grew into a friendship, and the friendship eventually blossomed into love. We started dating in high school and always talked about getting married. We got engaged six months ago, which was the happiest day of my life!"

John could see the glow in her face and hear the excitement in her voice as she described her relationship with Russell, but in the next instant, he witnessed the glow disappear as her tone became very somber.

"Then . . . a few weeks ago . . . I broke it off."

John was confused. "It sounds like you and Russell had a great relationship. So, what caused the breakup?"

Danielle's beautiful hazel eyes began to moisten. She took a deep breath and then explained. "Russ is a wonderful . . . *really* wonderful person. He's bright and hardworking. He graduated at the top of his class and has an excellent job in Boston, where he is on a fast track. He is kind, gentle . . . fun to be around. But Russ has one problem, a very big problem. He drinks too much. It started in high school, when he would sneak around with his buddies and drink beer. Then, when he went to college, he moved up to hard liquor. At first, it would only be on weekends. Then he started drinking heavily on some weeknights. And over the past few months, it has been every single night. I told him I was worried about him, but he would tell me there was no need to worry. He'd laugh and say, 'I work hard, so I play hard. I can stop drinking anytime I want.' So, I challenged him to stop. He would stop for a couple of days, but then, by the third or fourth day, he was back at the booze again. I finally gave him an ultimatum. I told him that he was an alcoholic and needed professional help. I warned him that if he didn't get it, we were through. That led to a huge argument and ended in my giving him his ring back. We haven't spoken since then."

She paused for a moment, gathering her composure. John was trying to figure out what he would say to all this, how he could possibly help, but thankfully, she continued, "You're probably wondering why I took such a firm stand with the man I loved . . . and still love. I had an uncle, Uncle Charlie—I never knew him, but I heard all the stories about him. He was handsome, outgoing, hardworking, and very successful. But there was only one problem—he drank too much. When people would confront him about it, he simply laughed and told them he could control his liquor. And he did for a long time, until one rainy evening. Charlie had too much to drink and was driving home from the tavern when he swerved into the oncoming lane and hit another car head-on. The driver of the other car was a young college student who was killed immediately. Uncle Charlie wasn't seriously injured. He was arrested for vehicular manslaughter, but before he went to trial, he committed suicide."

"Oh my God!" John said reflexively, truly taken aback. "I'm so sorry . . ."

Danielle shrugged. "Like I said, I never knew Uncle Charlie, but I knew my aunt Agnes, Charlie's wife. She always seemed to be very sad and depressed. Right up until the day she died, Aunt Agnes would blame herself for tolerating my uncle's drinking. My father says it was the guilt that eventually killed her. As much as I love Russ, I don't want to have the same experience as my aunt."

John was touched by Danielle's fortitude.

When she had finished speaking, he turned to her and said, "I appreciate you sharing all that with me, Danielle. It still is very painful for you, but you are an extremely strong and courageous person. Leaving Russ was difficult, but I can understand why you made that decision."

Danielle wiped a tear from her eye, smiled at John, and thanked him for his understanding. By this time, they were near the end of the trail, and she seemed to realize she'd spent so much time talking about herself that she hadn't learned anything about him.

"I'm so sorry. I took all of our time talking about me. I don't know anything about you."

John smiled and said, "No apology necessary. You had a lot on your mind, and like I said, I was pleased you felt comfortable sharing it with me. But if you really feel bad about it, you can make it up by joining me for dinner with my family tonight."

"That's very kind of you, but I'm afraid your family might not appreciate an unexpected guest."

"Nonsense! My father's house is always open to everyone. There is no such thing as an unexpected guest for him!"

"All right . . . I'll join you, and I look forward to meeting your father. He sounds like a very special person."

"Yes, he is." *And so are you, Danielle,* John thought to himself.

———∘∘∘◦❰◗❱◦∘∘∘———

On this particular night, Father Jason was making one of his favorite Italian dishes—braised lamb shanks over baked polenta. When John wrote down the address, he purposely didn't mention that it was actually a church rectory and that his father was a priest. He felt somewhat playful and was looking forward to Danielle's reaction. He was watching from the living room window and saw her pull up. It seemed to be taking an extra-long time for her to get out of the car. He smiled to himself as he thought, *She probably thinks she has gotten the address wrong . . . telling herself that I couldn't possibly live in a rectory.*

After a few minutes, she finally exited the car and headed to the front door, carrying a bottle of cabernet sauvignon. Just as she was about to ring the bell, John opened the door and greeted her. She handed John the bottle of wine and inquired, "Your family lives in a church rectory?"

John could see the curiosity on Danielle's face. He smiled and replied, "Well . . . yes, this is where my father lives, and this is where my brother and I grew up."

Almost as if on cue, Father Pat joined them, and John introduced the older priest as his father. He saw that Danielle appeared even more baffled. Father Pat gave her a warm smile and greeted her.

"Welcome to our home, Danielle. You're probably wondering how Johnny ended up with a priest for a father. Well, let's open up that wine, and I'll tell you the story."

They escorted her to the kitchen, where Father Jason was busy putting the finishing touches on the main course. He looked up and greeted Danielle.

"Welcome, Danielle. I'm Father Jason. Please have some appetizers while I finish getting dinner ready. There are roasted vegetables, Italian cheeses, and freshly baked bread."

Danielle tasted the appetizers and exclaimed, "These are so delicious! Now I know I'm in for an amazing meal tonight."

Father Pat poured everyone a glass of wine and proceeded to tell the story of how God blessed him with two special packages nearly thirty years before. John could see that his father loved telling the story. By the time he got to the part about adopting the twin boys, it was time for the first course. They moved into the dining room, and Father Jason brought out the salad plates and asked John to say grace.

The salad was a mixture of arugula, radicchio, fennel, and shaved Parmesan cheese, topped with a homemade Italian dressing. After savoring the salad and complimenting Father Jason, Danielle turned to Father Pat and said, "That is a wonderful story, Father Pat. Thank you so much for sharing it with me. It must have been very challenging raising two boys. I'd love to hear some of those tales, but I'm curious, where is your other son?"

The room went silent for a moment. John could tell from the look on Danielle's face that she regretted asking the question, and perceiving her uneasiness, he responded in a quiet, thoughtful tone, "My brother died. He was killed . . . tragically . . . a few years ago."

"Oh, I am so very sorry to hear that. It must have been very painful for all of you."

"Yes, Danielle, it was extremely painful . . . and it still is painful, but we're comforted by knowing that Jimmy is with God now, and someday, we will all be together again. It also helps when we remember that Jimmy sacrificed his life to do what was right."

Father Pat then went on to explain how James helped the FBI put an end to a major crime family. As he told the story, Danielle mentioned she recalled reading about it in the newspapers—and she also remembered that the victim had died in his brother's arms. She looked over at John, as though she could only imagine how difficult that must have been for him.

By this time, Father Jason brought out the lamb shanks. The meat simply fell off the bone, and the creamy polenta melted in her mouth.

Danielle exclaimed, "This is one of the best meals I've ever eaten! I'll be sure to come back to this restaurant."

Father Jason smiled with obvious pride and assured her, "Don't hesitate to come back. You are always welcome here."

Father Pat agreed that the dinner was excellent and added, "Father Jason's cooking skills are outstanding, and if he hadn't become a priest—a very fine priest—he probably would have been a famous chef working at some fancy restaurant in New York." Then he turned to Danielle and asked, "So, what do you do for a living?"

"I teach English literature at Amherst College. I've always loved Shakespeare and the other great playwrights." John noticed that her natural glow became more intense as she discussed her love of teaching. She went on to share with them, "I thoroughly enjoyed acting in college and seriously considered trying it professionally. I actually spent one year in New York, but I eventually realized that it was a very difficult career. There are a lot of talented actors but only a limited number of opportunities. That's when I decided to go to graduate school and teach at the college level."

After discussing her occupation, Danielle turned to John and asked, "And what do you do for a living, John?"

John smiled and said, "Well, Danielle, I'm in the seminary right now."

He watched the surprised expression on her face as she absorbed what he had just said. She regained her composure, laughed, and said, "Wow! That is amazing. I'm having dinner with two and a half priests. I really hope I didn't say anything inappropriate during our hike today."

John grinned and assured her, "Other than laughing at my falling in the water, you were very well-behaved."

After they had finished coffee and dessert, Danielle prepared to leave. She gave the two priests hugs and kisses and thanked them for the delicious dinner and the wonderful company.

John walked Danielle to her car and told her, "I'm so happy you came. You were a big hit."

Danielle smiled at John and told him that she was also glad she had come. She went on to say, "You know, this has been a very special day for me, John. It was so easy talking with you during our hike today. I shared a lot of stuff that has been bottled up inside of me. It felt like a giant weight was lifted off my shoulders. Then, to meet your wonderful father and be treated to an outstanding dinner by Father Jason—what an extraordinary day! I really enjoyed myself. Thank you so very much for inviting me. Let's stay in touch." She then kissed him on the cheek and gave him a warm hug.

They did stay in touch over the next year. Anytime John had a long weekend or a day off, the two of them would meet. Sometimes, she would stop in Boston on her way to visit her family in New Hampshire. When they didn't see each other, they would talk over the phone. Danielle teasingly nicknamed him "Sir John Falstaff" or simply "Falstaff" from Shakespeare's *Henry IV.* This was in reference to how they'd first met because Falstaff also had a habit of falling down in Shakespeare's play. He began calling her "the Belle of Amherst" from the play of the same name by William Luce about Emily Dickinson. John thought this nickname was appropriate, given that she taught English literature at Amherst College.

John had never felt this way with a woman before. He thoroughly enjoyed his time with Danielle and thought of her often. Anytime something special happened, he immediately wanted to share it with her. They clearly had developed a strong friendship, and after several months, John couldn't help but speculate if it was destined to be *more* than that. He wondered if this could be love. He would soon be ordained into the transitional deacon's role, which occurred one year before ordination to the priesthood.

He was feeling extremely confused and decided to speak to Father Jason. Father Jason listened as John explained how he was feeling about Danielle.

"I've been with other women, but I've never felt this way before. I find myself thinking of her in the middle of classes. I look forward to talking with her . . . seeing her . . . just being with her. I'm torn between being a priest and spending the rest of my life with Danielle. I don't know what to do."

"Johnny, I can see you are struggling with several emotions. It's understandable that you have strong feelings toward Danielle. She's a lovely and bright young woman. The positive attraction between the two of you was obvious the first time we met her. Recall that conversation Father Pat and I had with you during your final year of college. We said to you then that it was important for you to experience the real world before you went into the seminary. Well, your feelings for Danielle are another part of experiencing the real world. And remember, you are not committed to the life and work of a priest until you take your final vows and are ordained."

Father Jason stopped for a moment to let John absorb what he had just said. Then he continued, "I suggest you spend time alone at the chapel, praying to God for guidance and discernment. Trust that the Lord will guide you in the right decision. And, Johnny, whatever you decide . . . know that it will be all right with Father Pat and me."

John thanked Jason for his wise advice, and over the next few weeks, he spent every free moment at the seminary chapel, praying and asking God to give him a sign. It was a Thursday afternoon when John received a phone call from Danielle.

"Well, good afternoon, Falstaff. How's life at the seminary?"

"It's going great, Belle. What's up with you?"

"I'm driving to New Hampshire this weekend and wanted to meet you for lunch on my way."

"Sounds good to me. I always look forward to seeing you."

"And John . . . there's something important . . . very important that I want to share with you." John sensed the excitement in her voice and was anxious to hear what she wanted to share.

They met at a small restaurant in Newton Centre. She looked as beautiful as ever, but there seemed to be an unusual radiance in her appearance. They had not seen each other in nearly a month, so they spent most of the time catching up. John kept wondering when Danielle would share the "very important something." It was as they were having coffee that she gave him a big smile and shared the news.

"I told you that I had very important news to share with you. You've been my rock during this past year. You were the first person I opened up to about my breakup with Russ. You may not have realized it, but anytime I felt depressed, I remembered what you said about trusting in God. You shared your faith with me in a way that strengthened mine. You are going to be an amazing priest, John Donnelly. Thank you. Thank you for your unwavering support, your guidance, and most importantly, your friendship during this past year."

John wondered where this conversation was going. *This is a buildup to something, but what is it?*

"You were the first person I talked to about my breakup with Russ. Now, I want you to be the first person I speak to about *reuniting* with Russ."

John was more than a little stunned by the news, but he tried to hide it. He forced a smile and continued listening to Danielle.

"I hadn't seen Russell in nearly twelve months when I received a long letter from him. In the letter, he confessed that when we first broke up, he was very angry and hurt. Then, after a few weeks, he came to the realization that he truly was an alcoholic and that he had lost the most important person in his life because of his drinking. He knew that if he continued down that path, he would ultimately lose everything else that was important to him. So, he took a leave of absence from work and checked himself into an alcohol rehabilitation center in the Midwest. He said that he hadn't had a drink since entering the center. He wrote that he was back at work, and while he was still devoted to his career, he was making sure that he maintained the right balance in his life. He was exercising regularly and eating healthy. He asked if I would be willing to meet with him, and I agreed. When I saw him, I couldn't believe my eyes. He looked better than he had in *years*. And during the past few weeks, I've become convinced of two things. First, he will never let alcohol control him again. And second, I am very much in love with him. So, the very important news that I wanted to share with you—before I even tell my parents—is that Russ and I are going to be married."

It felt as though his chest had just caved in.

John stared back at her blankly for a moment—struggling to breathe—before realizing that he was supposed to respond positively to all this. A little too belatedly, he said, "Danielle, that's such wonderful news . . ."

"God works in mysterious ways, I suppose," she said with a smile. Her blonde hair fluttered into her eyes, and it was all he could do to resist stroking it out of her face, pinning it behind her ear, and kissing her.

But he didn't. Because he knew, in his heart, she was right.

Although there was a high degree of disappointment, John realized that his prayers had been answered in a very powerful way. God did indeed work in mysterious ways, and this seemed to be one of them—and he wasn't going to question it.

He gave Danielle a warm embrace and told her how happy he was for her. She insisted that she wanted him to meet Russell and also attend their wedding.

He promised he would.

# 31

# The Final Year

**John Donnelly**
**Saint John's Seminary | 1990–1991**

GIVEN THE POWERFUL message he had received from God regarding Danielle, John was even more devoted to his vocation. The sixth and final year of seminary was known as the practicum, or practical experience. This was when the seminarians were taught the art of celebrating mass and giving homilies. They were also trained on the other sacraments, including baptism and reconciliation. The seminarian was ordained as a deacon during this period. It was known as a transitional diaconate—that is, a transition to eventual priesthood. The deacon was assigned to a parish priest and was expected to learn the intricacies of running a parish. With this objective in mind, the pastor would delegate diverse duties to the deacon.

John was appointed to Saint Mary's Church, which was located in a poorer section of Boston. The parish was well attended by the lower-income families in the city. The pastor, Father Al, had been there for many years, and the parishioners all loved him. He was caring and sensitive, and he knew all of them by their first names, along with their family histories and backgrounds. Everyone seemed to come to him for advice and guidance. His homilies were always engaging and left the parishioners with a powerful message. The church community was extremely united and supportive. John saw strong similarities between Father Al and Father Pat.

Father Al provided countless examples of how to be an inspirational shepherd of God's people. One particular incident that would always remain with John was when a young woman died during childbirth. The infant also died. The father and his two young sons were heartbroken. They were angry at God and could not understand why he was punishing them. They felt that God had deserted them.

Father Al patiently listened to their tearful venting. Then he spoke to them in a gentle and soothing way. "You're feeling a lot of sadness, anger, pain, and confusion right now. That's human and very normal. God doesn't choose to hurt us, and he never deserts us . . . especially not during difficult times. Remember, God's way is much different than our way! He knows everything, but we cannot possibly know the mind of God. We know that Jesus felt pity for the widow who lost her only son. We know that he grieved when his friend Lazarus died. So, we know that the Son of God understands the pain we feel when we lose someone we care about. We also know that God the Father loved his son and was very proud of him. Yet, he allowed Jesus to die the most horrible death imaginable so that we all could be saved. Why would he do that? Wasn't there an easier way? Like I said, God's way is not our way. Sometimes, we just accept that it is his will! Even Jesus had this experience the night before he died. He knew that he was going to die a very painful death. So, he asked his father if it could be avoided . . . but only . . . only if it was God's will."

Father Al paused for a moment, gently touched the shoulder of each boy and their father, and then continued, "Your wife . . . your mother . . . was a wonderful person. It was always such a pleasure to see her. She had the ability to brighten a room with her mere presence. Her laughter was like beautiful music. We will all miss her! And your baby sister would have been just like her mother. Now both of them are in heaven with God. They are enjoying that beautiful banquet that Jesus described, and they are looking down and praying for each of you. They have become your *very special guardian angels*. Whenever you are troubled—like you are now—or struggling with some challenge, their spirit will be with you, helping to guide you and lift you up."

John listened to the words of Father Al and then observed how the anger and pain appeared to lift from the father and his sons. A warm calmness seemed to surround them. They hugged the old priest and thanked him. In that moment, John realized that his brother was his special guardian angel and remembered how his brother's image had flashed before him just before he was ready to attack Monsignor Mike nearly six years before. This had been the lowest point in his life, and his brother's spirit had lifted him up. This was an extremely powerful lesson, and he vowed to never forget it.

The final step before a seminarian was ordained into the priesthood was gaining the cardinal's approval. John's grades had been near the top of his class. He received strong endorsements from the faculty members, as well as from Monsignor Mike and Father Al. The cardinal knew about John's being raised by Father Pat and had actually met the old priest several times. Even with all these reasons to be confident, John was concerned that the cardinal might not approve him. Most young seminarians experienced similar feelings, resulting in many sleepless nights. Of course, John's fears were completely unfounded. The cardinal gave a very strong approval and was sure that John would be an outstanding priest.

The night before his ordination, John heard a knock on his door. When he opened it, Monsignor Mike was standing there with a bottle of scotch in one hand and two glasses in the other. He gave John a big smile and said, "So . . . you think you are good enough to be a priest! Well, so do I!"

John immediately hugged this man who had been a solid rock for him throughout the past six years.

# PART FOUR

# THE MOTHER

# 32

## Veronica

**Father John Donnelly**
**Rectory | 1993**

JOHN HAD BEEN ordained two years before and was the assistant pastor at a parish in Framingham—a suburb twenty miles west of Boston. It was Thursday afternoon, and he was in his rectory office, working on his homily for Sunday's mass. He would normally read through the Gospel passage a few times before he started writing his sermon. This scripture was from Mark, chapter 3, when Jesus is told that his mother and brothers are waiting outside to speak with him. He responds by saying, "Who are my mother and my brothers?" John smiled when he read this line. *I've got the brother part down, but I'm still trying to figure out the mother.* At that moment, the phone rang. It was Father Pat.

"Johnny, I want you to drive out here on your day off next week. There's someone I want you to meet."

"Of course, I'll be there. You know I always drive home on my days off. Who is it that you'd like me to meet?"

"Great! I'll see you late Monday morning, then." Father Pat quickly hung up.

John thought to himself, *That was a strange call. He knows I drive out there every Monday right after morning mass. And why was he so evasive when I asked him who it was?* Father Pat was in his mideighties, and John felt blessed to still have his father in his life. So, he purposely spent most of his free time with him.

John arrived at the rectory at just after eleven. Father Jason was on the front porch, reading the paper. As soon as he saw the younger priest, he put down the paper and greeted him.

"So, how's Father John doing today?"

"I'm doing great and looking forward to one of your excellent dishes tonight."

"You can count on it! But you better get into the house now. Your father has been anxiously waiting for you."

John noticed that Father Jason had a playful grin on his face.

When John entered the room, he saw that there was an attractive middle-aged woman sitting on the sofa, speaking with Father Pat.

"Hello, Father Pat. How's my favorite father doing today?" John gave him a warm hug and planted a kiss on his bald head.

"Johnny, my boy, it's so good to see you. We've been waiting for you."

John turned to the woman, smiled, and held out his hand. "Hello, I'm John Donnelly."

As she took his hand, he noticed that the radiance of her smile appeared to make her olive complexion glow. He immediately felt a strange sensation—as if he should know this person—and wondered, *Who is this lovely lady? She's smiling as if captivated by me and holding on to my hand like she doesn't want to let go.*

Father Pat, who was beaming, slowly got up from the sofa and placed his hand on John's shoulder. "I'd like you to meet Veronica."

The woman stood up. John watched his father, who was between them, stare at the painting hanging on the living room wall for several seconds. It was the depiction of the crucifixion when Jesus looked down at his blessed mother and the apostle whom he loved. The young priest was astonished by what his father said next.

"Woman, behold your son . . . Son, behold, your mother."

Then Father Pat walked out of the room and left the two of them alone.

"What . . ." John looked back at her, eyes wide. "What is Father Pat talking about?"

Veronica tucked a stray lock of brown hair behind her ear. "You've got the same deep-blue eyes as your father . . . You look exactly like him."

John was stunned. "What? Who are you?"

Veronica seemed to hesitate. It appeared to John that she was struggling with her response. Tears began flowing down her cheeks, and in that instant, John knew. He threw his arms around her. "Mom?" he said, and at first, the word was a question—but then it evolved into a statement. "Mom! Is it really you, after all this time?"

Veronica cupped her son's cheeks in her hands. "It's been a long time, hasn't it? I've got so much to tell you."

John nodded understandingly, visibly flustered. He moved back to the couch, patting the seat beside him, and said, "Well, I suppose that it's a good thing I don't have anywhere else to be."

"It's a long story," she warned him, but he only smiled.

"Start from the beginning."

# 33

## The Valedictorian

| Veronica Ruffo
| Woonsocket | 1958

VERONICA FELT THE tension wrap around her neck as her heart raced and tiny beads of perspiration formed on her forehead. She was worried that she was about to embarrass herself. She took a deep breath, inhaling the fresh summer air, and looked up into the brilliant blue sky. She could practically hear what her mother would say.

*Veronica, why are you so nervous about delivering this speech? You've spent hours writing it and have been practicing in front of the mirror for the past five nights. Every single word is memorized. Stop doubting yourself! You are going to be amazing!*

Her mother's wise advice had always calmed Veronica and instilled confidence within her. She wished her mom was there today, but she knew in her heart that her mother's guiding spirit would be with her forever. It had only been a few months since the cancer had taken Maria, and Veronica was still missing her mother's shining light in her life.

Just as she was envisioning her mother's loving encouragement, the high school principal's voice broke into her thoughts.

"It gives me great pleasure to invite Woonsocket's Class of 1958 valedictorian, Veronica Ruffo, to come up on stage and deliver her address."

Veronica slowly walked to the podium, radiating poise and sophistication. Her long brown hair and beautiful olive complexion presented a distinct contrast with the white cap and gown. Her address was powerful and inspirational, and it demonstrated a maturity far beyond her years.

"My fellow students, we are about to begin an amazing new chapter in our lives. Will we choose to *aim high*, or will we be satisfied with doing just enough to get by? Let's challenge ourselves to *reach for the stars*! Yes … we may not always achieve these lofty goals, but we can be assured that our accomplishments will consistently be above average."

Veronica was overwhelmed by the reaction from the audience. The entire graduating class, along with their families, stood up and enthusiastically applauded this motivational challenge. As the assembly took their seats again, Veronica acknowledged all of the parents for their guidance and support. It was during this part of her speech that she gave a touching tribute to her parents.

"I want to take a moment to say a special thanks to my wonderful parents—Angelo and Maria. This young couple left their family and friends in Italy and immigrated to America, ensuring a better future for their children. I will be forever grateful to them for providing me with this tremendous opportunity." Veronica stopped and looked up to the sky with a heartfelt smile on her face, which contrasted with the tears in her sparkling green eyes. "And, Mom, I know you are listening from your special place in heaven. I could not have accomplished anything without your loving encouragement. Thanks, Mom! I will always love you!"

As Veronica walked down from the stage, she saw that there were very few dry eyes in the audience.

# 34

# Boston University

**Veronica Ruffo**
**Boston | 1958**

VERONICA STARTED COLLEGE in August. Her guidance counselor had recommended Boston University to her because it was a prestigious school that had opened all its divisions to female students. Veronica's visit to the campus the previous fall solidified BU as her first choice. She felt both excitement and anxiety. She realized that this new chapter in her life was filled with wonderful opportunities.

At the same time, she had a nagging fear that she would not do well in college. Then she remembered the conversation she'd had with her mother just before she began high school. She had confided in Maria that she was worried about not doing as well in high school as she had done in middle school. Maria had smiled, held Veronica closely, and said, *Veronica, you've done well in school because you are an extremely bright girl who works hard. You always set high goals for yourself . . . and then you achieve them. So . . . just because you're going to high school now, do you think you've somehow become less smart? Do you think you are going to take it easy and decide to become lazy? You, my beautiful daughter, have the power within you to achieve whatever goal you set for yourself. I believe in you, and I know that God will always be there to guide you!*

As Veronica entered her assigned dorm room, she was greeted by a cheerful young lady with a welcoming smile.

"Hi there! I was getting worried that they forgot to assign a room-mate to me."

"Hello, I'm Veronica . . . Veronica Ruffo."

"Well, I guess they must have assigned us alphabetically. My last name also starts with an *R*—Roland. I'm Stephanie Roland. It's a pleasure to meet you, Veronica." Pulling back her shoulder-length auburn hair into a ponytail, she offered to help Veronica unpack. "Four hands will make the job easier. Then we can grab a Coke and enjoy the sunshine."

"Sounds like a deal. Thanks!"

"By the way, I chose this side of the room, but I am happy to switch if you'd prefer it."

Veronica noticed how Stephanie's hazel eyes twinkled when she smiled. "That's not a problem. I'm fine with this side."

The two new friends finished setting up their room and found a comfortable spot on the lawn to drink their sodas.

"So, I'm guessing *Ruffo* is Italian."

"You guessed right. We are from Naples."

"Were you born in Italy?"

"No, my parents immigrated to America shortly after my brother Joe was born. Tonia—my sister—and I were born here."

"So, where did you grow up?"

"In Woonsocket. My father worked in the textile mills there for several years, and when the factories started moving to the South, he switched to the GM plant in Framingham. How about you?"

"I'm from a small town in western Massachusetts. It's near Stockbridge. It's a gorgeous place to live. The Berkshire Mountains are unbelievably beautiful—especially in the fall. You'll have to come for a visit. My parents will love having you over."

Veronica sensed her roommate's natural warmth and found it very comfortable talking to her. Stephanie had a way of giving someone her full and complete attention. Veronica felt lucky because she realized she could have easily been placed with someone who was not as friendly. She thought that Stephanie was someone with whom she could develop a strong friendship.

They were enjoying getting to know each other so much that they lost track of time. Stephanie looked at her watch and exclaimed, "Wow! It's nearly six o'clock. No wonder I'm starving. Let's grab some dinner."

"I was wondering when you would suggest eating something. Seeing how slim you are, I was worried that you might be on a perpetual diet."

Stephanie laughed. "No way! I love food. I guess I just have a hyperactive metabolism."

As she finished chewing the first bite of her oversize burger, Stephanie asked. "I'm curious . . . how did you get your name?"

Veronica smiled, remembering the story her parents had told her. "Well, I was born a few weeks before Easter. My mom was attending Stations of the Cross services at our church when she went into labor. The priest had just begun the sixth station and—"

"Wait a minute. The sixth station?" Stephanie smiled knowingly. "That's when Veronica wiped the face of Jesus."

"You're right! My mother used to say that the Lord chose my name."

"That's a great story. Your mom must be a terrific lady and a tremendous cook. I can't wait to meet her."

Veronica swallowed hard and fought back the tears. "She . . . was . . . a wonderful person . . . and an excellent cook." Then she shared the story of her mother's ordeal with pancreatic cancer the previous year.

Stephanie hugged Veronica. "Oh, Veronica, I'm so, so sorry! I can't even begin to imagine how painful it was for you and how much you must still miss her. Whenever you are feeling down and need a shoulder to cry on or a hug to lift you up, I'm here for you."

Veronica smiled through her tears, realizing that she had found a true friend.

Her sister's husband—Ernie—had recommended that Veronica choose business as her major. He explained that it would provide her with excellent career opportunities. Veronica respected and admired her brother-in-law, so she followed his advice. One of her first classes was economics, taught by Dr. Elizabeth Horowitz. The class was given in a large lecture hall with over three hundred students. Dr. Horowitz was in her late fifties, with gray hair and horn-rimmed glasses, and stood barely five feet tall. Yet, she maintained complete control of the lecture hall. She thoroughly knew her material and explained it in a way that was easily understandable.

Another class was introductory accounting, which was taught by Dr. Herbert Cannon. This course was also conducted in a large lecture hall. On the first day of class, Dr. Cannon warned the students that if they were not willing to pay attention and devote the necessary time and energy to his class, they might as well drop it immediately. Although he was a tough taskmaster, he was also an excellent teacher. He was always well prepared for his lectures and provided several insightful examples. He set aside time at the end of each lecture for questions. His answers were always thorough. He never made a student feel that a question was foolish.

Veronica also took the obligatory courses, which included English and math courses, but the class that intrigued her the most was finance. The course was taught by Dr. Frank Coleman, who had spent nearly thirty years in a large investment banking firm. He had accumulated a sizable personal net worth, as well as an outstanding reputation in the world of finance.

Dr. Coleman taught the introductory finance course and one of the advanced classes. He joked with his students that this way, he could start them off on the right path and ensure they stayed on it. He was able to embellish what ordinarily would be considered dull topics by sharing his personal experiences in the industry. His classes became among the most popular ones for those students—like Veronica—who were interested in business.

It was not long before Dr. Coleman noticed Veronica in his class. At this time, very few women were interested in finance. Aside from the uniqueness of a female in his class, Dr. Coleman observed that Veronica possessed the same characteristics that had led to his success. It was clear to him that she was a hardworking and dedicated student. He was also impressed with her ability to easily grasp topics, ask insightful questions, and interact comfortably with the other students. He soon became a mentor for Veronica.

Veronica was home with Angelo for her Christmas break when her first-semester grades arrived. Her proud father was not surprised that she had achieved straight As. This was the first Christmas without Maria. While there was an understandable sadness, there was also laughter again. Joe and his new wife, Sandy, traveled from Texas to spend the holiday with the family. The more time everyone spent with Sandy, the more they loved her. The warm, engaging manner that had won Joe over was doing the same with the rest of the family.

Angelo and Tonia shared stories of Joe's youthful antics that had Sandy laughing until her sides hurt. One particular story seemed to stand out.

"One time, Joe and his friends decided to climb the grease pole at the Italian feast."

"Grease pole—what's a grease pole?" asked Sandy.

Tonia explained, "It's a telephone pole that's covered with thick grease. There is a prize taped to the top of the pole. It's usually around fifteen dollars. Then a team of five guys attempts to climb the pole so that they can get the cash. Each person stands on top of the other person's shoulders. Joe and his football buddies figured they'd have no problem, but this particular night, the organizers had put an extra coating of grease on the pole. So, there was plenty of slipping and sliding."

Sandy turned to her husband and asked, "Well, did you get the prize?"

"Yeah . . . after three tries!"

Angelo took over the story. "He was covered with grease from head to toe. When he tried to get into the house, Maria didn't recognize him. She locked the door and told me to call the police because a stranger was trying to break in."

Joe interjected, "I kept saying, 'Mom, it's me! It's Joe!'"

"Did she finally let you into the house?"

"No! She made Papa bring me out back and wash me down with the garden house. I had grease in my hair for the next few days."

Sandy also shared with them some of her more colorful courtroom cases. Sandy was a superb storyteller and had everyone on the edge of their seats as she described some of the more interesting trials. The two grandchildren—Angela and Michael, Tonia and Ernie's children—made Christmas extra special for everyone. Their excitement and joy were contagious.

And Joe beamed as he announced, "There's going to be a third grandchild at the table next year. Sandy is pregnant."

After the break was over, Veronica was excited and now confident about starting her second semester. She had taken Dr. Coleman's advice on which courses to select, including an additional three-credit course. The next five months seemed to fly by, and once again, Veronica had achieved straight As. Ernie, her brother-in-law, arranged a summer job for Veronica at the public accounting firm where he was a manager. She enjoyed working with the professional staff and looked forward to having a career after college.

Veronica also took some time off during the summer to visit Stephanie and her family in western Massachusetts. Not surprisingly, Stephanie's entire family was warm and welcoming to Veronica. The Berkshires were stunning during that time of the year, and the two friends enjoyed hiking in the mountains. While staying with Stephanie's family, she attended Sunday mass at a nearby church.

The Gospel reading was from Matthew, chapter 6, when Jesus told his disciples to depend on God for their daily needs. The priest gave an inspirational homily that seemed to bring the Gospel message home to all the parishioners.

"Brothers and sisters, Jesus tells us that we shouldn't worry about what we are to eat . . . drink . . . wear. Ha! Easy for him to say—he's God!" This comment was greeted with hearty laughter by the parishioners. "But don't miss his real message! God is always—yes, always—there for us. He watches over each and every one of us, and he knows exactly what we need . . . and it may not be what we think we need . . . or want! So, just trust in the Lord! Let go of all that anxiety! He says, 'Do not worry about tomorrow; tomorrow will take care of itself.' He is not saying, 'Live for today, for tomorrow you die.' Oh no! He is saying that we should live in the present moment. And in that moment, we should *seek God and his righteousness.* We should always put God first in our lives, love as he has loved, and trust in his infinite wisdom. He will guide us!"

Veronica felt like he was talking directly to her when he spoke. She was equally amazed by the way the families gathered around the priest after mass. It seemed like he had a very strong connection with each of them. All of the young children, as well as the teenagers, seemed to gravitate to him. His name was Reverend Patrick J. Donnelly, but everyone knew him as Father Pat.

Veronica expressed her thoughts about the priest to Stephanie. "What a great service, and your priest seems incredible!"

"Father Pat is one of the warmest, most caring, and most sincere human beings I have ever met," Stephanie agreed. "He never refuses anyone his time and is always able to make others feel comfortable, no matter the challenge or hardship. All of the parishioners love him."

Veronica had the opportunity to meet Stephanie's older brother, Christopher. He was in his senior year of college, majoring in business.

Christopher was dating his high school sweetheart, Lauren, who was a college senior in the teaching program. Stephanie told Veronica that Lauren was already considered part of their family and expected that she and Christopher would be married within a year after college graduation.

The summer break was quickly over, and Veronica began her sophomore year. Shortly after the school year started, the family received joyful news from Texas. Sandy had given birth to a baby boy, and both mother and child were doing well. They named the baby Stephen Angelo. Joe had a very close friend, Stephen Burns. They had met during the occupation of Japan and then shipped off to Korea together. Stephen was killed during the Battle of Heartbreak Ridge, and Joe wanted to name his firstborn son in honor of his friend, whom he considered a hero. Naturally, the middle name was in honor of his other hero—his father.

Veronica looked forward to meeting her new nephew during Joe and Sandy's next visit, which was planned for Christmas. She admired the loving relationships that each of her siblings had with their spouses. Veronica had grown up in a family where her mother and father were never embarrassed to show their love and affection for each other. She often wondered if she would ever find that special someone.

Once again, Veronica took the heavy caseload that Dr. Coleman had recommended. She found the second year slightly more challenging. Nevertheless, she focused on her objectives, devoted extra effort, and continued to impress her professors.

# 35

## David

MIDTERMS WERE FINALLY over. And now, Veronica had a few days off during which she could enjoy herself. Her plans were to take care of a few practical matters, but ultimately, she was really looking forward to enjoying the stunning October weather. Perhaps a hot bath and a good book were in order for the evening.

But her roommate clearly had other ideas.

"Look, Ronnie," Stephanie said, leaning on the countertop of their kitchen, "I've watched how hard you studied for all your midterms, and I'm willing to bet my left arm you aced each and every one of them. You haven't relaxed at all this entire semester. It would do you some good to give yourself a break."

"I'm having a break right now," Veronica argued feebly. Stephanie appeared unconvinced.

"Come to Tom's party with me tonight," she started, only for Veronica to immediately voice her objection—but Stephanie waved her away, pushing on. "It's just one night—not even a *full night*, if you don't want it to be. It could just be a few hours. But who knows—you might meet some good-looking guy at the party and decide to stay out longer. So, come on!"

Veronica surprised herself by reconsidering. Maybe a little socializing wouldn't hurt.

The party was at Tom Anderson's apartment in Boston. Tom, who was from New Hampshire, had invited some friends from his hometown and from college. Stephanie had confided to Veronica that she actually had a bit of a crush on Tom and thought that the feeling was mutual. Tom was a premed student in his junior year, had excellent grades, and hoped to be accepted at Harvard Medical School.

Veronica was glad that she had let Stephanie convince her to come. The atmosphere was relaxing, with friendly conversation, delicious food from a nearby Italian restaurant, and of course, some wine and beer. Someone had just put on Frank Sinatra's album *Come Fly with Me*. Sinatra had always been a favorite in the Ruffo household. Veronica poured herself a glass of cabernet, took a slice of pizza, and sat down next to Stephanie.

She smiled at her friend and said, "Thanks for pushing me to come. You're right—I do need to relax a little more. The people are friendly, the wine is good, the music is excellent, and this pizza is *almost* as good as my mom's."

Stephanie smiled and teasingly said, "And look at all these handsome men!"

Veronica simply rolled her eyes and took another sip of wine.

While Veronica had met Tom before, she wasn't familiar with many of the other guests. It was pleasant getting to know them. There was one young man in particular who stood out. He was tall and slim, with wavy black hair, deep-blue eyes, and a tan complexion. Veronica had a difficult time keeping her eyes off him. It seemed that every time she glanced his way, he was staring directly at her. It was easy to understand why any young man would have a difficult time not staring. Veronica had matured into a beautiful young woman with long brown hair, an olive complexion, and piercing green eyes.

She felt herself blush as he started to walk toward her. He smiled, held out his hand, and said, "Hi, my name is David . . . David Schwartz. I thought it was about time we stopped simply looking at each other and actually met. May I join you?"

Veronica smiled back at the handsome young man and shook his hand. "Hello, David. It's nice to meet you. I'm Veronica Ruffo. You can call me Ronnie." Then she slid over and made room for David to join her on the couch.

"Veronica is a beautiful name. Why would you change it?"

"Well, Steph—my roommate—started calling me Ronnie halfway through our freshman year, and it's kind of stuck."

"If it's okay with you, I'll stick with Veronica. I think it suits you." He smiled, and his blue eyes seemed to glisten.

Veronica was mesmerized by his eyes. They reminded her of the ocean, where she always felt a comforting calmness. She was having that same feeling with someone whom she had just met and thought, *What's going on here?* She decided to just go with the flow and enjoy the conversation. "I'm guessing you are a friend of Tom's."

"Tom's my closest friend! We've been inseparable since we were little kids. We got into our share of trouble together, but I'll save those stories for another time."

"So, you grew up in New Hampshire?"

"Yes. I love it there, especially hiking in the White Mountains. Tom and I have hiked the entire Presidential Range together." Veronica saw the glow in his face as he described his mountainous treks with Tom. "Actually, I'm still in New Hampshire, attending Dartmouth, and planning on law school after I graduate."

"That sounds great. Is your father a lawyer?"

"No, he runs a manufacturing company with my uncle. Dad and my uncle immigrated to America from Germany shortly after the Nazis took over. He experienced the early stages of anti-Semitism and was convinced it was only going to get worse. He couldn't convince his parents to leave. They believed Nazism was going to be short-lived and that the German people would come to their senses." David shook his head in obvious disgust. "We know how that worked out. My grandparents died in a concentration camp."

Veronica instinctively reached out and gently touched David's arm. "Oh, David, I'm so sorry!"

"Thanks, Veronica. I'm not sure why I laid all of that on you. I have to confess, it's just so easy to talk to you."

"I'll take that as a compliment."

"It was definitely meant to be! Now, enough about me. Tell me about yourself. You're attending BU, right?"

"Yes, I'm a business major in my sophomore year. My favorite subject is finance, and I'm considering a career in investment banking."

"So, you'll be making the big bucks someday!"

Veronica smiled. "I don't know about that."

"And what about your family?"

"My parents immigrated to America before the war. In fact, my brother, Joe, fought in the war. After hearing about your grandparents, I'm glad he played a role in defeating the Nazis. I cannot begin to understand how the German people allowed such atrocities to happen to their fellow neighbors just because they were Jewish. That was so . . . inhumane."

"I've often wondered that, too. It seems inconceivable even now. I guess that's why my grandparents were convinced that the German people would come to their senses. You mentioned your brother—what's he do now?"

"Joe decided to make a career in the army. After the war, he was stationed in Japan and then shipped off to Korea when that war broke out. My parents used to keep a small shrine in our dining room. We would pray for him every single day. Now he is at Fort Hood in Texas. He's married to a wonderful lady—Sandy. She's a successful attorney in Austin. They just had their first child."

"Do you have any other siblings?"

"Yes, my sister Tonia is ten years older than me. She's a nurse and is married to a wonderful guy—Ernie. He's a CPA for one of the large accounting firms. They have two beautiful children."

"Your parents must love being grandparents."

Veronica immediately thought about how much her mother had loved her grandchildren and felt a lump in her throat. From the expression on her face, it was obvious that something was wrong, but before David could ask, Veronica explained.

"I still get sad when I think about my mother. She passed away when I was a senior in high school. You are right, though; she loved being *Nonna*—that's Italian for *grandmother*."

This time, it was David reaching out and gently placing his hand on Veronica's shoulder.

"I'm so sorry, Veronica. It must have been very difficult for you."

"It was devastating for the entire family. Mom was full of love. She was our bright, shining light! We were all in a state of shock, asking why God took her from us. I'll never forget the young priest—Father Al—who sat with us. He assured us that she was now looking down from heaven and praying for us. He said that she had become our *very special guardian angel* who would be there for us whenever we were troubled or struggling with some challenge. And while the sadness never fully disappears, I feel a sense of warmth and comfort knowing that she is still there watching out for me."

"That's certainly a wonderful way to think of a loved one who has been taken from us."

They were so focused on their conversation that they had not noticed the time until Stephanie and Tom interrupted them.

"Hey, you two, it's nearly one o'clock, and everyone else has already left. Do you think we should break it up now?"

Veronica and David smiled at each other and laughed along with Tom and Stephanie.

David told Veronica that he had thoroughly enjoyed getting to know her and asked if she would like to have dinner with him the following night. Without hesitation, she said that she would love to join him. As she and Stephanie walked back to their room together, Veronica felt an energy and excitement running throughout her entire body. She turned to Stephanie and exclaimed, "I had the most wonderful evening! I'm so glad that you convinced me to come!"

"Well, look at you, girl. I've never seen you so animated. I watched the way you two were looking at each other. It was obvious that you made a great connection."

"I felt so comfortable talking to him. He's an amazing guy!" Then, grinning like the Cheshire cat, Veronica announced, "We're going to dinner tomorrow night!"

"Dinner? Wow! You two aren't wasting any time." Stephanie smiled back at her friend. "I'm really happy for you. Tom says David is a terrific person. They've been friends forever."

"I know. David told me they are the best of friends."

When they got to their room, Veronica hugged Stephanie. "Thank you, thank you, thank you! I feel something very special inside about David. If it wasn't for you, I might never have met him."

Veronica fell asleep, replaying the entire experience in her head.

The following evening, David took Veronica to Boston's North End for dinner. It was a small, romantic restaurant on Salem Street. The food was excellent, and the conversation was even better. They continued to learn more about each other and their career plans. David told Veronica about his goal of working for one of the large law firms, and she explained more about investment banking.

They walked to Quincy Market after dinner. David reached out to hold Veronica's hand, and she could not believe how wonderful it felt to be with someone whom she had only met the previous evening.

He drove Veronica to her apartment, parked in front, and said, "I had an outstanding time with you tonight, Veronica."

"So did I, David. Everything was perfect . . . especially the company!"

"Can I see you tomorrow morning before I drive back to New Hampshire?"

"I'd love that . . . but . . . I can't. You see, I spend Sundays with my father and my sister's family. We attend mass in the morning, and in the afternoon, my sister prepares a feast."

"A feast—what kind of feast?"

"She usually starts off with a homemade pasta dish that includes plenty of meatballs and sausage. Sometimes, she'll make baked lasagna or ravioli. The pasta is followed by a roast with potatoes and vegetables. Then we end the meal with espresso and Italian pastries."

"What an amazing banquet! I'm drooling just imagining it. How do you stay so trim after eating all of that delicious food?"

Veronica smiled and explained, "Well, I've learned to pace myself... and even so, I don't have much of an appetite for the next few days."

"Well, all right, I'm disappointed that I won't see you tomorrow, but I completely understand." Then, without skipping a beat, David asked, "What about next Friday night?"

"Next week? That's over a two-hour drive for you."

"The long drive is worth spending more time with you!"

Then he leaned over, gently caressed her cheek with his hand, and kissed her on the lips. Veronica smiled at David and agreed to meet him again the following Friday.

Not only the following Friday but every Friday night after that, the two of them met up. During the weekdays, they focused on their classes and studied late into the evening so that their weekends would be free to spend quality time together. They even started getting up extra early on Sunday mornings so that they could have more time before Veronica met with her family. They enjoyed being with each other and looked forward to David's weekly visits. Veronica remembered her mother saying to her, *You will know you're in love when you can't wait to tell the other person everything that has happened—the good things as well as the disappointments.*

That was exactly how Veronica felt about David. During the week, whenever something positive would happen, like a great conversation with a professor or a hilarious story about Tonia's kids—she wished David was there so she could share it with him. And she especially wished he was there when she was feeling anxious or challenged.

David sensed the same connection with Veronica. He had dated before, but he'd never felt such strong emotions for the other girls. He adored her. She was as smart as she was beautiful. She was focused and ambitious yet humble. She treated others with kindness and respect. She was everything he could have ever wanted, and he was definitely falling in love with her.

David was already thinking of how he would break the news to his family. He knew it would be a difficult conversation because his parents had strong convictions about him marrying someone within the Jewish faith. They had many non-Jewish friends, so clearly, it was not because they were prejudiced. One time, he had joked about marrying Tom's younger sister. His parents loved Tom and were very friendly with his entire family, but David could still recall his mother's reaction.

*David, don't you ever . . . ever say anything like that again! Tom's sister is very nice, but remember—she's not Jewish!*

Their disapproval of intermarriage had more to do with the fact that they had lost so many family members and friends during the war. According to Jewish law, the religion is passed down through the mother, so if one of their sons were to marry a non-Jewish woman, then the children would not be considered Jewish. David knew that this would be a very emotional discussion and that he would have to find the right time and right way to break the news to them. Nevertheless, he felt that once his parents met Veronica and got to know her, they would fall in love with her just as he had. David was honest with Veronica about his concern. She understood his parents' perspective, and they agreed to hold off on family introductions until the time was right.

Veronica finished her sophomore year of college with straight As again. Dr. Coleman arranged for her to get a summer internship at a prestigious investment banking firm in Boston. She worked in the analysts department, and although she was assigned the most menial tasks, she was exposed to every aspect of the organization and found it exhilarating. Veronica looked forward to a career in investment banking. She impressed everyone with whom she worked. They found her to be bright and energetic. By the end of the summer, Dr. Coleman's former associate, who was a director at the firm, told Veronica that they wanted her to return the following year.

As he did during every summer break, David, along with his younger brother, Barry, worked at his father's factory. He told Veronica that he enjoyed his job there because the employees were like family to him, and he was able to spend quality time with both his father and brother. Veronica was grateful that the factory was located in Salem, New Hampshire. That shortened David's trips to Boston by over an hour. So, he would drive to Boston during the week. She would get to see him on at least one or two weeknights, as well as on the weekend.

Angelo turned sixty-five that year and retired in June. He had worked hard all of his life, and the last few years at the factory seemed especially draining for him. He had aged considerably since Maria's death. The family arranged a retirement party for Angelo. Many of the neighborhood friends, along with some close colleagues from the GM plant, attended the party. Joe and Sandy made the trip from Texas to surprise Angelo. He was especially delighted to meet his new grandson, Stephen.

After the party, Tonia shared some exciting news with the family.

"Ernie has been promoted to partner at his accounting firm, and the managing partner has asked him to relocate to the Houston office. It's growing, and they need talented young leaders like Ernie." Veronica could see that Tonia was extremely proud of her husband.

"And now that he has retired, Papa has agreed to move to Texas with us."

"Houston sounds great! You'll only be a three-hour drive from us in Austin," exclaimed Joe.

Veronica had mixed feelings upon hearing the news. She would definitely miss her family, but she was very excited for Ernie. She also thought the change would be good for her father.

Veronica's facial expressions gave away her thoughts. Tonia put her arm around her younger sister and said, "We love you and will miss you. I want you to promise to spend your Christmas breaks with us!"

Veronica smiled back at her sister and assured her, "You can count on it. Escaping the Boston winters for even a few weeks will be an easy promise to keep. I'm so happy for Ernie. He deserves this opportunity."

Veronica started her junior year and seemed to relish the challenge of another heavy course load. The summer internship at the investment bank had reenergized her and given her a clear career path. Having David in her life made her feel that she could take on the world. David was in his final year at Dartmouth and had already started preparing his applications for law school. Like Tom, Harvard was David's number one choice.

Now that her family had relocated to Texas, Veronica and David had more time together on Sundays. She still attended mass, and then they would have brunch together before David drove back to New Hampshire.

David even joined her at church on a few occasions. Afterward, he would good-naturedly tease her about all the kneeling, standing, and sitting that went on during the mass. They would usually spend time with Stephanie and Tom on the weekends.

The loving relationship between Veronica and David continued to grow. David was the one who brought up marriage first, although Veronica had been thinking about it already.

"Veronica Ruffo, I want to spend the rest of my life with you!"

Those words sent exhilarating waves of happiness throughout Veronica's entire body. She wrapped her arms around him and said, "Oh, David, I love you so much!"

"We'll have to wait until I finish law school to get married."

"I'll wait as long as it takes . . . I don't want to marry anyone else!"

"I think it's time that you met my family."

"Are you sure? How are they going to handle my not being Jewish?"

"Look . . . they're going to see how much I love and adore you, and they're going to fall for you, too. Don't worry—they'll get over this Jewish thing."

"Are you sure?"

"I'm positive. We'll arrange for you to meet them in December, just before you fly out to see your family."

"That sounds wonderful! And then you can fly to Texas and meet my family."

"Looking forward to it!"

Their warm embraces and long, sensuous kisses were exciting, but they were always able to stop before going all the way. They promised to hold off on sex until after they were married. This commitment was extremely difficult during some of their evenings together, but they had been able to control their physical desires, until one Saturday evening.

Then, it happened.

They had enjoyed a wonderful day—a perfect September day. The cloudless sky was a rich blue; the trees were still green; the temperature was comfortable, with a slight, pleasant breeze. They packed a picnic lunch and headed to the Boston Common. After lunch, they walked all over town. It was an exhilarating time to be in Boston. The handsome young senator from Massachusetts, John Kennedy, was running for president, and there were political signs everywhere.

After walking for hours, they ended up in the North End and had dinner at the same restaurant where David had first taken her. David ordered a bottle of Chianti. Veronica selected the chicken parmigiana, and David chose the pasta Bolognese, which he devoured. For dessert, they enjoyed cannoli. The delicious ricotta filling oozed out with every bite.

They arrived at Veronica's apartment shortly after eight o'clock. There was a note from Stephanie saying that she was out with Tom and not to wait up for her. This meant that she would probably spend the night with Tom. So, they opened another bottle of wine, put on some Sinatra, and relaxed on the couch. Veronica smiled at David and then shared what she was feeling.

"I had such a wonderful day today! It was the perfect day . . . with the perfect person. I love you so, so much, David . . . Oh, how I wish I could simply snap my fingers and make these next few years just fly by so that we can be together forever."

He smiled back at her and said, "I feel the same way, Veronica." And then, without warning, he pulled her close to him and began kissing her. The kiss was long and lingering. It excited the deep emotions in her. He began unbuttoning her blouse, and she pulled his shirt over his head. He gently touched her all over, and she enjoyed the sensation it gave her. She felt as if she was in a trance as he picked her up and took her into the bedroom. At this point, they took off the rest of each other's clothes and got into bed together. They held each other tightly. It felt so good and so natural to have their naked bodies next to each other. Their lovemaking was not rushed. David was a very thoughtful and sensitive lover. Veronica responded by slowly caressing and holding him tightly as he entered her. They both climaxed at the same moment and wished that it could go on forever.

Afterward, they just held each other closely. There were no feelings of guilt or regret because they loved each other and intended to spend the rest of their lives together.

David looked into Veronica's eyes and said, "I love you so very much, Veronica. There is absolutely no reason for us to wait until I finish law school. Instead, we'll get married right after you graduate. You'll be employed, and I have money saved from working at my dad's company. It may be difficult financially for the first couple of years . . . but we will be together. And afterward, between the high-flying investment banker and the powerhouse attorney, we'll be rolling in dough."

Veronica stared into his deep-blue eyes and asked, "David, do you really mean it? Do you really . . . really want to marry me?"

By now, David's smile had grown wider. His mind seemed to be racing. "Do you actually have to ask that question? Of course . . . of course! I mean every word. I never, ever thought I could love someone as much as I love and adore you. I want to spend the rest of my life with you! In fact, when I fly out to Texas to meet your family, I'm going to ask for your father's permission to marry you."

Tears of joy welled up in Veronica's eyes, and she could not say another word. She just hugged David as if she would never let him go. It was one of the happiest days of her life.

The next morning, Veronica woke up next to David, who was simply staring at her with a warm smile on his face. He kissed her cheek and said, "We should get ready for mass. If we're going to have a church wedding, then I better get used to all of your crazy rituals."

After mass, he insisted on making her breakfast. He bragged that he was a master omelet maker. The omelets were delicious, but what mattered most to Veronica was that she was with the man of her dreams, her future husband.

As they were cleaning up the breakfast dishes, Stephanie and Tom walked into the apartment. Their facial expressions revealed that they sensed something different with their two friends. Veronica was bursting to announce their decision to get married. They had even decided that Stephanie would be the maid of honor and that Tom would be the best man. Nevertheless, they had agreed not to say anything until after David received Angelo's permission.

The rest of the day was a blur, and Veronica did not want it to end. It started raining, and she was worried about David driving back on a dark, stormy night.

"It's ugly out there. Why don't you stay over and leave in the morning?"

"I'd really love to, but I can't. I have an early class tomorrow morning."

"Then I'm walking you to your car!"

"You'll get soaked."

"I don't care! I insist!"

Reaching his car, they hugged each other for a very long time. As he kissed her, David whispered in her ear, "I love you more than anything else in the world, and I can't wait until I see you again!"

"I miss you already!" Veronica squeezed him as if she wouldn't let go.

Then David got into his car and drove away. Veronica stood in the rain and watched until she could not see his car any longer.

When Veronica got back inside the apartment, she was wet from head to toe, but she didn't seem to notice.

Stephanie teased, "You could've at least taken an umbrella!"

Veronica gave her friend a big smile. "Why? Is it raining outside?"

Stephanie playfully threw a pillow at her. "Somebody has it really, *really* bad!"

Veronica laughed. "No . . . no way! Somebody has it really, really *good*. I am completely in love with David, and I know he's in love with me. I feel happier than I have ever felt in my entire life!"

Veronica changed into some dry clothes, and then the two of them shared warm soup together. Afterward, they studied and then went to bed.

# 36

## Tragedy

**Veronica Ruffo**
**Boston | 1960**

IT WAS AFTER midnight when Veronica was awakened by loud banging on the apartment door. Stephanie was the first one out of bed. She ran to the door and was visibly surprised to discover that it was Tom. Veronica ran up beside her, peering out at their doorstep. Tom had tears running down his cheeks.

"Tom . . . Tom, what is it? What's wrong?" Stephanie asked.

Tom struggled to get the words out. He seemed to look only at Veronica, temporarily at a loss for words, before saying, "It's—it's David! There's . . . there's been a terrible . . . *horrible* accident. He's . . ." He shook his head, looking at Veronica. "David has been killed."

Veronica felt as if a sledgehammer had just smashed her heart into tiny pieces. She dropped to her knees and began screaming and sobbing uncontrollably.

"Oh, no . . . no, no! It can't be! Oh God, oh God . . . not my David! It must be a mistake!"

Stephanie and Tom immediately ran to her and wrapped their arms around her. They remained that way for a very long time. Finally, they led Veronica to the couch, and Tom somberly explained what had happened. "David's brother, Barry, called me. He said that David was nearly back at school when his car was struck head-on by a drunk driver. David was . . . was killed immediately. The other driver only suffered minor injuries."

Veronica, still crying and in shock, began to blame herself. "It's my fault, all my fault! If I hadn't made him stay longer, this would have never happened! Oh . . . David, my David . . . please forgive me!"

Tom, who was brokenhearted over the loss of his closest friend, put his hands on Veronica's shoulders, looked into her eyes, and said, "Ronnie, don't say that! Don't ever blame yourself! This was definitely not your fault! That miserable bastard who was driving drunk—*he* was responsible for David's death! You didn't force David to stay. He relished every single moment that he spent with you. My friend . . . my best friend loved you with all of his heart. I am so, so very sorry that he is no longer here for you . . . for us . . . but don't ever, ever blame yourself! I know, in my heart, that David would never want that."

Veronica was unable to respond. She just stared into Tom's eyes, began crying again, and collapsed into his arms. The three of them spent the rest of the night together, sitting on the couch and holding each other. Each of them would doze off for a few minutes, then awaken to the realization that the nightmare was real.

The next day, Veronica felt that all the life had been drained from her. As horrible as it had been to lose her mother, the pain she was feeling now was even worse. She clutched David's picture next to her heart and quietly continued crying. She thought of the first time she had seen him and how she couldn't keep her eyes off him. She remembered that once they started talking, it was as if the two of them were the only ones in the room. The memories of their first date and every wonderful moment that they had spent together raced through her mind. They were going to spend the rest of their lives together, and now she would never be able to hold him again . . . touch him . . . kiss him . . . laugh with him. She wanted to curl up and die. Stephanie begged Veronica to eat or drink something.

Tom called Barry to get the funeral information. In the Jewish tradition, the funeral generally took place within one day of the person's death. David's family had decided that the services would be held on Tuesday morning. Tom arranged for the three of them to stay at his parents' home on Monday evening.

Stephanie helped Veronica pack, and the three of them drove to Tom's family home in Salem, New Hampshire. They arrived at the house shortly after five. Tom's parents, Rose and Arthur, greeted them at the door. They had seen Stephanie on several different occasions. They knew that she and Tom were in love and were very pleased that their son had found such a wonderful person. Tom's parents had never met Veronica. Tom explained to them that she and David had been dating and in love with each other. Seeing how deeply affected she was by the loss of David, Rose and Arthur were particularly considerate and attentive to Veronica.

When they sat down for dinner, Tom asked Stephanie to say grace. She closed her eyes, thought for a moment, and then began, "Dear Lord, we thank you for this wonderful meal that Rose prepared. We are grateful that we are together to support and comfort each other during this difficult time." Then, with tears welling up in her eyes, Stephanie continued, "And we pray that David . . . will be welcomed in your heavenly kingdom. Amen."

Veronica made a valiant attempt at her dinner, but she had very little appetite. Arthur did his best to encourage some light conversation.

Then Rose, who rarely held things inside, stated exactly what she was feeling.

"I have very strong faith in God. And yet, I find myself asking, *Why, God? Why would you take such a wonderful young man like David?* We've known him since he was a little boy. He was like family to us. He had his whole life ahead of him. And yet . . . God allowed this terrible, terrible tragedy to happen!"

Veronica was reminded of the same questions she'd asked when her mother died. She remembered the words of Father Al, and that seemed to give her an inner strength she didn't realize she possessed. Then she looked at all four of them and said, "I don't know the answer, either. I do know that David was a wonderful . . . amazing person. I loved him, and I will continue to love him with my whole heart and soul for the rest of my life! When I lost my mom a few years ago, there was a priest who comforted us. He said that God's ways are not our ways and that we can't possibly know or understand God's mind. I was especially blessed to have David in my life, even for just a short time. I will cherish each moment that we shared. My memories of him will keep his spirit alive in my heart. I absolutely believe that God has a special place for David in heaven. And now David has become my very special guardian angel. No matter what challenges I face in life, his spirit will be right next to me—guiding me and giving me the support I need. I'm going to miss having David next to me every single day for the rest of my life, but I'll be comforted by knowing that his spirit—his gentle spirit—will always . . . always be with me."

After saying these words, Veronica felt a tremendous sense of peace. She recalled the words of Father Pat—*God is always—yes, always—there for us . . . Just trust in the Lord!* It was almost as if Jesus were there with his hand on her shoulder, saying to her, *I will carry you through this, my child.* Rose got up from her chair, walked to Veronica, and hugged her.

After dinner, Stephanie asked Veronica to take a walk with her. They walked quietly, arm in arm, through the neighborhood. Each street was lined with tall maple trees. The lawns were well manicured, and there were several colonial homes with huge wraparound porches. It was exactly the way that David had described it to her. Veronica thought to herself, *These are the streets where my David grew up. This is where he said we would live someday.* She felt a tear run down her cheek. Stephanie must have noticed and handed Veronica a tissue.

"You are such an amazing person, Ronnie. I can only begin to imagine the horrible pain you are feeling right now. And yet, what you said in there gave all of us an enormous amount of peace and comfort. I'll never forget those words!"

"You know, at first, David's death ripped my heart apart. I was feeling numb and just wanted to die. It was at the exact moment when Rose asked the question, 'Why, God?' that it seemed like God whispered in my ear, and I remembered the words of the priest when my mom passed away. I know that there will be tough days ahead . . . days when it will seem like the whole world is closing in on me . . . times when I won't know what to do. Those are the times that I'll have to just trust God, knowing that he has given me two very special guardian angels to help me through it."

"I'll never compete with your angels, but I want you to know that I will always be there for you."

"I know you will."

They hugged each other and slowly walked back to the house.

Everyone was up early the next morning. Rose served a light breakfast, and then they drove to the cemetery where the funeral service was to be held. There was very little conversation. They parked the car and walked to the Memorial Chapel, where they were ushered to their seats. Veronica sat between Rose and Stephanie. She held hands with each of them for comfort and support.

Unlike the Catholic funerals that Veronica had attended, there was not a public viewing of the deceased in the Jewish tradition. A plain wooden casket sat closed in the front of the chapel. Although the building was large, it filled up quickly. David and his family were well-liked by the entire community. Veronica's eyes were focused on the casket that now held David's body—the body that she had caressed and held just a few days before.

After several minutes, the rabbi, along with David's family and relatives, entered the chapel from a private room. Veronica immediately recognized David's father. He was in his early fifties, tall and slim, with wavy hair that was just beginning to turn gray. He had the same deep-blue eyes that had drawn her to David. He had his arm wrapped around David's mother, who was weeping sorrowfully. She was an attractive woman of average height with a slim figure and dark hair. David's younger brother, Barry, followed his parents to their seats. While there was some resemblance to David, Barry was shorter and slightly heavier.

Once the family and relatives were seated, the rabbi began reading from scripture. He read from Psalm 23. Veronica felt her chest tighten up when the rabbi recited the words, "Though I walk through the valley of the shadow of death, I fear no harm, for you are with me."

Tears began to run down her cheeks.

Stephanie and Rose each wrapped an arm around Veronica.

After a silent prayer, the rabbi gave the eulogy. He was a close family friend and knew David well. When he shared stories about David, he had tears in his eyes and took a few moments to regain his composure before continuing. As the rabbi spoke, Veronica could not stop thinking of her last two days with David. They had been the happiest days of her life, and now she was at his funeral. It felt like a weight was crushing her heart. Then, once again, she pulled from her inner strength and recalled what she had said the previous evening. She realized that her guardian angel was next to her and would give her the support she needed.

After the eulogy was finished, some additional prayers were recited in Hebrew. Then the parents and relatives were escorted back to the private room. The pallbearers moved the casket from the chapel to the hearse for the short drive to the graveside. The rest of the guests were guided to the burial site by the funeral director. Additional prayers were said as the casket was lowered into the grave. Another important Jewish custom was to shovel dirt on top of the casket. This tradition provided closure and was a way of saying goodbye for the last time. Tom accompanied Stephanie and Veronica to the gravesite and then handed the shovel to Veronica. She picked up some soil and threw it on top of the coffin. As she did this, she whispered, "Goodbye, David. I will always, always love you."

After the service, they slowly and silently walked to the car and drove back to Tom's parents' home. They shared a quiet lunch together. Veronica was thinking about the funeral service and the stories that the rabbi had shared. She did her best to fight back the tears, but the pain was still overwhelming. Arthur had arranged for all of them to make a shiva call later that day. Shiva was a seven-day period of mourning, and the shiva call was a way of paying respect and providing support to the family. Rose prepared an entire dinner to bring to the Schwartz home.

It was a huge, stately house with a brick front. After entering the house, Arthur and Tom carried the meal to the kitchen, and all six of them were escorted to the formal living room, where the family was sitting shiva. Tom's parents approached the family first to give their condolences. David's mother looked up at Rose, smiled, and thanked her for coming. The two women hugged each other. David's father stood up and shook hands with Arthur. They spoke briefly, and then Tom's parents walked to the side, where chairs had been set up for guests.

Next, Tom walked up with Stephanie and Veronica. Mrs. Schwartz looked up at Tom and said, "Tommy, you and my David were so very close. He loved you like a brother."

Tom, with tears in his eyes, could barely speak. "I loved him, too. I will miss him so much!"

Then Mrs. Schwartz asked about his two friends. He introduced Stephanie and explained that she was his girlfriend. Next, he introduced Veronica. David's mother smiled at Veronica and asked, "How did you know my David?"

Veronica took a deep breath. This was a big moment—one that David had warned her wouldn't be well received, but considering the tragedy of his death and the circumstances, it only felt right to be honest. And perhaps, in her grief, David's mother would see things for what they really were instead of being blinded by prejudice.

"David was my boyfriend," Veronica announced. He felt like so much more than simply a boyfriend to her, and she wished there was a way to convey that, but there wasn't. "We loved each other very, very much. We were planning on marrying." At this, there were a few gasps, but she didn't let that stop her from adding, "I will love him for the rest of my life."

Upon hearing what Veronica said, Mrs. Schwartz's composure changed completely. She stiffened, her smile was gone, and her eyes turned very dark. It seemed like all of the anger and emotion from losing her child immediately boiled over, and she screamed at Veronica, "You lie! You're a liar! My David would never date a non-Jewish girl! He knew how we felt about that. Get out! Get out, you shiksa!"

And then Mrs. Schwartz started sobbing uncontrollably. David's father took his wife into his arms, turned to Tom, and quietly said, "I think you should take your friend out of our house, Tommy."

Tom quickly escorted Veronica and Stephanie from the living room, and the three of them walked briskly to the car. Rather than breaking down, Veronica remained stoic as she relied on her inner strength again.

Tom was apologetic.

"I'm so sorry, Veronica. Mrs. Schwartz is hurting right now. Let's give it a few weeks, and then I'll go and speak with her. I will explain how much David truly loved you."

Veronica looked at Tom and then responded in a strong and determined voice, "No, Tom, absolutely not! Whether Mr. and Mrs. Schwartz believe me or not isn't going to change how David and I felt about each other. It's not going to bring him back! His parents are in pain right now and will never get over losing their son. They don't need any more hurt. Let it go! Let them believe what they want."

She opened the car door and sat in the back seat. Tom's parents were not far behind. Rose looked at her son with compassionate concern for Veronica. Her eyes told him that she wanted to say something, but he shook his head, and she understood. So, she quietly got into the car next to Veronica and simply held her hand.

Tom and the girls drove back to Boston that evening and arrived at the apartment shortly before ten o'clock. Veronica told them that she was exhausted and was going to bed. Stephanie and Tom talked quietly for a while, and then he left.

Veronica quickly got back into her normal college routine—rising early each morning, diligently attending classes throughout the day, and studying late into the evening. She appeared to be even more focused on her schoolwork. Stephanie seemed to understand that it was Veronica's way to take her mind off losing David. Veronica shared her thoughts and feelings with Stephanie and was grateful to have her strong and supportive friendship. That support enabled Veronica to get through the next few weeks.

# 37

# The Pregnancy

| Veronica Ruffo
| Boston | 1960

IT WAS THE end of the month when Veronica realized something was not right. She had always been regular with her menstrual cycles, but now she was two weeks late. She had been feeling extremely tired lately and had initially assumed it was because of the excessive amount of time she was devoting to her studies. Her first reaction was panic. *Oh my God, could I be pregnant? What am I going to do? I'm still in college. There is no way that I can support a child!* Next came disbelief. *It's impossible. We only had sex that one time! I couldn't have gotten pregnant!*

Then, the rational Veronica with formidable inner strength took over. *First, I have to schedule a doctor's appointment before I jump to any conclusions. Then I'll determine the next steps.*

Veronica confided in Stephanie but made her promise not to share anything with Tom. Stephanie naturally agreed to honor her friend's wishes, but she admitted that it would be extremely difficult. Veronica scheduled an appointment with Dr. Burke in Boston, whom she met the following Tuesday afternoon.

Dr. Daniel Burke was in his late fifties. He had wavy gray hair and a well-trimmed mustache. It was obvious that he had been a handsome young man. In fact, he was still quite attractive, and when Veronica first saw him, she thought he resembled the movie star Clark Gable.

Dr. Burke greeted Veronica with a pleasant smile and gently shook her hand. He offered her a seat and then sat down next to her. He asked, "So, Veronica, why are you here today?"

She took a deep breath before responding. "I . . . I think that I might be . . . pregnant. I've always been regular with my periods, and now I'm over two weeks late."

Dr. Burke asked more questions before he began his physical examination of Veronica. *When was your last period? When did you have sex? Are your breasts tender to the touch? Do they feel swollen? Have you felt nauseous? Have you been overly fatigued lately?*

As part of the examination, the doctor asked her to provide a urine sample and explained that it would take approximately two weeks before he would have the actual results. So, they scheduled a follow-up visit. Based on her answers to his questions, Veronica knew in her heart what the test would say. It was the longest two weeks of her life. Stephanie's support was never more valuable or appreciated as it was during this time. In fact, Veronica asked Stephanie to come to the next office visit with her.

The day arrived, and the appointment was scheduled for three o'clock. Veronica's last class ended at noon. She met Stephanie at their apartment, and they left for the doctor's office. Upon arriving, they were greeted by the receptionist, who asked them to take a seat in the waiting area. After a few minutes, the nurse called Veronica's name. Veronica reached for Stephanie's hand, forced a smile, and said, "I'm so glad you're here with me. You've been an outstanding friend. Please . . . please say a prayer for me."

Veronica walked into Dr. Burke's office. He was reading from a file when she entered his office. As soon as he saw her, he took off his glasses and smiled at her. Then he got up, shook her hand, and asked her to have a seat. Just as he had done on her first visit, he sat down in the chair next to her. Looking directly into her green eyes, he asked, "How are you feeling?"

"About the same . . . extremely tired . . . and a little nauseous."

"Veronica, the test results indicate that you are definitely pregnant."

Although Veronica had been expecting this answer, it still felt like someone had punched her in the stomach. Upon seeing her reaction, Dr. Burke immediately reached out and held her hand to comfort her.

She regained her composure and asked, "Is the baby healthy?"

The doctor—who had probably heard the same question thousands of times before—looked at her sympathetically and explained, "It is really too early to tell, but there is no reason to suspect otherwise."

"When will the child be born?"

"Near the end of May." He went on to explain what she would be experiencing throughout her pregnancy, the schedule of appointments that they would set up, and things to avoid eating and doing during her pregnancy. Although he had been through these discussions countless times before, he spoke with a tremendous amount of care and empathy. His sensitive, kindly manner helped Veronica feel comfortable. Next, he asked, "Will the father be coming to any of the visits?"

A tear started slowly falling down Veronica's cheek as she shook her head.

Dr. Burke did not pursue it any further; instead, he asked, "Do you have any other questions?"

"Not now, but I'm sure that I'll have more later on."

"I'll be with you throughout your entire pregnancy."

They both got up, and he walked her to the door.

Stephanie stood up as soon as she saw her friend walk down the corridor. Veronica simply nodded, and Stephanie seemed to know what that meant. She walked toward her, and the two friends hugged each other. Stephanie whispered to Veronica, "I'm here for you, Ronnie. It's going to be all right!"

They were both quiet on the way back to the apartment.

Once they got settled, Stephanie boiled some water for tea, and they sat on the couch together. Stephanie reached out for Veronica's hand and held it in hers. Then she asked, "Veronica, do you think . . . you should speak to David's parents now?"

Veronica felt her posture stiffen. *After the last ordeal?*

"Absolutely not," she said definitively. "They wouldn't believe me, anyway. You saw how David's mother reacted. She was ashamed and angered by the mere thought that David would date someone who wasn't Jewish. How do you think she would handle being told that David actually fathered a child with that same non-Jewish woman? Like I told Tom the day of the funeral, David's parents do not need to hurt any more than they already do. They definitely don't want me or my baby in their lives."

Stephanie listened to what Veronica had just said and seemed to know her friend well enough to realize that she wouldn't change her mind. So, instead, she asked, "What will you do?"

Veronica sipped her tea slowly and swallowed it. "I've given it a lot of thought over these past two weeks. I am going to finish this semester and then take a leave of absence for the spring semester. I'll fly to Texas to be with my family. At first, they'll be shocked and upset . . . but I know they'll be supportive. My father loves children, so he'll be very excited to have another grandchild in his life. My sister, Tonia, is a nurse and a wonderful mother, just like my mom. So, she'll be able to guide me through the pregnancy and help with a newborn baby. Her daughter, Angela, is five, and her son, Michael, is two. They'll be my little helpers with their baby cousin. My brother, Joe, and his wife, Sandy, have a new baby also. So, my child will be able to grow up with cousins and a loving family. Dr. Burke said that my child would arrive by the end of May. I'll transfer to a college in Texas to finish my degree. I'm sure that I'll be able to get a good job in Houston after I graduate."

Now that Veronica was certain of the pregnancy, she was ready to implement her plan in full measure. Stephanie looked at her in awe and said, "I think that's what I like most about you, Ronnie." Veronica raised her eyebrows and tilted her head to one side, wondering what her friend meant. Stephanie leaned closer to say, "You've got this ability to step back, become very focused, and organize a rational course of action, regardless of the circumstances."

"Thanks, Steph. That means a lot to me."

"I'm going to miss you so, so very much!"

"I'll miss you, too!" Veronica hugged her friend, knowing that she would always have Stephanie's unconditional love and support.

# 38

# Alzheimer's

**Veronica Ruffo**
**Boston | 1960**

VERONICA DECIDED IT would be a good idea to speak with her sister first. She thought that Tonia could help prepare the rest of the family for the news. Veronica waited until the weekend to call her sister. She dialed the number and heard her father say hello on the other end. It felt so good to hear his voice, and she immediately said, "Hello, Papa! It's Veronica. How are you doing?"

Angelo responded slowly, "I am . . . fine. How are you?"

Angelo's response seemed almost robotic to Veronica. It was not his usual upbeat, friendly way of speaking. She thought that she might have surprised him, so she tried again.

"I'm doing great, Papa! What have you been up to?"

Again, it was a strange response. "Oh . . . just the same old thing."

Then Veronica heard her sister in the background ask who was on the phone. She was shocked by Angelo's response to Tonia. "I'm not sure ... who it is on the phone. I think it's one of your neighbors."

Tonia took the phone from her father, and Veronica overheard her ask Angela to "take *Nonno* into the living room." She spoke into the phone, "Hello, may I help you?"

Veronica was completely confused at this point. "Tonia, it's Veronica! What's going on with Papa?"

There was a long, uncomfortable silence before Tonia answered. "I'm so sorry, Veronica ... I should've called you sooner. It's been a difficult ... very difficult time."

"What do you mean, difficult?" Veronica asked, sitting down. The same terrible gut feeling she got when Tom showed up on her doorstep emerged again.

"Shortly after we settled into our new home, we noticed that Papa seemed confused and disoriented. Initially, we chalked it up to a new environment and a different routine ... but then it kept getting worse. One night, we were awakened around three o'clock in the morning by Papa walking down the hallway. Ernie got out of bed to see what was wrong and found Papa fully dressed and ready to walk out the front door. Ernie asked him where he was going, and he said he was going to the factory. Ernie was shocked and explained to Papa that he was retired, that we lived in Texas now, and that it was the middle of the night. Papa just stared back at Ernie and then started hitting his head with his fists while saying, 'My head! My head! I don't know what's wrong with me!' We made the decision to take him to a doctor as soon as possible. I spoke with a physician at my hospital, and he arranged for an appointment with a highly regarded neurologist. He gave Papa a thorough examination. He looked at his medical history, asked what types of medicines he was taking, and inquired about the symptoms. Then he conducted several tests and requested blood work and X-rays. The neurologist wanted to be sure that there wasn't another condition—like a stroke—causing these problems.

"After all the tests were completed, the neurologist met with us and explained that Papa has dementia caused by a disease called Alzheimer's. He told us that the dementia would only get worse. Initially, Papa will become even more disoriented and confused. Then his behavior will change. He will begin to forget things and ask the same questions over and over. Eventually, he will forget who he is and who we are. His speech . . . his ability to swallow . . . even his ability to walk will be impaired. There is no cure.

"Oh, Veronica, I'm so, so sorry to break the news to you this way. I know I should've called you sooner. It's just that we . . . are still trying to wrap our heads around it, and we know you have been through so much already. Just a year ago, Papa was so vibrant and full of life. And now . . . now he seems like a shadow of himself. There are times that he is lucid, but then he goes back into a fog."

Veronica was in complete shock. She could not believe what she was hearing. Her father had always been the solid rock of the family. Now they were losing him. She thought about her reason for calling and knew that she could not even broach the subject now. Instead, she asked about care for Angelo.

"I gave up my part-time job at the hospital so that I can be with him. Right now, with Ernie's help, we can manage. Eventually, we'll have to hire someone to help us. Both Ernie and I have decided we don't want to put Papa into a home."

Veronica struggled with what to say and then asked, "Tonia, what can I do? Should I leave college and come there to help you?"

Her sister's response was quick and firm. "Absolutely not, Veronica! Papa would never want you to give up college! He was so, so very proud of you. You continue with your studies. Keep getting those high grades, and then land that top job in finance. That's what our father would want for you. That's what we all want for you!"

Tonia paused, as though thinking something over for a moment, and then added, "The most important thing that you can do is pray for Papa. Then fly out here for Christmas and spend quality time with the entire family."

Veronica had a huge lump in her throat and could barely get out the words "I-I love you, Tonia. I will pray for Papa . . . and for you!"

The emotion in Veronica's voice was obvious to Tonia. "I love you, Veronica. I've dropped a lot on you and never even asked how you are doing. Are you okay?"

"Everything is fine . . . just fine." Veronica needed her sister so much right now, but she realized that she couldn't put yet another burden on Tonia.

Stephanie was sitting in her room reading when Veronica came to the door with tears in her eyes. Clearly sensing that the phone call did not go well, Stephanie got up from her chair, walked to Veronica, and asked, "What happened?"

Through tears, Veronica explained everything to her friend. Stephanie had met Angelo on several occasions and could not believe what was happening to him. She told Veronica how deeply sorry she was to hear about Angelo, and she thought to herself, *Dear God, how much more can Veronica take? She lost David, she's pregnant, and now she is losing her father!*

Stephanie did her best to support Veronica during the rest of the weekend.

Veronica focused all of her energy on her studies during the following week. She believed that she needed to formulate a different plan because it would be impossible to raise her child with Tonia's family as she had planned. *Tonia has enough on her plate caring for Papa. I can't possibly add to that burden.* She was overwhelmed with emotion and thought it would be best to simply concentrate on school. After her last class on Friday, Veronica walked to Saint Cecilia's Church. It was only fifteen minutes from the campus. She blessed herself with holy water, walked to the front pew, genuflected, and then knelt down. There was a painting of the Last Supper above the altar. She stared for a long time at the image of Jesus surrounded by his apostles. She wondered what thoughts went through his mind, knowing what he would face in just a few hours. Then she began to pray.

*Dear Jesus, please give me strength and guide me. I feel lost and don't know what to do. I am putting my troubles into your sacred hands. I trust that you will guide me.*

She finally glanced down at her watch and realized that she had been in the church for over an hour. She looked up one last time at the Last Supper painting, picked up her books, and slowly walked back to her apartment. While she did not have a solution yet, she felt like a burden had been lifted from her shoulders. She trusted that God had a plan.

When Veronica returned to the apartment, Stephanie suggested that they drive to her parents' house and spend the weekend there. She said it would be good to get some fresh air and a few home-cooked meals. She seemed pleasantly surprised when Veronica agreed. They packed their bags and left for the two-hour drive.

Stephanie's mother had prepared a huge meal, and she was at the door welcoming the two girls. She gave each of them a hug and a kiss.

Stephanie's father was opening a bottle of wine when they walked into the kitchen. He smiled and warmly embraced the two young women. Veronica was happy she had come. The kindness and love she felt in Stephanie's home helped her to forget about her troubles for just a little while.

The next morning, after a hearty breakfast of pancakes and sausage, Stephanie and Veronica went hiking in the nearby Berkshire Mountains. It felt great to be in the fresh, crisp air. They talked and laughed just like old times. When they got back to Stephanie's house, her brother, Christopher, and his wife, Lauren, were there. As Stephanie had predicted, they'd married soon after Christopher's graduation. He had taken a job in Hartford with one of the major insurance companies, and Lauren was teaching school in the Connecticut town where they lived. Stephanie's mom insisted that Chris and Lauren stay for dinner. They did not need too much convincing. In fact, it almost seemed like they were expecting an invitation.

As usual, dinner at Stephanie's home was delicious. Just as his mother was setting a homemade pie on the table, Christopher picked up his spoon, tapped his glass, and asked for everyone's attention. He looked at Lauren, and they both had huge smiles on their faces. Then he turned to the rest of the family and announced, "We have some great news to share with you! Lauren and I are expecting a baby."

Stephanie's father jumped out of his chair and hugged both his son and daughter-in-law. With tears in his eyes, he told them how thrilled he was to finally become a grandfather. Stephanie's mom, who also had tears running down her cheeks, could barely get her words out. "I am so happy . . . so blessed!"

Stephanie was naturally excited and asked when the baby was due.

"The doctor said around the end of May," responded Christopher.

At that instant, Stephanie seemed to realize that it was the same time Veronica's baby was due. Her expression conveyed a twinge of guilt as she turned to her friend—and to her surprise, Veronica had a big smile on her face and congratulated the young couple. "Once again," Stephanie whispered to her friend when nobody was looking, "I am amazed by your inner strength, Ronnie."

Stephanie's father decided to open up a bottle of champagne to celebrate. Her mother insisted that Christopher and Lauren spend the night rather than drive back to Connecticut. Once again, they did not need much convincing, especially after the wine and champagne.

Later that evening, as they were getting ready for bed, Stephanie asked, "How are you doing, Veronica?"

Veronica thought about her friend's question before responding.

"Honestly, I have mixed emotions. It's clear how much Chris and Lauren love each other . . . and I'm very happy for them. At the same time, it hurts . . . It hurts terribly that David isn't here with me. I know in my heart that he would've been a wonderful husband and a tremendous father. Together we would have figured out a way to raise our child, but now . . . now I'm not sure what to do. I spent a long time at Saint Cecilia's on Friday afternoon. I put my troubles into God's hands, and I'm trusting that he will guide me to a solution."

The family rose early the next morning for Sunday mass. They arrived about fifteen minutes before the mass actually started. Stephanie's father said that was the only way to ensure that they would all sit together in one pew. Veronica remembered from her previous visits how impressed she had been with their pastor, Father Pat. And there he was, walking down the aisle, stopping at nearly every pew and greeting each of the parishioners. It was evident to Veronica that this priest sincerely cared for his congregation and had a strong connection with each of them. When he arrived at their pew, Stephanie's father whispered in the pastor's ear. Father Pat's smile got even wider, and he immediately congratulated Christopher and Lauren.

As usual, Father Pat gave an inspirational homily. It was after she received communion that Veronica realized God had answered her prayers. She knew *exactly* what she was going to do with her child.

The rest of the semester went quickly. Veronica concentrated on her studies and once again achieved straight As. Before she left for the Christmas break, she met with Dr. Coleman.

"Some urgent family matters have come up, and I will not be returning for the spring semester."

She could see the concern on his face and quickly added, "I will be back for the fall semester. Fortunately, with all of the extra courses you've advised me to take over the past two years, I will still be able to graduate on time."

"I'm so sorry to hear about your family situation. It must be very serious. Is there anything . . . anything at all that I can do for you?"

"Well . . . there is one thing. Would you be willing to call Mr. Johnson at the investment banking firm and explain to him that I will not be able to return there this summer?"

"Of course . . . and if there is anything else, please . . . just ask!"

"Thank you for being so understanding and supportive."

Veronica left for Texas a few days later. She was looking forward to seeing her family but was also experiencing a lot of anxiety. She did not know what to expect when she saw her father, and she felt guilty about keeping her pregnancy from the family. She was just starting to show, but with slightly larger clothes, it wasn't noticeable.

Ernie and the children were waiting for her when she arrived at the gate in Houston. Angela ran to Veronica and hugged her. Ernie, who was holding Michael, smiled and kissed her on the cheek. Angela could not stop talking to Veronica during the drive home. When her niece finally took a breath, Veronica turned to Ernie and asked him about her father.

He explained, "He has good days and bad days. There are moments when he is very lucid and almost seems like the old Angelo, and then he lapses back into confusion. During those lucid moments, he remembers what the doctor told us. He tells us that he is going to fight to hold on to every memory as long as he can. He tells us not to feel sorry for him because he believes he has had a wonderful life."

Veronica could see that her brother-in-law was getting choked up as he continued, "He says that we all have to bear a cross before . . . before we can get to heaven. And then . . . then he actually apologizes and tells us how sorry he is for being a burden to us. Can you imagine . . . can you even imagine? Your father is amazing! I love him as much as I love my own father, and I will miss him. Actually . . . I *already* miss the man I knew!"

Veronica could hear the emotion in Ernie's voice and realized how difficult the situation must be for him and her sister.

They pulled into the driveway, and Veronica braced herself. Tonia opened the front door and gave her sister a long, heartfelt hug. It was as if she did not want to let go, and Veronica felt the same way. It felt so good to be with her big sister. Then, Tonia walked arm in arm with Veronica down the hallway to the living room, where Angelo was sitting, staring at the television.

Tonia said, "Hey, Papa, look who's here."

Angelo looked up, immediately smiled at Veronica, and said, "My little angel . . . my little Veronica!"

Veronica ran to her father. She hugged him and kissed him several times. She was so pleased that he recognized her and that he seemed like himself. She wanted to hold on to this moment as long as possible. Ernie put his arm around his wife and smiled at her as they both fought back tears.

The next few days were filled with a lot of activity as they prepared for the Christmas celebration. Veronica helped her sister finish wrapping presents. Next, they began getting the seafood ready for Christmas Eve. This was a Ruffo family tradition that they had brought from Italy. In the Catholic faith, Christmas Eve was a day of abstinence from meat. So, at the evening meal, a seafood feast was served. Some Italians call it the "Feast of the Seven Fishes." Tonia and Veronica cooked *baccala*, clams, mussels, calamari, octopus, eels, and smelts. The entire house smelled like a seafood market.

Joe, Sandy, and baby Stephen arrived that afternoon. After plenty of hugs and kisses, Tonia teased her sister-in-law, "Well, now that you're an honorary Italian after marrying this guy, let's get an apron on you so that you can help prepare our dinner."

Sandy laughed. "Absolutely! Just tell me what to do. It'll be a pleasure to be helping in the kitchen rather than dealing with some pompous judge or manipulative lawyer."

Joe and Ernie spent the rest of the day keeping Angelo occupied. Joe saw the changes in his father since his last visit.

"So, Joey, how is the war going? Have you defeated those damn Germans yet?"

Joe placed his hand on his father's shoulder. "Papa, the war was over a long time ago. We defeated the Germans in 1945. It's 1960 now."

Angelo bowed his head and placed his hand on his chin as if in deep thought. Then he shook his head and said, "I don't know what's wrong with me. Sometimes, I forget things. I'm so sorry!"

Joe made eye contact with Ernie, who simply closed his eyes and swallowed hard. "It's okay, Papa. There's no need to apologize."

When the seafood feast was ready, everyone gathered in the dining room. Ernie said grace, and the adults quickly began enjoying the various fish. Angela and her little brother wanted no part of the "smelly stuff." There was much laughter around the dinner table, and even Angelo seemed to be enjoying himself. Tonia brought out the dessert after dinner. When Veronica tasted the homemade cookies, she immediately thought of Maria and remembered how much her mother enjoyed baking. Ernie brewed espresso and brought out the sambuca.

On Christmas morning, they got up early for mass. Angela was anxious to see what Santa had left her, but Tonia explained to her, "Before we can open our presents, we must go to church to wish happy birthday to baby Jesus."

"Okay, Mommy . . . but as soon as we come back home, we can open presents, right?"

"Well, honey, we'll have breakfast first, and then it will be time."

Veronica smiled, remembering a similar conversation between Maria and her several years ago. After mass, the family returned home for a light breakfast. Then it was time to open the presents. Veronica loved the tradition that her parents had started many years ago. Angelo would take his time handing out the gifts. Each person opened their present before the next one was handed out. Initially, her parents did this because there were very few presents, but even as the number grew, they continued this practice. Veronica was pleased that Tonia and Ernie had embraced this custom within their household. Tonia said, "It's an excellent way to teach Angela and Michael to be grateful and appreciate each gift."

With the Santa hat on his head, Ernie handed the first gifts to each child. Veronica smiled as she watched her niece and nephews open their presents. Then, in the next moment, she had a sorrowful thought. *My child will never be able to experience this!*

This process went on for the rest of the morning. The most emotional moment occurred when Ernie handed a large box to his father-in-law. Angelo lifted it, shook it, and asked what was inside. Tonia encouraged him to go ahead and open it up. Angela helped her grandfather rip off the wrapping paper. When Angelo finally opened the box, he lifted out several photo albums. He seemed somewhat confused. Tonia walked over to him, put her arm around his shoulder, looked into his beautiful green eyes, and said, "You told us that you are going to do everything possible to hold on to all of your memories. So, we wanted to help you hold on to them. We gathered all the old photos that we could find. We even wrote to our cousins in Italy and got pictures of you and Mama with our relatives back in Naples. Then Ernie organized them and wrote a description under each picture."

Tonia opened the first album and pointed to the picture of a young Angelo and Maria on their wedding day. Angelo stared at the picture for several moments. Then, with tears running down his cheeks, he smiled and hugged Tonia. Veronica felt as though a faucet had been turned on in her eyes and couldn't stop crying. Sandy wrapped an arm around her shoulder and softly whispered, "I know, Veronica, it's hard . . . so hard."

Spending the next few weeks with her family meant the world to Veronica. At times, Angelo became anxious, confused, and disoriented. She was grateful that she was there to give her sister help and support, but she worried about how her sister would handle their father as his dementia worsened. Seeing her father's condition and the strain it was already placing on her sister confirmed Veronica's decision. *I was right! Tonia has enough on her plate caring for Papa. I can't possibly ask her to help me to care for an infant.* Nevertheless, there were times that she wanted to talk to Tonia about David and their unborn child, but she resisted the urge. This conflict must have been apparent on her face. One day, her sister asked, "Veronica, you look so sad and distracted. What's wrong?"

Rather than telling her sister everything, Veronica told her sister a half-truth. "I'm just so heartsick about Papa."

There were tearful goodbyes the day Veronica left for Boston. She spent most of the morning sitting with Angelo, going through the photo albums with him. It was extremely emotional when she kissed and hugged her father goodbye. She did not know if he would even remember her when she returned. Once again, Veronica embraced her big sister as if she would never let go.

The plane landed late in Boston. Stephanie and Tom were there to greet Veronica. Seeing her closest friends helped ease the pain of leaving her family. It had been a long flight, and by the time they arrived at the apartment, Veronica was thoroughly exhausted—both physically and emotionally. She said goodnight and promised Stephanie that she would fill her in the next day.

Veronica sat with Stephanie the next morning and, over coffee, told her about the visit. She shared how emotional it was saying goodbye to her father. Stephanie expressed that she could only imagine how painful it would be to lose a parent to such a terrible disease. Then, Veronica was quiet for several moments before taking a deep breath and sharing her new plan with Stephanie.

"I'm taking this semester off. I've already spoken to Dr. Coleman and completed the necessary paperwork. I've said that there is a family emergency and I'll be unable to attend classes during the spring semester. I'll attend summer school after the baby is born. With the extra credits I've already accumulated and the summer classes, I'll still be able to graduate on time. I'm going to move out of the apartment—"

"*What?*" Stephanie immediately interjected, but Veronica was ahead of her.

"I can't stay here! Too many people know me. I don't want anyone feeling sorry for me because I'm pregnant and unmarried. I will definitely not go to one of those maternity homes that I've read about. They sound like prisons. I'll get a small apartment away from campus where no one knows me. If any of the new neighbors ask, I'll simply tell them that my husband is in the army and stationed overseas. I'll wear my mother's wedding ring. Not only will it prevent unwanted questions, but it will also be a reminder that my mother is still looking out for me . . . and my baby. I'll continue to see Dr. Burke, and when my baby is due, I would really like you to be there with me. I'll make sure that my baby is healthy . . . and then . . . I will give the baby up for adoption."

Stephanie quietly listened to everything Veronica said. Finally, she looked at her friend and said, "You shared a lot with me, Veronica. I'm really trying to process all of it right now, but the one thing that stands out for me is . . . is giving up your child. Are you sure . . . are you *absolutely certain* that you want to give this baby up?"

With tears running down her cheeks, Veronica responded in a soft, trembling voice, "No, it's actually the last thing that I want to do! I love this baby, this child that's growing inside of me. He or she is a living part of David. No, I don't want to give up my baby . . . but more importantly, I want this child to have a good life with a mother and father, with sisters and brothers. I can't . . . can't *give* that to this baby. It breaks my heart, but I know that it's the right thing to do."

Stephanie nodded, acknowledging the emotion combined with the strong determination that stood behind Veronica's decision. She simply wrapped her arm around Veronica and said, "Veronica, I'll do whatever you need me to do! I love you like a sister."

Nothing more needed to be said. Veronica gave Stephanie permission to tell Tom about the pregnancy.

But there was one piece that Veronica had not shared with Stephanie. She was not going to give the baby to an adoption agency. Instead, she was going to leave the baby with Stephanie's pastor—Father Pat. She recognized that he was a kind, loving, and sincere priest who knew everyone in the parish. She was confident that he would be able to find a loving home for her child.

# 39

## Twins

Veronica Ruffo
Waltham | 1961

VERONICA FOUND A small furnished apartment in Waltham, which was about a half hour from Boston. Tom and Stephanie helped her move in. Once again, Tom offered to speak with David's parents, but Veronica adamantly refused. He never raised the issue again.

Veronica settled into a routine during the next several weeks. She attended daily mass at the local church several days each week. Looking up at the crucifix, she always recited the same prayer.

*Dear God, please protect the child growing inside of me. Accept David into heaven and give peace and comfort to his parents. Help Papa in his debilitating illness and give strength and comfort to Tonia and Ernie. And dear God, please give me the support and guidance that I need during this challenging time. Amen.*

Then Veronica would walk back to her apartment and eat a healthy breakfast. She knew it was important for her and her child that she remain well nourished. It was an unusually mild New England winter, so she took long walks several times each week. She found these walks were beneficial both physically and mentally.

Except for her doctor appointments, Veronica spent the rest of her time reading. She borrowed books that dealt with pregnancy and babies from the local library. She was focused on doing everything possible to ensure a healthy baby. She also obtained a reading list for her planned summer classes in order to keep up with her studies. At five o'clock, she would put her books aside and prepare dinner. Afterward, she would treat herself to a little television and then go to bed.

But despite it all, there were days when she felt overcome with depression and sadness. On those days, she would pull from her inner strength and her unshakable trust in God to get through these emotional periods. Stephanie visited a couple of times each week, and sometimes Tom would accompany her. These moments with her closest friends meant everything to Veronica.

The visits with Dr. Burke continued to go well. He was always compassionate and supportive. He assured Veronica that her baby was doing well. It was during one of these visits that she received unexpected news. Dr. Burke began his normal examination. He listened for the baby's heartbeat and then measured the size of her uterus. He did this by laying a cloth measuring tape on her abdomen and measuring from her pubic bone to the top of her uterus.

During this particular office visit, it appeared to be taking longer than normal, and he repeated the procedure multiple times. Then he picked up his notes from the previous visits and began rereading them. At this point, Veronica became concerned and asked, "Is . . . is something wrong with my baby, Dr. Burke?" *Oh my God! He's going to tell me that the baby has some kind of defect!*

He put his notes down, took off his reading glasses, and sat down beside her. Then he looked directly at her. "Veronica, everything is absolutely fine . . . but there is something I need to share with you."

At this moment, Veronica did not know what to expect. *If my baby is fine . . . what could it be?*

"You are having twins."

His words felt as though another heavy weight had been dropped on her shoulders. She was completely unprepared for this news and was in a state of shock. *Twins? Am I going to be able to deliver both babies? Will they both be healthy?*

Dr. Burke could see how disturbing the news was for her, and he immediately reassured her, "Veronica, listen to me. Both of your babies are healthy! You've done an excellent job in caring for yourself and them. You are going to be fine, and so will they. I'll be here for you every single step of the way."

It took a while, but eventually Veronica regained her composure, and then she had several questions for the doctor. "Are my babies the same size? How will I deliver them? What are the potential complications? How long will my labor last? What should I do differently now that I'm expecting twins?"

Dr. Burke answered each question in the same calm and comforting manner with which Veronica had become familiar. By the time she left the doctor's office, the shock was beginning to wear off, and Veronica was in a better state of mind. Once again, she was able to pull from that amazing inner strength and decided she would continue doing everything she had been doing to ensure the health of her babies. Her decision regarding adoption made even more sense now that she was expecting twins. She was convinced that she would be unable to give these infants a good home at this stage of her life. She wanted the best for her children. Although her rational side told her this was the only choice, her emotional side wanted to keep these babies. These were the times when she felt the most torn about her choice.

The babies continued to grow, and by the end of February, it looked as though Veronica had a basketball under her blouse. Stephanie teased her about it, and they both had a good laugh. She began to experience the babies' movement during March, and by April, she was feeling extremely large and anxious to deliver them.

It was a lovely spring morning in May. The air was fresh, the cloudless sky was a perfect blue, the trees were in bloom, and the grass was a deep green. Veronica woke up early. She was finding it difficult to get a good night's sleep as the babies grew larger. Veronica had a light breakfast and then decided to walk to the local Italian market. Stephanie and Tom were coming over to her apartment at noon, and she wanted to prepare a special lunch for them. Tom would be graduating the following week, and he had been accepted at Harvard Medical School. So, naturally, she wanted to acknowledge this wonderful accomplishment with a celebratory meal. She also wanted to thank her two friends for their unconditional love and support. Most recently, they had offered to purchase bassinets for the babies.

Veronica enjoyed the walk. The fresh air felt good, and there were plenty of people outside enjoying this beautiful spring morning. The store was only a few blocks away, and the owner was friendly. He would always ask how she was feeling and insisted on adding a little extra to each of her orders. He would wink and say, "No charge—it's for the baby."

She returned to the apartment and prepared the antipasto. As she placed Italian cold cuts and cheeses on the platter, she was reminded of the many times her mother had created an antipasto masterpiece. Veronica found herself thinking about her mother often lately. She assumed that it was because she would soon become a mother. It was at these moments that she felt extremely conflicted. She loved these two babies. Every time they would move, she became excited, knowing that she was carrying two human beings inside of her. Veronica wanted so desperately to keep these children and raise them, but she realized she couldn't provide them with the home they deserved. She hoped that Maria was looking down on her and understood.

Tom and Stephanie arrived just as Veronica finished setting the table. Not only did they bring two beautiful white wicker bassinets but also blankets, diapers, and baby bottles. When Veronica saw all these gifts, she was overwhelmed and tearfully said, "You two have done too much! How can I ever repay you for everything that you've done, for all of your wonderful support?"

Tom smiled at Veronica and said, "Don't talk about repaying us! We wanted to do this for you and for your babies." His face grew sad, then, but only for a bit. "I figured I owed it to David, too, as his best friend and all."

"We love you so much," Stephanie said, closing in for a hug.

They arranged the bassinets and other gifts in Veronica's bedroom. Then they sat at the table for lunch. Stephanie saw what Veronica had prepared and exclaimed, "This is an absolute masterpiece! It looks way too good to eat."

Tom quickly interjected, "Well, then you can watch as I eat it because I'm starving, and it looks delicious!"

Stephanie laughed. "Then we better say grace quickly."

Veronica prayed, "Dear Lord, thank you for the food before us and the many blessings you have given to us. Thank you for giving me such wonderful friends. Please—oh, please—bless and protect my babies. Amen."

Tom filled his plate and broke a huge chunk of crusty Italian bread from the loaf. He sliced the bread and filled it with the Italian cold cuts and cheeses. Stephanie teased him, "Are you going to leave anything for us, mister?"

He simply ignored her and savored his first bite. Veronica smiled and thought to herself how nice it felt to share a meal with her closest friends. She thought about how good it would be when she moved back in with Stephanie in the fall. Then she immediately realized that in order to do that, she would have to say goodbye to her babies. At that moment, a certain sadness gripped her. Although she forced a smile, the heartache was apparent in her eyes. Both Stephanie and Tom saw it and gave each other a knowing glance.

Halfway through lunch, Veronica excused herself. She explained that she found herself making more frequent trips to the bathroom lately. After what seemed to be an excessively long time, Veronica shouted from the bathroom, "Stephanie, Stephanie . . . please come in here—hurry!"

Stephanie sensed the panic in Veronica's voice and rushed to the bathroom. Veronica was bracing herself by the sink. Stephanie immediately asked, "Veronica, what's wrong? What is it?"

Veronica's face was flushed, and she had perspiration dripping down her forehead. She turned to Stephanie and said, "My water . . . it's broken! I—I think it's time!"

At that moment, she felt her first contraction and cried out. Once the pain subsided, she instructed Stephanie, "Call . . . call Dr. Burke! His number is by the phone."

Tom had come to the doorway, and he immediately rushed to place the call. He reached the answering service and explained what was happening. Dr. Burke called back within a few minutes and asked to speak with Veronica. She was able to tell the doctor what had happened and rate her degree of pain. He told her to have her friends bring her to the hospital and that he would call ahead to arrange for her admittance. He assured Veronica that he would meet her there.

Tom and Stephanie helped Veronica into the car. Stephanie got into the back seat with Veronica, put her arm around her, and tried comforting her.

"It's going to be all right, Veronica. Don't worry! We'll get you to the hospital, and Dr. Burke will be there for you."

Just then, Veronica felt another powerful contraction and yelled out. They seemed to be getting closer and lasting longer. Tom put the car in gear and raced to the hospital. Fortunately, the traffic was light since it was a Saturday, and Tom made it there in record time. Stephanie helped Veronica out of the car and walked her into the hospital. The staff was expecting her, and she was quickly admitted. A nurse was already bringing Veronica to her room by the time Tom parked the car. He went to the waiting room in the maternity ward.

Veronica took off her clothes so that she could put on the hospital gown. Stephanie helped her adjust the gown in order to make it as comfortable as possible. Then she asked, "How are you feeling, Veronica?"

Veronica said that she was nervous and concerned about her babies.

Stephanie reassured her, "Veronica, you've taken excellent care of yourself and of these babies. They are going to be fine!"

Just then, she heard another voice behind her. It was Dr. Burke. He had on a blue polo shirt and a pair of khaki slacks. Then, in that same calm and soothing voice that Veronica had become accustomed to, he said, "You are absolutely correct! Veronica has done a superb job, and these babies will be just fine."

Then he walked over to Veronica, smiled, took her hands in his, and said, "Well, it looks like these two kids want to come out a little earlier. That's fairly normal for twins. I'm going to examine you, and then we'll keep a close eye on you. The contractions will get more intense and closer together."

He went on to explain that once her cervix was fully dilated, it would be time for the babies to be delivered. Dr. Burke had met Stephanie previously when she had accompanied Veronica to office visits. He smiled at Stephanie and told her that he was glad she was there for Veronica.

The next few hours were a blur of activity. The contractions continued getting closer and closer together. At times, Veronica did not think she could handle the pain. The nurses would check in on her regularly, and Stephanie never left her side. Finally, it was time to bring Veronica into the delivery room. Dr. Burke assured her that she was doing great and that she would soon be holding her babies. Stephanie kissed Veronica's cheek and told her that everything was going to be all right. Then she joined Tom in the waiting room.

Barely an hour later, a smiling Dr. Burke walked into the waiting room and exclaimed, "She was fantastic! Veronica delivered two beautiful and healthy baby boys! They are twins, *identical* twins! And even though they're identical, it's going to be easy for Veronica to tell them apart. The first one to be born is so peaceful and easygoing. The second one . . . that one is a real fighter. He gave me a hard time coming out."

Stephanie was thoroughly relieved and gave Dr. Burke a big hug. Then she introduced Tom to him and proudly shared that Tom would be entering medical school in the fall. Dr. Burke congratulated Tom.

"That's wonderful, Tom. You'll find medical school to be one of the most exciting and challenging times in your life. I'm so, so very happy for you. If you ever need someone to talk to—to be a sounding board for you—please don't hesitate to reach out to me."

The following day, Stephanie visited Veronica in the hospital. She held one of the twins while Veronica held his brother. It was obvious to her what Dr. Burke meant when he had said that one child was peaceful and the other was a fighter. Stephanie realized that she had the fighter in her arms. He was in constant motion. The baby Veronica was holding was lying quietly in her arms. It looked as though he was staring at her and just smiling. She listened as Veronica spoke gently to the baby.

"Hello, my little angel. You are such a beautiful baby. Mommy loves you with all of her heart. You look just like your daddy, with your dark hair and your beautiful blue eyes."

Stephanie could see the tremendous amount of love Veronica already had for these babies. She wondered how Veronica would be able to bring herself to give them up for adoption. She could only imagine how painful it would be for her friend. Stephanie tried to block these thoughts from her mind for now and instead asked, "So, have you chosen names for these two angels yet?"

Veronica was quiet for a moment and then answered Stephanie, "Well, I told the nurses that I haven't decided on their names yet. So, they've written down Baby Boy #1 Ruffo and Baby Boy #2 Ruffo." Then Veronica closed her eyes for what seemed a long time. It was as if what she was going to say next hurt so much that she didn't even want to speak. Finally, she said, "I know that the . . . the adopting parents will want to give them their own names. So, I didn't think I should name them."

Stephanie wasn't sure what to say, so she didn't speak and compromised by reaching for her friend's hand and taking it in hers.

Veronica smiled and tearfully said, "But I find myself calling this one 'Little Angelo' and his brother 'Little David.'"

At this, even Stephanie had to shed a tear.

Tom and Stephanie helped Veronica bring the babies home a few days later. Stephanie remained with Veronica during the first week to help her with the newborns. Over the next several weeks, Veronica spent her days completely engaged with her sons. She loved holding them, feeding them, listening to them, and simply *watching* them.

She was struggling with her decision to give them up for adoption. Her plan had seemed so right before the babies were born. Her head kept telling her that it was the best thing to do, but her heart did not agree. She continued trying to think of a way she could keep the babies and provide them with a wonderful life, but she always came to the same conclusion: no matter which way she twisted it, she'd never be able to provide for them the way they deserved.

It was a dark, cloudy Saturday in July when Veronica decided that this was the day. It was an unusually cool day, and they were predicting heavy rains for the late afternoon. Veronica thought that the weather matched what she was feeling inside. She sat at the table and began writing a letter.

*Dear Father Pat,*

*You don't know me, but I have attended mass many times at your church. You are definitely one of the best pastors I have ever seen. I know that you love your parishioners, and they, in turn, adore you. You seem to know every one of them. So, I am going to ask you for a very, very special favor. Please, oh, please, find a loving home for my two babies. It is breaking my heart to give them up. I love them with all of my heart and soul. I can honestly say that they were conceived in love—a very deep and meaningful love. Circumstances changed dramatically and tragically. I am unable to provide them with the home that they deserve. I want them to have every opportunity for a wonderful childhood and a fulfilling life. I pray that God will always bless and protect them. And I pray that someday, I can reunite with them and that they will forgive me! Please find a good home for my babies!*

*Thank you and God bless you!*

She finished the letter, and as she reread it, tears welled up in her eyes. A teardrop fell on the letter. A little later, she fed each baby and put them down for a nap. When they woke, she bundled them up and placed them in the bassinets. Then she brought them down to the car. Just as she began to drive, the skies opened up, and the rain began to fall.

# 40

## Meet the Family

| Father John Donnelly
| Rectory | 1993

VERONICA FINISHED HER story, and John remained silent for several minutes. Veronica broke the silence.

"I've been watching you process everything that I shared. It reminds me of the way that David . . . your father . . . would quietly digest large amounts of information. You have such a strong resemblance to him—the dark hair, deep-blue eyes, and tan complexion. I know that he would be very proud of you."

John smiled at Veronica and said, "I was remembering when Father Pat first read your letter to us. We reread it so many times that eventually, we had every word memorized. We would even dream about you! Father Pat always said something terrible must have caused you to give us up. Now I understand the tragic circumstances that forced you to make such a painful, difficult decision. We were convinced that some way, somehow . . . someday . . . we would be reunited with you. We forgave you a long, long time ago."

John stood up, held both of Veronica's hands, and then wrapped his arms around her. Veronica began to cry.

"What's wrong?"

"Nothing is wrong. These are tears of joy! I had been so anxious and apprehensive about meeting you, but Father Pat assured me that everything would be all right. Your compassion and understanding mean so very much to me."

After their long embrace, John walked over to a table and picked up a framed portrait. It was a picture of him and his brother taken shortly after college. He brought it to Veronica and pointed to his brother, saying, "I wish he was here to share this wonderful moment. I know that he would have been as overjoyed as I am."

John thought for a moment, smiled, and then added, "You know something . . . I can feel his spirit with us right now!" After placing the picture back, he asked, "I am so grateful that you are here today, but I am curious . . . Why did you decide to reach out now?"

"For many years, I kept the pain—and the shame—of giving up my children deep inside of me. I didn't think I could ever love anyone else again or that anyone could love me. Then, about seven years ago, I fell in love with a wonderful man. He asked me to marry him, but before I said yes, I told him that I needed to share something with him. I also assured him that if he did not want to marry me after hearing my secret, I would completely understand. I told him the entire story, and when I finished, he responded with unbelievable tenderness and warmth. He said he was grateful that I had shared my secret with him. Then he asked me again to marry him. It felt so good to finally speak openly with someone about it. There have been several times that I wanted to come forward . . . wanted to speak to you . . . wanted to meet my sons . . . but I didn't have the courage. Christopher—that's my husband's name—reassured me that I would know when the time was right. A few months ago, I had a medical scare. I found a lump in my breast."

John immediately became concerned. *Oh no! I've just found her . . . Now I'm going to lose her again!* The worried look on his face broadcast John's thoughts. Veronica placed her hand on his shoulder and said, "It's all right . . . I'm fine. Fortunately, it turned out to be a benign tumor. That experience brought me to the realization that I didn't want to leave this world without meeting my sons. So, that is why I am here today."

Before Veronica left, they agreed on a date when John would meet her husband, stepson, and the rest of her family. She explained that both her brother and sister, along with their families, had moved back to the Boston area. She said that her closest friends, Stephanie and Tom, would also be there.

Veronica and Christopher lived in Newton Centre. When John parked the car and looked at the huge house, he was reminded of the many times that he and his brother had walked down this same street from Boston College. He recalled how they would wonder who lived in these large homes and even joked about visiting here someday. Now he knew someone who actually lived here. The house was a magnificent brick Georgian colonial with a meticulously landscaped lot.

Surprisingly, John felt no apprehension about meeting Veronica's family. In fact, after listening to her story, he was looking forward to getting together with them. He heard a familiar voice as he walked toward the front door.

"Hey, John, what are you doing here? I didn't know Aunt Veronica would need a priest at this family dinner!"

John turned to see his good friend Stephen, and in that instant, he remembered that Stephen's last name was Ruffo. He immediately connected the dots and smiled at Stephen, realizing that their relationship was much deeper than either of them could have imagined. He shook Stephen's hand and said, "I was introduced to your aunt recently, and she invited me to meet your entire family."

Although John had already figured it out, he decided to maintain the element of surprise. So, he asked, "Exactly how is Veronica your aunt?"

Stephen, who seemed to still be wondering where his aunt would have met John, answered, "My father is her older brother."

Veronica had already opened the front door by the time the two friends got there. She immediately wrapped her arms around John and kissed his cheek. Stephen appeared surprised by the warm embrace for someone she had only met recently. Veronica then hugged and kissed her nephew and walked them to the massive living room, where everyone else had already gathered. Michael and Francis immediately walked over to Stephen and John. They had the same reaction as their cousin. Veronica made sure that all of her guests had a glass of wine in their hands before announcing, "Everyone, we have a very special guest joining us tonight. I would like you to welcome Father John Donnelly."

Veronica then proceeded to introduce John to each of her family members, starting with her husband, Christopher. After the introductions, Veronica said that she had something very important to share with all of them. Then she took a deep breath and looked at Christopher. He nodded his encouragement, and she placed her arm around John and then said, "I would like you all to meet my son, John Donnelly."

There was complete silence and obvious confusion. Then, Veronica proceeded to explain everything to them. When she had finished, her sister, Tonia, got up from her chair, walked over to John, and hugged him as she said, "It's so wonderful to meet you, John. Welcome to our family!"

Then, turning to Veronica, she said, "I'm so sorry that I wasn't there for you when you needed me the most."

"There's no need for you to apologize! Papa needed you much more at that time."

One by one, each of the family members gave John a warm embrace as they welcomed him. When it came time for the three cousins, Fran smiled at John and said, "So, Johnny, I guess we're stepbrothers now!"

Michael chimed in, "And it's the *four cousins* from now on!"

A grinning Stephen joked, "So . . . let me get this straight. We have an Irish priest who is half-Italian and half-Jewish! Now I'm *really* confused!"

# 41

## Living Memorial

Father John Donnelly
New Hampshire | 1993

A FEW WEEKS after the family dinner, John met his mother for lunch.
He explained to her that Father Pat, whom he loved dearly, would always
be his father. Nevertheless, he wanted to learn more about David—his
biological father. Veronica looked at him with understanding and then
reached into her purse. She took out a photograph and handed it to John.
It was a picture of her and David. John looked at the two of them smiling,
their arms wrapped around each other. It was obvious that they were very
much in love. Veronica had not changed that much in thirty years. Her
hair was shorter now and had a few streaks of gray. John could see that
he closely resembled his father. After a brief silence, Veronica began to
describe her first love. She talked about David's wonderful personality, as
well as his humorous idiosyncrasies. John could see Veronica's face glow
as she spoke about David.

After she had finished, he reached across the table, held her hand, and expressed what he was feeling. "Thank you very much for sharing that with me. While I never met him, you have described David in such a way that I feel like I know him now. It's so gratifying to learn that my—I mean *our*—father was such a wonderful human being. It's also very evident that the two of you were deeply in love and that you still love him."

Veronica smiled at John and then asked him if he was up for a drive. They finished lunch, got into Veronica's Mercedes, and drove to New Hampshire. Veronica shared more stories about David during the ride. The traffic was light, and they arrived at the cemetery in under an hour. Veronica took John's arm in hers and walked him to David's grave. John read the inscription on the gravestone.

*In Loving Memory of*
*David Schwartz*
*1939–1960*
*Beloved Son & Brother*

Mother and son knelt down at the grave and said a prayer. Then Veronica placed her arm around John's shoulders. She smiled, looked up to the sky, and said, "David, my love, I want you to meet our son John. You would be so very proud of him! He's a fine young man who has chosen the priesthood as his vocation. I'm guessing you've already met his twin brother, James, and know that he sacrificed his life to do what was right for others."

Veronica asked John to drive on the way back to Boston. As they drove, he was quiet for several minutes, digesting everything he had learned about his father.

"John, I've been thinking about a way to honor David's memory. I want it to be a living memorial and have considered various options. One thought was to establish a scholarship at Dartmouth in his name. Another idea was a charitable fund in Israel to honor his Jewish heritage. I even considered building a wing at Harvard Law School, where he would have attended. Then Christopher came up with an excellent suggestion."

John was intrigued and asked, "What is it?"

"Christopher proposed a drug and alcohol rehabilitation center. He said that too many people have died due to addictions. While David certainly was not an addict, he was the victim of one. How many lives could be saved if we could help people overcome their addictions? How many relationships and families could be rebuilt? So, we thought of creating a center in David's name where the most advanced, proven, and emotionally sensitive methods are employed to help those who are addicted to drugs or alcohol. The staff would consist of doctors, healthcare workers, social workers, and counselors. We want each person to rebuild his or her life physically, mentally, emotionally, and spiritually."

John could hear the passion in Veronica's voice. After listening to what she described, he shared his thoughts.

"It is an amazing idea! When I was in the seminary, I spent time working in homeless shelters and met many individuals who were battling some form of addiction. Each person had a unique and touching story. I did my best to support them, but I always felt incapable of giving them the type of help they truly needed. I would pray for a more powerful solution. This rehabilitation center that you and Christopher have envisioned would be an extremely effective and dynamic answer to my prayers. I promise you that I'll devote my time and talent to this program. I'm confident that I'll be able to recruit several of my priest friends, seminarians, and parishioners to volunteer."

"I am overjoyed by your response. Christopher and I will make the initial investment to get the program started. Then I'll approach my wealthy colleagues and banking clients to obtain ongoing funding. Christopher is also investigating available government resources."

The next family dinner was at Joe and Sandy's home. They lived in a large colonial in Wellesley. During dinner, Veronica and Christopher shared their vision of a drug and alcohol rehabilitation center to honor David's memory. The family's response was overwhelmingly positive.

Veronica's brother, Joe, who had spent the majority of his career in the army, shared a personal experience. "I saw a significant amount of drug abuse during my time in Vietnam. Addiction and homelessness are serious problems for many Vietnam veterans. And now that we're retired, Sandy and I will be able to volunteer at the center. This will be a meaningful way to help my fellow vets and all those other lost souls who are suffering from some form of addiction."

Stephen seemed touched by what his father had shared and offered his thoughts. "I know that the individuals serviced by the center will benefit from my mother's legal experience, and I'll ask the DA about establishing a pro bono program."

Veronica's brother-in-law, Ernie, spoke next. "We'll handle all of the financial recordkeeping through my accounting firm. And this will also give Tonia the opportunity to use her nursing skills again."

Tom and Michael both said they would volunteer their services as physicians and believed that other doctors and medical professionals would do the same. The David Schwartz Rehabilitation Center was established six months later. Over the next decade, it became one of the most successful centers in the nation.

# PART FIVE

# CANCER IN
# THE CHURCH

# 42

## Brian Andrews

**Archbishop John Donnelly**
**Boston | 2016**

THE ARCHBISHOP WAS working in his office when Jackie, his secretary, knocked on the door.

"Your Excellency, you have visitors—Mr. and Mrs. Brian Andrews."

Archbishop John smiled when he heard that Brian had come to see him.

"Please show them in."

Brian walked into the archbishop's office with his wife, Nancy. Brian was a handsome young man with blond hair and blue eyes. He had recently graduated from law school and was an associate at a large Boston law firm.

"Brian, it is so good to see you. And Nancy, you're looking as lovely as ever." Pointing to the couch and cushioned chairs, the archbishop said, "Please, let's sit over there. How about some coffee?"

"That sounds great if you have the time."

"I always have time for you. I'm glad you stopped by."

"Your Excellency, we are both so happy about your elevation to cardinal. Congratulations!"

"Thank you, Nancy. I feel especially blessed."

"We wish we were able to attend the ceremony in Rome, but with the demands of the new job, I can't get away. I'm really sorry!"

"There is absolutely no need to apologize. I completely understand. So, tell me, how's life as a lawyer?"

"It's a lot of work, but I'm loving it."

"That's great. Who knows, maybe someday you'll end up being elected governor, like my cousin Stephen."

Brian laughed. "One step at a time . . . one step at a time." Then, handing a package to the archbishop, he said, "I selected a special gift—a fourteen-year-old bottle of single malt scotch. I did it for two reasons. First, I know how much you enjoy your two fingers each evening."

Archbishop John smiled and nodded in acknowledgment.

"And the second . . . and probably the more important reason . . . is because you were God's answer to my prayers fourteen years ago."

The archbishop closed his eyes, remembering the painful encounter that had created his lasting bond with Brian Andrews.

# 43

## Painful Encounter

**Father John Donnelly**
**Boston Suburb | 2002**

FATHER PAT HAD passed away nearly five years before. He had lived a wonderful life and died peacefully at the age of ninety. John and Father Jason were with the old priest when he passed. He died a "happy death," just like his patron saint, Saint Joseph. John promised himself that every single day of his life, he would strive to be as good a priest as his father. He believed that this would be the best way to honor Father Pat and keep his wonderful spirit alive. His father was his role model and guide as a pastor. Whenever he had to make an important decision, he would consider how Father Pat would have approached the situation.

John was now the pastor of his own church in a small town outside of Boston. The parishioners easily warmed to Father John. They told friends who had strayed from the church about the new pastor and encouraged them to attend at least one mass. Many of these lapsed Catholics began practicing their faith again. They were inspired by this young priest who had a tremendous amount of empathy, understanding, and compassion. His homilies made the Gospel message come alive. Father John was able to explain how these teachings from two thousand years ago were still relevant in today's world. The other characteristic that attracted them to the young priest was that he always made himself available to his parishioners. He gave each person his undivided attention. John made every effort to listen to what the individual was saying and sometimes even to what they were not saying. With this ability, he helped guide them to the right decision.

One of the examples that Father John followed from his father was to spend time after each Sunday mass speaking with the parishioners as they left the church. Sometimes it would be a simple "Have a great week!" or "What did you think of last night's game?" Other times, families wanted to share good news with their pastor—such as a new baby on the way or an engagement. On this particular Sunday, the Andrews family approached Father John. It was Laurie Andrews who smiled at the priest and said that their son, Brian, had an important question for Father John.

Brian was a good-looking eleven-year-old with wavy blond hair and blue eyes. He had two younger sisters who adored their big brother. Father John smiled at Brian, shook his hand, and asked, "So, what can I do for you, Brian?"

The young boy responded enthusiastically, "Well, Father, I really want to become an altar boy! Will you accept me? What do I have to do?"

Father John had anticipated the request because Brian's father, Bob, had mentioned it to him after one of the parish council meetings. So, he was ready with his response. "Brian, that is such great news! I would definitely love to have you as an altar boy!"

John went on to describe the training that was involved and how Brian would be paired with an experienced altar boy for his first few masses. Brian promised the priest that he would work extremely hard—and he kept this commitment. Within no time, he learned every aspect of the altar server's role. Brian became one of the most dependable and dedicated altar boys. Whenever he was scheduled for mass, he would always arrive early to ensure the altar was set up properly. He lit the candles, filled the cruets with water and wine, and still had time to say his prayers. Brian was usually the first to volunteer for Holy Day masses. He was also a reliable server for weddings and funerals. As John observed Brian, it brought back memories of the Donnelly twins as altar boys.

The assistant pastor, Father Jeremy, who had been at Father John's parish for the past three years, had recently been assigned to another church in the suburbs. John had enjoyed working with Father Jeremy, who reminded him of a young Father Jason. He was sorry to lose Jeremy, but he was happy for the younger priest since he was being assigned to the new church as a pastor. John believed that this was a well-deserved promotion and fully supported the transfer.

The new assistant's name was Father Stewart Long. He was in his midfifties and had served at several other parishes throughout the diocese. Father Long was relatively short and slim with dark-brown eyes, a somewhat pale complexion, and a receding hairline. He seemed pleasant but reserved. John wondered why Father Long had never been assigned as a pastor. After listening to a few of his dry homilies and watching his tentative interactions with the parishioners, John concluded that his new assistant lacked the leadership skills necessary to become a successful pastor. Although the relationship was not like the one he had with Father Jeremy (or what Father Pat had with Father Jason), it was cordial and respectful.

Father Long seemed willing to help when asked, but he rarely volunteered on his own. There were two notable exceptions. He offered to take over the training and assigning of the altar boys and also stepped in as the chaplain for the local Boy Scout troop.

Father John was impressed with the newer altar servers, who appeared to be well trained. When he mentioned it to Father Long, he learned that the priest had recruited Brian Andrews to assist in the training of the newer boys. Brian took on this new assignment with the same enthusiasm he had previously shown. John made it a point to thank Brian for his excellent work.

It was a weekday afternoon when Father John remembered he needed to replace the candle in the sanctuary lamp. He had noticed that it was very low after the morning mass. The sanctuary lamp was a reminder that Jesus was present in the tabernacle. Rather than asking Stanley, the church custodian, to take care of it, John chose to do it himself. This was another habit that he learned from Father Pat, who would say to his sons, *Now, boys, never ask anyone to do something that you're not willing to do yourselves. Remember, our Lord even washed the feet of his apostles. So, a little humility is always a good thing!*

The candles were kept in the storage area in the basement of the church. John entered the church and walked down the steps from the vestibule. He unlocked the storage closet and picked up the candle. As he was closing the closet door, he thought he heard someone crying. It seemed to be coming from the opposite side of the basement, where there was another set of stairs leading to the sacristy of the church. As he got closer to these stairs, the cries became even louder. Then he heard someone in a pitiful voice cry, "Oh . . . oh, dear God, please help me . . . help me! I don't know what to do!"

When John arrived at the bottom of the stairs, he was shocked to see Brian Andrews. The boy was sitting halfway up the stairs. His face was buried in his lap, and he was crying uncontrollably. John quickly leaped up the stairs, placed his hand on the boy's shoulder, and asked, "Brian . . . Brian, what is it? What's happened, son? Are you hurt?"

The boy looked up at the priest. He seemed both stunned and frightened. His eyes were filled with tears as he stammered, "I-I can't . . . can't tell you. He said that I couldn't tell you or my parents . . . He said that if I did . . . something really, *really* terrible would happen to you or to them."

Now, John was extremely concerned and confused. He could see that Brian was terribly upset and frightened. He could not imagine what the boy was talking about. Intuitively, John knew that he had to be extremely sensitive and patient in asking the boy questions. So, he sat down next to Brian and handed him a handkerchief. He patted the boy's back and just sat quietly with him for several minutes. Eventually, the boy stopped crying and just stared into space. That's when John decided to speak.

"Brian, I'm not sure what's wrong, but I'm here to help you. Absolutely *nothing* is going to happen to me if you tell me. I heard your prayer to God. You asked him to help you. Well, he listened to you and sent me. His Holy Spirit is with us right now. He is watching over us and protecting us. So, you can talk to me."

Brian turned to the priest and then slowly and painfully revealed everything that had occurred. Father Long had been very friendly toward Brian over the past several months. The priest often praised Brian for how well he served at mass. Eventually, he asked Brian to help train the newer altar servers. Brian fully embraced this opportunity to teach the others. Father Long always seemed completely satisfied with Brian's performance. He would take Brian to lunches as a way of thanking him for his dedicated efforts. This time with the assistant pastor made Brian feel special. Whenever they were together, Father Long was very congenial and seemed to take a sincere interest in Brian. He even began calling the boy his "little buddy."

Father Long had asked Brian to meet him for a training session after school that day. When the boy arrived at the church, he was surprised to see that there were no other altar servers present. When

Brian asked about the others, Father Long explained that this was a special training class for Brian only. The terrified boy described what happened next. John was shocked by what he heard and became viscerally upset. His blood began to boil as he listened to the story of how this innocent child was molested and abused by someone he trusted. John had not felt this much fury since his brother was killed. He forced himself to use every ounce of his self-control so that he would not upset Brian any further.

When Brian finished telling him everything that had transpired, John responded in a quiet and sensitive manner. "Brian, I am so, so sorry for what has happened to you. You didn't do anything wrong . . . but what was done to you was *terribly* wrong. Father Long will be punished for what he did. I promise you that! I am going to call a very close friend of mine who works with the police. Father Long will never hurt you or anyone else ever again!"

Father John took Brian home. Laurie Andrews opened the door, and when she saw the look on her son's face, she immediately knew something was seriously wrong.

"Brian . . . Father John . . . what's wrong? What's happened?"

Brian wrapped his arms around his mother and began sobbing. Bob Andrews ran into the entranceway. He looked at his son and then turned to the priest. "What—"

Before he finished asking his question, John said, "Bob, Laurie, I think it's best if we sit down."

"Let's go into the dining room."

As John sat down, he thought of Father Pat. *Help me through this!* He took a deep breath and began, "Something terrible . . . very terrible has happened to Brian." Then, with as much consideration and sensitivity as he had within him, John described everything to them, starting with the moment he had heard Brian weeping in the stairwell.

As he told them what had happened, he saw their expressions turn from confusion to shock and horror. Brian continued clinging to his mother. Tears were running down Laurie's face as she hugged Brian, kissed his head, and said, "My poor baby."

Bob's eyes became as dark as coal, and his face turned a deep red. He slammed both fists down on the table so hard that the whole room seemed to shake. He bolted up as if he were going to run out. "I'm going to kill that bastard!"

John stood up and grabbed Bob by his arms. "You have every right to feel the way that you do. Honestly, I had the same thought when Brian told me what had happened to him." Looking into Bob's eyes, John continued, "It took every ounce of self-control not to go after Father Long. I realized that was not the answer . . . but this monster will pay for his horrific crime!"

Although still agitated, Bob Andrews had calmed down slightly. He looked at his son, cradled in his wife's arms, and then turned back to John and roared, "You're damn right!"

"As soon as I leave here, I'm going to drive directly to the district attorney's office. My cousin is an assistant district attorney. I know he will take the necessary steps to make sure that Long is brought to justice. Trust me . . . I know he will! Then I will go to the cardinal to tell him about this dreadful crime."

"Are you sure that they'll arrest this animal?"

"Yes . . . yes, definitely!" John thought to himself, *How could they not?*

"And what about your cardinal . . . what do you think he'll do?"

John thought about that question for a moment before answering. "Well, I suspect that he'll be angry and upset. Then he'll take the necessary steps to defrock . . . and excommunicate Long for this horrendous sin."

By this time, Bob had sat back down. John also returned to his chair and looked at Brian with a deep sense of concern. "I believe that it would be a good idea for Brian to see a counselor. If you'd like, I can ask one of the psychologists at the David Schwartz Center to recommend someone."

Laurie Andrews wiped away her tears and, in a voice still filled with emotion, said, "Thank you . . . thank you for all you've done, Father John. Yes, please get us the name of a very good counselor for Brian." Bob reached for his wife's hand and nodded his agreement.

Before he left, John looked directly into Brian's eyes and reassured him, "Brian, remember you did nothing wrong! What Father Long did to you was terrible. It was a horrible sin, and he will have to pay for it. Your parents love you very much. And never forget that God loves you."

John sped to the district attorney's office in a daze. He needed a moment alone, a moment to *think*—but it seemed that as soon as he'd turned the ignition of his car, starting the engine, he'd already arrived.

What was he going to say? How could he say it? A wash of shame bled up into his cheeks, a wave of heat. This had happened under *his watch*.

He went inside, and just as the drive had gone, everything passed in a blur. Stephen listened calmly and neutrally—as one might expect of a lawyer—and responded quickly with an action plan. John wasn't to return to the rectory until they'd gotten Father Long into custody, and after that, their investigators would do the rest.

"You're not to go back there, John," Stephen reiterated firmly, walking John to his car. It was clear to them both that John wanted nothing more than to go back and exchange a few strong words—and God knew what else—with Father Long. "Promise me."

"I've got to go inform the cardinal of what's happened," John replied with gritted teeth, shutting his car door halfway. "And I'll stay with Mom until you've given me the go-ahead."

With that, he started his car and headed in the cardinal's direction.

—∘∘∘❧❦∘∘∘—

John drove to the cardinal's residence. He felt that it was important to bring this horrendous news directly to the top. Cardinal Richard Clark was an extremely powerful figure in the Catholic Church and was well-connected with several American politicians. He had been very close with the previous pope, and many had speculated that Clark would be elected pontiff when the pope died. They were surprised when a lesser-known cardinal from Ireland was selected instead.

John had only met the cardinal once before, and he doubted that Clark would remember him. Upon arriving at the cardinal's residence, John was told that unless he had an appointment, it was highly unlikely that Cardinal Clark would see him. John insisted that he had extremely disturbing information that the cardinal needed to hear directly. He was adamant that he would not speak to anyone except the cardinal. John was told to wait in a small room off the foyer. During that time, John rehearsed exactly what he was going to say. Finally, after nearly an hour, someone came for John and brought him to the cardinal's study.

Cardinal Clark sat behind a large ornate desk. He had a full head of white hair, with not one of the hairs out of place. The cardinal had dark-brown eyes and a tan complexion. His suit jacket looked like it had been custom-made. He had the appearance of one of those actors who was always cast as a senator or president in the movies. The cardinal's initial facial expression appeared to communicate the message, *What are you doing here, and why are you interrupting my evening?* Then, with the skill of a gifted politician, he quickly gave John a warm smile and welcomed him.

"Father Donnelly, welcome to my humble home. It's a pleasure to meet you. I've heard a lot of nice things about you."

John seriously doubted that the cardinal had heard anything about him, but he appreciated the gesture. "Your Eminence, thank you for agreeing to see me on such short notice. I apologize for interrupting your evening plans. I have uncovered something terrible … absolutely horrible that needed to be brought to your attention immediately."

John's well-rehearsed opening statement captured the cardinal's attention, and he asked John to sit down and explain.

John described how he had found young Brian in the stairwell of the church basement. Then he relayed everything that the boy had told him. The cardinal listened with intense interest.

When John finished, Cardinal Clark asked in a condescending tone, "You believe that this boy was telling you the truth? Isn't it possible that he was simply upset at Father Long for something and made up a story?"

John was thoroughly stunned at the cardinal's reaction and could feel his emotions rising. Nevertheless, he maintained his self-control and calmly responded, "No, Your Eminence, I do not think Brian made up the story. There is actually *no way* that a boy his age could possibly be aware of this type of abuse unless he was a victim of it. I saw and felt this boy's emotion when I found him. He was hurting—hurting terribly, both physically and emotionally. No, no … absolutely not! He didn't simply create a story. He was telling the truth … a very painful and hurtful truth!"

The cardinal backed off from his initial comment. "Please don't misinterpret my question, Father Donnelly. We simply need to ensure that we have the facts before we pursue an investigation and falsely accuse one of our priests. Of course, we will look into it and then take appropriate measures."

John informed the cardinal that he had already gotten the authorities involved and that an investigation was underway. The moment Cardinal Clark learned that John had already involved the district attorney's office, his demeanor completely changed. His face turned beet red, and he raised his voice. "Who gave you the authority to go to the police, young man? You had absolutely no business doing that! We take care of our own! We protect our own!"

At this point, given everything that had occurred that day—and now hearing Cardinal Clark's protest—John was no longer able to control himself. His voice rose, riding the tidal wave of his emotions, as he shouted, "That's *exactly* what I was doing—protecting our own! He's a child! An innocent child—and he has been terribly abused. A crime has been committed, and when a crime is committed, the police need to be involved. We can't cover this up!"

All decorum vanished as the cardinal sprung from his chair and yelled at John, "Do you have any idea to whom you are speaking? Why, you insubordinate little twit . . . Get out! Get out of here immediately! *Immediately!*"

John was in total disbelief and consternation as he drove the short distance to his mother's home. He'd never imagined that type of reaction. Why had the cardinal responded in such a manner? Had he mishandled the situation?

It was nearly ten o'clock when John arrived. Veronica opened the door and saw the distraught look on her son's face. John was so upset that he could barely eat the meal she had saved for him. Christopher poured scotch for all three of them. John began to share the disturbing events that had taken place that day. Veronica seemed aghast as she listened and expressed that she found it so difficult to fathom how a priesthood that consisted of such outstanding individuals like Father Pat and her son could also include such monsters as this Father Long.

It was nearly midnight when Stephen knocked on the door. He apologized for arriving so late but explained that he wanted to communicate the news personally. Stephen had a grim look on his face as he said, "John, the good news is that Father Long confessed. The bad news is that it's much worse than any of us could have imagined."

All three of them were stunned by Stephen's statement.

John cleared his throat and asked, "What could possibly be worse than the molestation of an innocent child?"

"He not only confessed to sexually abusing the Andrews' boy but also nearly twenty other victims throughout his priesthood. He provided us with names, dates, and parishes. It appears that the archdiocese had been warned about his behavior but chose to ignore it. Instead, they transferred him from parish to parish."

Now John understood the angry reaction from Cardinal Clark. He remembered that the cardinal had exploded when John had mentioned a cover-up. Then, Stephen dropped another bombshell. "Based on our interrogation of Long, we believe that the archdiocese has done this with other priests over the years. The DA has authorized a full-blown investigation."

John was sickened by what he heard. How could it be that church leaders, that men of God, would simply *move* suspected sex offenders from parish to parish? He and his fellow priests would all be tainted from now on, it seemed—and it was clear that his actions that evening would create a massive explosion within the Catholic Church. Another fear struck him in the chest—might he face punishment for igniting this eruption? Then he remembered the wise counsel of Father Pat when he learned about James's work with the FBI. The old priest had said, *Maybe... as bad as this all seems... God has a plan for you. These are clearly evil people. They do terrible things. It's possible that God is using you to put an end to this evil.* These words from his father resonated as much now as they had then and gave the young priest comfort and strength.

The investigation was expanded over the next several weeks. There was an extensive pattern of sexual abuse and cover-ups throughout the diocese. The media jumped on this breaking news. In addition to criminal prosecution, lawyers for the alleged victims began civil lawsuits. Cardinal Clark defended his actions. He claimed that he had relied on the advice of mental health professionals. His words fell flat, and he quickly went from being a powerful, well-connected leader to someone who was despised and shunned. The pope summoned Clark to Rome and asked for his resignation as both archbishop and cardinal.

# 44

## The Baptist

**Father John Donnelly**
**Rome | 2002**

JOHN RECEIVED A call from the Vatican a few weeks after Cardinal Clark's dismissal. He was instructed to be in Rome on the following Friday morning. Would he be asked to resign due to the firestorm he'd ignited? He arrived at the Vatican promptly at eight o'clock. He had expected to be meeting with a bishop from the Curia, the church's central bureaucracy. Consequently, it came as a surprise when he was led to the pope's private apartment in the Apostolic Palace.

They walked past a ceremonial hall where six Swiss Guards stood at attention. He followed his escort down a long marble corridor with richly decorated arches. John had never seen anything as ornate in his entire life. Then they entered the apartment. The priest who escorted John to the apartment introduced him to the pope.

"Your Holiness Pope Daniel and Your Eminence Cardinal Peter Longo, may I introduce Reverend John Donnelly."

Pope Daniel was in his late fifties. He was over six feet tall and ruggedly built. He had a full head of curly red hair with just a touch of gray. He wore a white cassock, a cape across his broad shoulders, and a white sash around his waist. The zucchetto, or skullcap, seemed lost in his mound of hair. A pectoral cross hung around his neck. Standing next to the pontiff was a cardinal John did not recognize. The cardinal wore a red cassock, and his appearance was a distinct contrast to the pope's. He was thin and nearly a foot shorter than the pope. He was bald and wore horn-rimmed glasses.

John could feel his heart beating at a rapid pace. He attempted to overcome his surprise and awe as he knelt down, kissed the fisherman's ring on the pope's finger, and addressed him as "Your Holiness." John then turned to the cardinal and greeted him as "Your Eminence."

The pope smiled at John and thanked him for traveling to Rome. He then pointed to a beautifully upholstered chair with lustrous white satin fabric and golden arms and legs. There was also a large matching couch and an elaborately carved mahogany coffee table. John waited until the pope and cardinal sat before he took his seat. Beverages had been set on the coffee table, and the pontiff offered John Italian coffee. The pope explained that being Irish, he had grown up drinking tea all of his life, but that changed when he came to Rome to study for his doctorate. He said he got hooked on espresso and never drank tea again.

The pope poured coffee for all three of them and then asked, "Donnelly is an Irish name. From which part of Ireland did your ancestors emigrate?" John smiled and said, "The Italian and German sections." When he saw the puzzled look on the pontiff's face, John explained, "My brother and I were adopted by an Irish priest—Patrick Donnelly—but our biological parents were of Italian and German heritage."

The pope placed his hands under his chin and leaned forward in his chair. "Adopted by a priest? Please . . . please tell me what it was like being raised by him."

John became more comfortable as he described life with Father Pat. It was as if the calming spirit of his father was there with him now. After listening to John's story, the pontiff smiled and said, "Father Pat was a remarkable individual. You were truly blessed to have him in your life. Actually, he reminds me a lot of the priest who influenced my life—Father Daniel Kelly. I had a wild spirit when I was younger and made some bad choices, but Father Daniel saw something in this pub owner's son and guided me in a far better direction. I've never forgotten that wonderful man. In fact, that is why I chose the name *Daniel* when I became pope."

The pope's story brought back memories for John. *Wild spirit . . . bad choices . . . sounds familiar.*

He went on to tell the pontiff about reuniting with his mother and the strong relationship he had developed with her and his newfound family. John felt a pang of sorrow when the pope asked about his brother. Even after all these years, John still felt a huge lump in his throat when he described the circumstances of his brother's tragic death.

When John finished talking about his personal life, Cardinal Longo asked him about his assignments since being ordained as a priest. John's enthusiasm and passion became evident as he described his work as a diocesan priest. He also talked glowingly about his volunteer work at the rehabilitation center that was established in honor of David. As John spoke, he wondered where the conversation was headed. He had come to Rome fully expecting to be removed from the priesthood. Now he was having an extremely pleasant meeting with the pope and sharing his life story.

Next, the pope changed the topic to Brian Andrews. The pontiff wanted to hear everything and asked several probing questions. There was a distinct change in the pope's demeanor and in the intensity of his questions. The cardinal also had several inquiries related to the incident, as well as John's explosive meeting with Cardinal Clark. John thoroughly described every detail and responded to each of their questions with complete candor.

When John finished, the pope's disposition became relaxed again. He then asked John another personal question. "How did Father Pat arrive at the names for you and your brother?"

John smiled and recounted the story that he'd heard from his beloved father.

The pope looked amused and said, "So, you were named after John, the beloved apostle."

John nodded.

Then, Pope Daniel shook his head and exclaimed, "Well, it sounds like Father Pat was an outstanding priest and father, but I'm afraid he got the source of your name wrong. I don't think you are like the apostle John. No, I believe you are more like John the Baptist!"

John's brow furrowed. Was he missing something? *John the Baptist?*

"John the Baptist was 'a voice crying out in the desert.' When he saw a terrible sin, he was not afraid to call it out, no matter whom he upset," the pope said, and John's heart steadied in his chest. This seemed to be a favorable comparison. "You also uncovered a terrible sin and were not concerned about whom you upset. You certainly angered quite a few people in authority, especially Cardinal Clark!"

The pontiff glanced at Cardinal Longo, who nodded. It appeared that the cardinal was doing more than agreeing with Pope Daniel's opinion about John's similarity to John the Baptist. There seemed to be a deeper understanding between the two men. Then, the pope continued, "It sounds like you thoroughly enjoy shepherding your parishioners."

John smiled in agreement.

"I am afraid," the pope added, his tone shifting, "that your parishioners are going to miss you as their pastor."

It was as though his legs had just been cut off from underneath him.

He'd suspected that he'd be forced to resign from the priesthood, but to have it actually take place, to be discharged by the pope himself… He immediately felt a combination of emotions that ranged from complete helplessness and sorrow to frustration and anger.

Pope Daniel seemed to notice the reaction on John's face and quickly clarified, "Father Donnelly, I can see that I was not very clear and have caused you some distress. I am very sorry for that. Let me explain. The reason that your parishioners will miss you is because I want you to take on an important assignment."

Now John was completely confused. He could not imagine what the pope meant.

"You discovered a horrible sin. It should have never been tolerated or covered up! The investigation that you instigated has enlightened us about the widespread nature of this abuse throughout the Boston diocese. I am not naive enough to believe that this cancer only existed in one diocese, and I am very concerned that it has metastasized to other areas of your country. In fact, I believe that it may be present in other countries as well."

John could feel the emotional energy and passion in the pope's voice.

"I asked you earlier how you were given your name. My given name is Michael. My parents named me after Michael the archangel. He was the leader of God's army who defeated Satan and the forces of evil. The devil has now entered our church. Unless we expose him and destroy him, we will lose the moral authority to lead God's people!"

The pope stopped for a moment, pointed to Cardinal Longo, and added, "I mentioned to you that when I was studying in Rome, I became addicted to espresso. I also met Peter during this time. I was impressed by the scrawny priest from Pittsburgh. We became fast friends and have remained close ever since. There is no one I respect or trust more than Peter. That is why I have asked him to leave Pittsburgh and relocate to Boston. He will become my commanding general as we pursue this battle against Satan. And you, Father Donnelly, will be his top lieutenant. You were probably wondering why we put you through this inquisition. Well, it was what you might call a job interview, and you passed with flying colors. Peter will become the archbishop of Boston—and *you* will be named his auxiliary bishop."

# 45

# The Battle

Father John Donnelly
Boston | 2002-2006

THE NEXT FOUR years of Bishop John Donnelly's life were entirely devoted to battling the cancer of sexual abuse within the Catholic Church. He worked closely with the public authorities to identify and investigate all allegations as they aggressively pursued each situation to ensure that it was addressed in a timely and effective manner. Given his personal experience with Brian Andrews, John was always extremely sensitive and empathetic to each of the victims. In addition to prosecution and civil suits, the guilty priests were defrocked and required to spend the rest of their lives in prayer and penance for their sins. Any religious leader who ignored or covered up these crimes was forced to resign.

The civil suits brought against the Boston diocese amounted to nearly one hundred million dollars. Liability insurance was insufficient to cover all of these payments. Therefore, John was forced to close and consolidate numerous churches so that property could be sold and proceeds from these sales could be used to pay the remaining liabilities. As a former pastor and the adopted son of a pastor, he found the closing of parishes particularly painful. However, he had no remorse when he sold Cardinal Clark's lavish mansion.

John collaborated with many individuals, including victims groups, public authorities, attorneys, mental health professionals, and clergy, to develop strict policies and procedures that would prevent this type of atrocity in the future. He spent considerable time working with the rector at the seminary to develop more thorough evaluation tools for applicants to the priesthood. Working with Cardinal Longo, John succeeded in updating the penal code of the Catholic Church so that sexual abuse of a minor by any member of the clergy would now be classified as a crime.

John's efforts were not restricted to the Boston diocese. He and the cardinal worked closely with other church leaders throughout the country. Pope Daniel had been correct in his suspicion that the cancer had metastasized. This required extensive travel within the states. Additionally, Cardinal Longo and Bishop Donnelly made periodic trips back to Rome to apprise the pontiff of their work. These two leaders made every effort to communicate regularly with the press. They wanted to be completely transparent in the hopes of regaining the public's trust.

John hadn't seen Veronica in over two months. He was finally able to break away for a few hours to have a quiet dinner with her and Christopher. When his mother opened the door, he saw the stunned look on her face and then heard the alarm in her voice.

"John, you look . . . terrible! Aren't you eating? You're nothing but skin and bones! How much sleep are you getting? Those circles under your eyes are as dark as coal!"

He hugged her and attempted to brush aside her concern. "Well, it's nice to see you, too, lovely lady."

"Hey . . . I'm very worried about your health! You've got to take better care of yourself!"

"I know . . . I know! You're absolutely right. It's been a tremendous grind—the late hours and all of the travel. I have to admit, there are days that I'm physically and emotionally drained. What helps me to continue this battle is the knowledge that we are destroying this cancer in the church."

"I am so proud of you, and I know in my heart that your two fathers are looking down with enormous pride at your relentless efforts in putting an end to this evil."

John smiled at his mother, remembering that Father Pat had used these same words on a different occasion.

"But, John, you are not going to be of any use to those victims if you get yourself sick!"

"I promise that I will take better care of myself."

Eventually, John was able to slow his pace and take his mother's advice regarding his personal health and well-being.

## 2006–2010

Cardinal Longo observed how his auxiliary bishop was transforming into an accomplished and highly respected leader. On several occasions, he let the pope know that they had chosen the right person for this challenging assignment. As the years passed, John became involved in various other endeavors for the cardinal. He enthusiastically handled each of these engagements in a skilled manner. He viewed each new project as an opportunity for growth and development. It was obvious to many observers that Bishop John Donnelly was being groomed for a more expansive role.

That bigger role came nearly eight years after finding Brian in the stairwell of the church. It happened during one of their trips back to Rome. Although they usually traveled together, Cardinal Longo left Boston a few days before John. When John arrived at the Vatican, he was escorted to the pope's private apartment. As he walked down the ornate corridor of the Apostolic Palace, he recalled his first visit here. *It certainly feels much more comfortable now than it did back then. What a whirlwind it has been!*

Upon entering the pope's apartment, he was warmly greeted by Pope Daniel.

"Ah, the Baptist has arrived!"

John, who had gotten used to the pontiff's affectionate nickname for him, smiled. "Your Holiness. It's a pleasure to see you again."

As if he had read John's earlier thoughts, the pope responded, "Much more pleasurable than your first visit here, I'm sure! Please sit down and join us for some freshly brewed espresso."

Cardinal Longo greeted his protégé. "I trust that you had a good trip?"

"Yes, no problem, Your Eminence."

"The cardinal has been singing your praises—not only were you highly effective in addressing the sexual abuse scandal, but you have successfully handled some other challenging assignments. I call the two of you my dynamic duo!" The pontiff took a sip of his espresso before continuing. "Unfortunately, I am going to break up this team."

John felt his muscles stiffen as he turned to Cardinal Longo. *What does the pope mean?*

It was obvious from the expression on John's face that he was blind-sided. The cardinal simply nodded to Pope Daniel.

"I can see that you are surprised. Please, relax. You see, I have another disaster on my hands. The Vatican Bank has been mismanaged for years. My predecessors and I have tried to patch it here and there, but these piecemeal efforts have not been enough. The bank needs a complete housecleaning. It's full of corruption. I want it cleaned up once and for all! And I want Peter to take it over."

"As you can see, John, His Holiness gives me all of the easy jobs. I will certainly miss working with you. In fact, I even tried negotiating with him to have you join me in Rome, but he has other plans. And I must confess . . . better plans."

*Better plans? What better plans?* John wondered as he turned to Pope Daniel.

"I've decided that the most capable person to replace Cardinal Longo in Boston is the bishop who has proven himself so indispensable in battling the cancer in the church. So . . . Bishop Donnelly, you are to become the archbishop of the Boston diocese. Congratulations!"

"I . . . I don't know what to say. I am so . . . humbled . . . so gratified . . . thank you . . . thank you!"

# PART SIX

# GOD'S PLAN

*Everything Happens for a Reason*

# 46

## Diana

**Archbishop John Donnelly**
**Boston | 2016**

ARCHBISHOP DONNELLY MADE regular visits to the David Schwartz Rehabilitation Center. He had promised Veronica that he would offer his time and talent to this drug and alcohol rehabilitation program many years ago. Even now, with all of his other responsibilities, he still kept his promise. In addition to meeting with the director and her senior staff, he would take considerable time speaking to the clients and the frontline workers. His ability to listen with empathy and share comforting words with each person was abundantly powerful and greatly appreciated.

Naturally, everyone was pleased that their archbishop would soon become their cardinal. Each person with whom he spoke enthusiastically congratulated him. Upon leaving a client's room, he nearly bumped into Diana Wyman, a young clinical psychologist.

"Oh, I'm so sorry, Your Excellency."

The archbishop smiled. "Diana! It's so good to see you." He still found it amazing how much she resembled her mother, with long blonde hair, large hazel eyes, and high cheekbones.

"Congratulations on your elevation to cardinal. My parents are looking forward to attending the consistory in Rome."

At that moment, the archbishop recalled a meeting that he'd had with her mother nearly twelve years ago. Looking at how far Diana had come, he thought, *God has a reason for everything that happens—both the good and the bad. That certainly applies to me as well!*

# 47

# Addiction

**Auxiliary Bishop John Donnelly**
**Boston | 2004**

BISHOP JOHN DONNELLY was still intensely focused on the church's sex scandal, but the pace had slowed to a more manageable, less exhausting level. He was working in his office when his assistant announced that he had a visitor. With a somewhat confused look on her face, she said, "The visitor said to tell Bishop Falstaff that the Belle of Amherst had arrived."

John laughed out loud, recalling how they had given each other those nicknames so many years before. When Danielle walked into his office, they hugged each other with the warmth of close friends. Due to his travel schedule, it had been over a year since they had seen each other—but she was still as attractive now as she had been the first time John met her during that memorable hike in the Berkshires. He smiled as he recalled the creek he'd tripped into, the light sound of her casual laughter, and the way she'd captivated him immediately.

After some pleasantries, Danielle began to fidget with her hands, which John had learned meant she was about to speak about something serious. He reached forward, holding her hands to keep them still, and looked her in the eyes. "What troubles the Belle of Amherst?"

Danielle smiled slightly, but there were tears in her eyes. "I've got a couple of heavy things to talk to you about, John." He directed her to the nearest sofa and offered to pour her a glass of sherry—which she declined. "Thank you for offering, John . . . but my family has struggled with that substance for too long. Feel free to pour yourself one, though. After what I've got to say, you might need it . . . or something even stronger."

John raised his brows. "What is it, Danielle?"

"John, I have heard amazing things about the David Schwartz Rehabilitation Center. You and your mother must be extremely proud and gratified."

Danielle and John had spoken about the center shortly after it opened. "We are."

"John, I'm not sure how else to say this, so I'm just going to come out with it," she said, the words coming out in a whoosh of breath. Her hazel eyes widened, tear filled, as she whispered what seemed to be a confession. "I looked into my uncle Charlie's manslaughter case. I honestly don't even know what prompted me to; I just felt—"

"Called to," John said, knowing God worked in mysterious ways.

"Called to," she agreed, nodding. "John . . . It was my uncle Charlie who killed your father all those years ago. He was the drunk driver."

John merely stared back at Danielle. Yes, he was shocked—but he'd also never known his father and thus, in a way, couldn't fathom the gravity of his loss. "Danielle," he went on, moving to sit beside her on the couch, "if there's one thing God has taught me, it's that everything in life happens for a reason. Who am I to argue with his ways?"

"I need you to forgive me, John," Danielle said a little harshly. "I know it's easy to give it all to God, but I need *you*—"

"Of course, I forgive you. And I also forgive your uncle Charlie." He waved a hand in the general direction of the David Schwartz Rehabilitation Center. "That's why my mother and I chose to create our rehabilitation center—not because we condemn those who are struggling but because we forgive and understand their struggle."

Danielle blinked back at him, tears shaking free from her lashes. "If that's true, John, then there's one more favor my family must ask of yours," she said, reaching forward to rest her hand over his. He held it, nodding. "I need your help in having someone enter the rehabilitation program at the center."

"Russ?" he asked, perhaps too preemptively.

"No, it's not Russ. He kept his promise to me and hasn't had a drink since we reunited. We have a wonderful . . . amazing life together," she confirmed, tears welling up in her eyes all over again now. "This is about my daughter."

John nodded subtly, maintaining a neutral expression. "How can I help?"

"Diana always loved school. She seemed to excel in every subject and always achieved the highest grades. She was also a tremendous athlete. With her intensity and natural skill, she mastered every sport that she attempted. She was truly a scholar athlete. And to top it all off, she was always extremely positive and outgoing. We were so very proud of her."

John had met Diana several times over the years. Why was Danielle describing her daughter in the past tense?

"Russ took us skiing in Colorado about a year ago. Diana was having a wonderful time as she skillfully took on the most challenging slopes. Then, on the afternoon of our last day at the resort, she had a terrible accident. She struck a large rock, lost control, and slammed directly into a tree. She sustained compound fractures in both her legs and arms, along with multiple broken bones throughout her entire body. She spent several weeks in a Denver hospital and was in constant pain. The doctors prescribed strong doses of codeine to alleviate the pain."

"Danielle, I'm so sorry," he interjected. "Is she all right?"

"She's recovered from the accident, yes," Danielle replied, and he couldn't help but notice that there was a strategy behind those carefully chosen words. "Twelve months later, my daughter's body is healed, but she isn't the same person. She has lost interest in both college and sports. She skips classes, and her grades have suffered. She quit her sports teams. She has become completely introverted and highly temperamental . . ." She threw up her hands, shaking her head. "It became clear to Russ and me that Diana had become addicted to the pain medication. We thought we could handle it ourselves with unconditional love, patience, and understanding, but she just keeps getting worse. She has broken into locked medicine cabinets and stolen cash and jewelry from us to purchase drugs and alcohol. The final straw was when we couldn't find her for three days. Eventually, the police discovered her sleeping on a street corner several towns away. She was severely hungover and completely disoriented. That is when Russ and I came to the realization that we were incapable of doing it on our own. Diana needs dedicated professional help. It was actually Russ who suggested your center. So that's why I'm here today. I'm asking you to accept her as a patient so that we can get our bright, shining daughter back. Please, help me, John!"

"Of course," John said, immediately standing to get started on the paperwork. "Is she ready to accept treatment, though? You know as well as I do that it's important to make sure they're ready to receive help, that they're committed to recovery."

"She's ready," Danielle confirmed. "Thank God!"

"Then we'll get the process started and admit her as soon as possible," John said, turning once again to face his Belle of Amherst. "If you and Russ need anything—"

"Thank you, John," she interjected. With that, she stood up from the couch, wrapped her arms around his shoulders, and whispered, "I don't know what I did to deserve you, but I'll be forever grateful to God that you tripped into that creek one October afternoon—and that I didn't hold back on making fun of you for it."

He smiled. "Me too."

Diana was one of the center's most challenging clients. Despite agreeing to her treatment, she was terribly argumentative and combative—but the staff members at the center were not intimidated by her behavior. They responded with skill and professionalism while being firm and compassionate. After several months, the persistence of the staff was rewarded. Diana responded in a positive way and eventually became one of their greatest success stories.

So grateful was she to the psychologists who had worked with her that she decided to dedicate herself to others who were dealing with addiction.

Now, Diana was a talented and dedicated psychologist at the center. Her personal experience combined with her excellent education gave her the ability to treat each client with knowledgeable understanding and compassionate expertise.

# 48

## Gabriel

**Archbishop Bishop John Donnelly**
**Boston | 2016**

ONE WEEK BEFORE departing to Rome, the archbishop visited the parish where he had served as a deacon prior to his ordination as a priest. Father Al had passed away several years before but was still fondly remembered by many of the older parishioners. Saint Mary's Church had expanded through consolidations and now served a diverse community. Naturally, John had a genuine desire to return to his first church, but the underlying catalyst was to see the youth minister—Gabriel Lopez.

The archbishop saw the young man's face light up as soon as Father Mark—the pastor of Saint Mary's—escorted him to Gabriel's office.

"Your Excellency! It's so good to see you. Congratulations! We are all so happy for you!

John gave Gabriel a warm hug. "It's good seeing you, too!" Then, stepping back, with his arms still on the young man's shoulders, he said, "You look great! I trust that Father Mark is treating you well?"

Turning to the pastor, he smiled and replied, "Oh yes! I couldn't ask for a better boss. And I'm loving this job. I believe that we are really making a difference . . . especially with the high school students."

"That's excellent! They are the future of our church. It's so important that we keep our teenagers fully engaged in their faith."

"And I am taking your advice about not rushing into the seminary right after college."

John smiled, remembering the guidance from Father Pat and Father Jason. "That's right! Live in the real world for a while before making any permanent decision about the priesthood. God clearly has a plan for you, and he will let you know what it is; you just have to listen."

"I know that, and Father Mark has reinforced that message."

"My visit to Saint Mary's was precipitated by a congratulatory card from your mother. It sounds like she and Sebastian are doing well. I can't believe that your two brothers are in college and your sister is a junior in high school."

"Yeah, they're doing great."

The expression on the young man's face changed, and tears began to form in his eyes.

"What is it, Gabriel? What's wrong, son?"

"I . . . I just want you to know how grateful I will always be to you! The words *thank you* don't seem adequate! If it wasn't for your kindness, your compassion, and your lack of judgment toward my mom . . . I might not even be here!"

The archbishop embraced Gabriel in his arms again as he remembered a phone call over twenty years ago.

# 49

## Isabella

**Father John Donnelly**
**Boston | 1994**

SHORTLY AFTER HIS reunion with Veronica, John received a phone call. He had just finished the morning mass and was having a light breakfast in the rectory's kitchen when the phone rang.

"Hello, may I help you?"

"Hello, Father Donnelly?"

"Yes, this is Father Donnelly. How can I help you?"

"Father, this is Michelle Connors from Birthright."

Michelle was the director of the local Birthright Center. Birthright was started in Canada during the late 1960s. Several centers had been founded throughout the United States since then. The philosophy of Birthright was that any pregnant girl or woman had the right to whatever help she may need to carry her child to full-term.

"Hello, Michelle. How are you doing? And please, call me Father John."

The young priest had met her a few weeks before and shared his personal story about being raised by a parish priest and recently reuniting with his biological mother.

"Well, Father John, you told me that you valued the work we do and offered to assist us whenever we might need you. I'm calling to take you up on your offer."

"Of course! What can I do for you?"

"There is a young woman—Isabella. She is only eighteen years old, and she is struggling with an unplanned pregnancy. She is distraught, scared, and confused. Her parents have disowned her, telling her that she is nothing but a whore and that she has disgraced their family. She has considered getting an abortion and even contemplated suicide. After much encouragement, a friend convinced her to speak to someone at Birthright. I happened to be the person on call that evening. She shared her whole story with me. She was in love with her childhood sweetheart—Gabriel. They planned on marrying as soon as he returned from serving in the army. They were overcome with emotion and were careless the night before he shipped off. He was killed in a training exercise less than a month later. Isabella was devastated by losing the love of her life. A few weeks after the funeral, she realized she was pregnant."

John closed his eyes and exhaled slowly before saying, "That sounds awfully familiar."

"I thought you'd understand. My intuition tells me that she is open to adoption. I really think she would benefit from meeting with you . . . given your personal experience."

"Yes . . . yes! Tell me where and when. I'll help in any way I can."

"I've got to warn you, she was hesitant about meeting with a priest. She was raised in a very strict Catholic household and is afraid you will condemn her for her 'sinful ways.' I assured her that you were not like that. She finally agreed, but she is still very anxious."

"I completely understand her apprehension. You know what . . . I'll dress in my casual clothes when I meet with her. Facing someone with a priest's collar and a dark suit can be intimidating."

"Thank you, Father John. I knew I could count on you."

John arrived at the meeting wearing a polo shirt and blue jeans. He greeted Isabella with a smile and a warm handshake. Rather than sitting behind a desk, he pulled up a chair and sat next to her. The young woman shared her story with John. He listened with empathy, remembering everything that Veronica had shared with him.

When she had finished, Father John said, "Isabella, God loves you no matter what has happened! You've been through a lot, and you are feeling many different emotions. That's completely understandable and normal. Would you mind if I shared a story about another young woman who was in a similar situation?"

Isabella readily agreed to listen to the story. John proceeded to tell her about Veronica and the babies that she left at Father Pat's doorstep. He described how the two brothers were raised with an abundance of love and support. John shared that Veronica never stopped loving her sons and that, eventually, they met and began a wonderful relationship. Then he surprised Isabella by telling her that he was one of those sons. He went on to explain, "We were thoroughly grateful that my mother didn't choose to end her pregnancy. Thanks to Father Pat's wise counsel, we understood that something terrible had caused her to give us up. We forgave her long before being reunited."

John paused for a few moments to let Isabella reflect on what he had just shared with her. Then he asked, "What do you truly want to do?"

"In my heart . . . I want to keep my baby! This child was conceived in love . . . and by keeping him or her, I will be keeping a part of Gabriel in my life." She shook her head while taking a deep breath and then continued, "But I can't provide for this child. I have nowhere to live . . . no job . . . no support at all!"

John thought he had a possible solution for this young woman, so he asked, "Isabella, would you be interested in a place that could provide a home for you and your child?"

"Yes . . . yes, absolutely!"

"A wealthy couple felt abundantly blessed that God had given them six healthy children for whom they were able to provide a wonderful home. They realized that it was extremely difficult for unwed, young mothers to do the same. They understood that was the reason why so many young women decided to end their pregnancies. So, they established a center with the objective of providing a meaningful alternative to abortion."

She interrupted him and, in an excited tone, asked, "You mean that there would be a place for my baby and me to live?"

"Yes! You and your baby would have a place to live for the next three to four years. You would have a private room, and both of you would be provided with nutritious meals and proper medical care. You would also have an opportunity to learn a skill or take college courses. In return, you would be expected to share in the household chores and abide by the rules of the center."

John could see that a tremendous weight had been lifted from the young woman's shoulders. He decided that now was the opportune time to share something else with her. He smiled and said, "There is one other thing, Isabella. The center was named after the angel who announced to Mary that she would give birth to Jesus. That angel's name was . . . Gabriel!"

Isabella's eyes filled with tears, and she hugged Father John.

He made arrangements with the director of Gabriel's House, and a few days later, he drove Isabella there.

She gave birth to a healthy baby boy six months later and named him after his father, Gabriel. Father John visited on a regular basis and thoroughly enjoyed spending time with little Gabriel as he grew up. He would jokingly tell the boy that this huge house was named after him. Being with Gabriel reminded John of the wonderful time he and his brother had spent growing up with Father Pat.

Isabella earned an associate's degree over the next four years. One of Father John's parishioners was a senior vice president at a large corporation. John reached out to this parishioner and arranged an interview for Isabella at his company. She was hired as a customer service representative. This enabled her and Gabriel to move into their own apartment. Isabella excelled at her work and was promoted within a few years. Her manager was completely impressed and encouraged her to obtain a bachelor's degree. She followed his advice and continued to progress at the company.

During this time, Isabella also met a wonderful man, Sebastian Lopez. He fell in love with her and with her son. They asked Father John to marry them. After the marriage, Sebastian formally adopted Gabriel. The couple had three more children, each of whom John baptized. When Gabriel was considering the priesthood, he spoke to his mentor and friend, Archbishop Donnelly. Recalling Father Jason's advice, John suggested that Gabriel work for a few years in the real world before making a decision about the seminary.

## PART SEVEN

# TRANSFORMATION

# 50

# The Special Guest

**Archbishop John Donnelly**
**Holy Cross Rectory | October 2016**

IT WAS LATE afternoon on the day before the archbishop's flight to Rome. Veronica, along with the other family members, had departed a few days earlier so that they could do some sightseeing prior to the ceremony. In addition to Paul and his wife, there was a special guest who would be flying with the archbishop. Paul was bringing this individual to the archbishop's residence, and John was looking forward to seeing his old friend. The guest's favorite meal—steak and mashed potatoes—was being prepared, and the archbishop planned on opening the scotch he had received from Brian.

Archbishop Donnelly watched as his guest exited the car. Although his hair was completely white and he was slightly stooped over, he still projected a towering presence. John bolted down the steps and warmly greeted Monsignor Mike. The older man raised an eyebrow, grinned, and said, "So . . . you think you're good enough to be a cardinal, huh? Well, so do I! And it's about time that Irishman did it. It's long overdue!"

Throughout dinner, the monsignor had John laughing as he shared stories from his retirement home. One that the archbishop considered particularly hilarious was a tale about the widows flirting with Monsignor Mike.

"You wouldn't believe it, John. I've got all of these old ladies coming on to me. There's one in particular—Mary O'Rourke—she won't let up! So, finally, I said to her, 'For the love of God, Mary, I'm a priest!' And at that, she turns around and says, 'Yes, Michael, but you're retired. So, it's okay for you to fool around now!'"

They moved to the living room after finishing dinner, and the archbishop poured a glass of scotch for each of them. The monsignor became uncharacteristically quiet and gazed at his glass with a slight smile on his face. John could tell that he was thinking about something. After a few more moments of reflection, the older man shared his thoughts.

"I was just remembering the night before your ordination to the priesthood. We shared some very good scotch whisky then, too."

John smiled as he recalled what transpired that evening. It had resulted in an unshakable bond between the two men.

# 51

## The Choice

John Donnelly
Saint John's Seminary | 1991

MONSIGNOR MIKE POURED the scotch that he had brought to the seminarian's room. They reminisced about the young man's six years at the seminary. By the time they began their second glass of scotch, the monsignor looked intently at the young man and declared, "Your brother, John, would be very proud of the person you've become!"

The seminarian was slightly puzzled and teasingly responded, "You must have had too much scotch, old man! You mean my brother, *James*, would be proud."

The monsignor leaned forward, looked directly into the young man's eyes, and stated with conviction, "I know exactly what I said!"

At that very moment, John realized what the monsignor was telling him. He put down his glass of whisky and somberly asked, "When . . . when did you realize that I wasn't John?"

The monsignor explained, "I began to suspect it shortly after you returned to the seminary. I noticed the distinct difference in your personality. There was a certain amount of rage right under the surface . . . sometimes, even *above* the surface. You struggled with most of the basic material that we had covered during the first few weeks of class. It was the night that you exploded and were ready to kick the crap out of me. Then, you suddenly broke down in my arms. That's when I was certain that the young man in front of me was not John Donnelly."

"Why . . . why did you continue to support me?"

After a brief silence, the monsignor said, "Saint Paul has always been one of my favorites. He was an intense young man who supported the death of our first Christian martyr, Saint Stephen. He went on a murderous rampage, persecuting the early Christians. Then one day, as he was on his way to Damascus, a traumatic event changed him forever."

Monsignor Mike quoted from the Acts of the Apostles. "'The Lord said that I have chosen him to be an instrument of mine to carry my name before the Gentiles, Kings and Israelites.'"

The monsignor was quiet for a few moments before adding, "You are also a very intense young man. You experienced your Damascus when John was killed instead of you. God has a purpose for you! And just as Ananias helped Saul to become Paul, I knew in my heart that I could help James . . . become John. And I know that with your intelligence, drive, and intensity, you will be an outstanding priest and a powerful leader!"

James just looked at the monsignor for a long time. Then tears welled up in his eyes as he shared what happened on that fateful day. "I planned a wonderful weekend with Johnny in the Berkshires. I knew it would be the last time that we would ever see each other. The night before the shooting, he described the seminary and how much he thoroughly enjoyed it. He even talked about this monsignor who was like a tough drill sergeant but had a heart of gold."

James stopped and smiled at Monsignor Mike before continuing. "Johnny literally glowed as he spoke about the seminary. He would have been an outstanding priest! Eventually, he asked me what I planned on doing with my new life. I had already decided to become a lawyer, but I teasingly told him that I was going to become a priest, too. After he stopped laughing, he asked me what I was *really* going to do. That's when I shared that I intended to get a law degree. Johnny thought it was a wonderful idea and told me how proud he was of me."

James poured each of them another glass of scotch before going on. "Johnny got up before me the next morning. The smell of freshly brewed coffee eventually woke me up, and as I was getting out of the sleeping bag, I noticed John's cassock hanging in the tent. As a gag, I put it on and strolled out of the tent. He burst out laughing as soon as he saw me. I told him that I had reconsidered and had decided on the seminary over law school. He practically choked on his coffee. He handed a cup to me and warned me not to spill anything on his brand-new cassock. Johnny cooked a breakfast of scrambled eggs and sausage for us. We planned on doing some hiking right afterward. As we were clearing the plates, I heard the FBI agent's voice on the two-way radio and bent down to answer it."

James became silent as tears ran down his face. The monsignor placed his hand on James's shoulder and, in an unspoken way, gave him the support he needed to regain his composure.

"That's when the shots rang out. There were three of them. When I looked up, Johnny was clutching his chest, and then he collapsed onto the ground. I went to him and held him in my arms. He knew he was dying. He smiled at me and repeated what he had said to me the night before, 'Love never dies, Jimmy . . . I will always be with you . . . You will do great things with your life.'

"Our last words to each other were *I love you*. Then Johnny died in my arms. I kept screaming, 'No . . . no, not Johnny, Lord! Take me . . . not him!'

"It was about this time that Joe Atkins, the FBI agent, reached our campsite. The other agents had overpowered the assassin. When Joe saw me in the cassock holding my brother, he naturally assumed James had been killed. I told him that it was Johnny! Initially, he seemed stunned by the revelation. When he saw the other agents running toward the campsite, he waved them off and told them to call for a helicopter and search the surrounding area. Then, Joe Atkins looked directly at me and made a statement that chilled every bone in my body: 'You have to become John,' he said.

"I argued vehemently with him and said that I wouldn't steal my brother's identity. He challenged me by saying that if I didn't make the choice to become John, then Father Pat would lose both of his sons. If I kept my own identity, then I would need to go into the witness protection program and never see Father Pat again. I protested that I wasn't good enough to become a priest. Joe told me to stay in the seminary for at least a year and then do whatever I wanted.

"So, I made the choice . . . the choice to take Johnny's identity. I planned on leaving the seminary after the first year. Then something changed inside of me that night I broke down in your arms. You repeated practically the same words that Johnny had said to me while he was dying: 'Love never dies.'"

James shook his head and then said, "Johnny was right after all."

Monsignor Mike looked as though he was not exactly sure what James meant. The young man saw the confusion on the monsignor's face and then explained, "Johnny got really angry with me when I said I was going to work for the Martoni family. He insisted, 'If you work for a crook, then you are a crook.' Well, it turns out, I really am a crook. I stole my brother's identity! And every single waking moment of my life, I will always try to live up to Johnny's expectations of me."

# 52

## A Toast

**Archbishop John Donnelly**
**Holy Cross Rectory | October 2016**

THE ARCHBISHOP AND the old monsignor were quiet for a long time as they reflected on that evening so many years ago. Finally, Monsignor Mike said, "I'm sure that your brother, John, is looking down and smiling right now. You have certainly lived up to his expectations. And because of that, I think a part of John has continued to live on in you."

The archbishop closed his eyes, smiled, nodded his head as if he'd just realized something, and then said, "I was just thinking... about what you said that night. You said that you could help James become John. Well, Pope Daniel has a tendency to call me 'the Baptist' after John the Baptist. And what you just said about a part of John continuing to live in me made me remember John the Baptist saying, 'He must increase, and

I must decrease.' Maybe . . . just maybe, over these many years . . . John was increasing in me, while James was decreasing."

Then the archbishop and the monsignor raised their glasses to John Donnelly.

**The End**

# ACKNOWLEDGEMENTS

I am grateful to my wife, sons and daughters-in-law for their enthusiastic support throughout the process of writing my first novel. Special thanks to my son Stephen for developing the powerful image for the book cover.

Thanks to Father Jason Giombetti for ensuring that my description of the life as a seminarian was accurate.

Thanks to Joseph Altman, a retired FBI agent, for providing insightful knowledge and experience.

Thanks to the entire Bublish Team, especially the editorial staff for their skillful guidance and support.

Printed in the USA
CPSIA information can be obtained
at www.ICGtesting.com
LVHW080435150224
771864LV00001B/1/J